Color Blind

PENNY MILLER

Penny Miller
#whatcolorisyourmagik?

Not AR

Color Blind

Indie Gypsy

IG
Indie Gypsy
PO Box 511002
Livonia, MI 48151
http://www.indiegypsy.com

ISBN-13: 978-0692374696
ISBN-10: 0692374698

Library of Congress Control Number: 2015933977

.   ©2015 by Penny Miller
Cover Photo by Penny Miller

Dedication

In memory of Sue Campbell, my English teacher five grades in a row and the first person to tell me, "You should be a writer". And for my children; Robert, Amy and Cheyenne—believe in your own greatness. There are no limits to what you can achieve.

Chapter One

THE HALLWAYS WERE JAMMED with students rushing to make their first period class. Standing at my locker, rummaging and rooting around, I delayed the inevitable as long as possible. I'd be late, again. Get another lunch detention from Ms. Idlewilde, again. I hated Paranormal History, but it's a required class for all sophomores during their third semester.

Almost catching my fingers, I pulled my book from my locker seconds before the door slammed. Startled, I jerked back as wide shoulders leaned against the painted metal. Challen Parks' menacing smile demanded attention.

He's the most handsome boy in my school and the biggest jackass I knew. We'd had a mutual hate-hate relationship since the first grade. Sadly, he managed it much better than I. I lacked the clout to back up any emotions I might have against him, and he saw it.

"Are you planning on hanging out here all day, Gray?" A predatory gleam filled his eyes, well aware I loathed to be called that cruel nickname.

"I'd hate to have to give you another tardy slip. As lead hall monitor, it's my duty to report suspicious kids trying to skip class." The sarcastic dog lied with a smile like a shark; way too many teeth.

"Leave her be, Parks." A familiar voice came to my rescue.

Tesch, my best friend in this Para-purgatory of a high school, stepped up. Honestly, he was my only friend. Though, I wondered if being my friend was good for his social or survival aspirations, particularly in this instance.

Challen moved broad shoulders off my locker door, turning to face my champion. Other kids either hurried to get out of the way or jostled for a better view. Challen's pack of flunkies formed a loose circle around us.

"Or what, water boy?"

Tesch's oblong eyes narrowed to slits at the racial slur. He walked up to Challen, facing off with him nose to nose.

"Or the next time you decide you want to take a dip in the pool, you might find yourself in hot water."

"Are you threatening me siren?"

"And if I am?"

"I think it's time I showed you who's the alpha around here...."

A deep growl emanated from Challen's throat. Small changes

occurred in the flesh around his eyes; thickening skin and heavier brows. His light irises darkened. His fingers grew longer and curled into loose claws.

Tesch stood his ground. *Oh crap! Had he lost his freaking mind?*

"What seems to be the problem here?" The concerned but firm tone of Mr. Bellfwigg, the vice-principal, interrupted the building tension.

Stretching myself, I'm almost five foot two. The balding, paunchy male barely reached my shoulder, but I felt his power surrounding us. The coarse hair covering his jawbones and neck ruffled with a surge of magik as he moved into the ring of male dominance.

The opponents were forced smoothly apart. Moments before, they were close enough to smell each other's toothpaste then magikally separated by four feet. Mr. Bellfwigg stepped into the void between them.

"Mr. Parks? Mr. Wight? I believe first bell has rung, and it's time you both moved on to class."

I have to give Mr. Bellfwigg props for bravery. Wading into the middle of teenage Paras bent on showing supremacy is a foolhardy thing to do. But I've heard Brownies are made of tough stuff.

Tesch relaxed his stance first. Without another word to Challen, he picked up my book bag and looped it over his shoulder.

"Come on, Harmony. We don't want to be late."

I curled my Para-history book to my chest and fell into step beside him. Behind us, Mr. Bellfwigg shooed spectators and instigators on to their respective classrooms.

"Whew... that was intense." I mumbled. "Why did you have to provoke him like that?"

"Provoke him?" Tesch choked out. "Harmony, he could have cut your fingers off with that locker door. I saw him waiting for you! A split second difference or you hesitating and bye-bye digits; you would have been crippled for life."

It warmed my heart he cared. Tesch had always been there for me. I peeked up at him as we walked to first period.

Tesch forced his wild, shadowy curls into a punk porcupine hairdo. No telling how much gel he used to achieve those spikes. He had a nice face with a strong, rectangular jawline. Slightly pointed ears poked upward and were pierced six ways from Sunday.

His wide mouth currently turned down in a stern frown. I wished I could see the color of his eyes.

Heck, I wished I could see the color of my own, but a trick of fate left me without any color perception. None, nada, zip. I could see light and dark and shades of what I thought was gray, but I couldn't be sure.

"Well? Would you rather he maimed you for life?" Tesch demanded.

"At least I would have an excuse for skipping Idlewilde's class." The thought escaped my mouth before I could stop it.

"You'd rather be permanently disfigured than sit through an hour of Para-history?" He looked at me with a grimace.

We were outside the door of that very subject. I felt the pout coming on.

"I don't know. Ask me in an hour."

Pulling the door open, we shuffled inside. Tesch stayed behind me all the way. It's one of his many endearing or aggravating habits, depending on my mood.

As we headed to our seats, I contemplated life without fingers versus an hour of pixie torment. I came to the conclusion I could do without pinkie fingers. Or ring fingers for that matter. Just need thumbs and indexes really.

We weren't late, barely. Ms. Idlewilde floated near the front of the class. Her wings buzzed rapidly, angrily at me, as I crossed the front of the room to my desk.

She hates me. I knew it. It wasn't like she tried to hide it either. Since the first day, when I contradicted her lesson on the history of the Fae, she'd had it in for me. I'm barely scraping a "D" in her class.

That's a sad statement considering Charlie, my adoptive father, is as well versed in Para-history as American. He teaches at the University of Oklahoma. American history that is, not Para.

No way! Normals didn't know about us. Our governing Council aimed to keep it that way.

Charlie tried to tutor me in Ms. Idlewilde's class but got disgusted. He said she teaches a version that is more subjective than objective. I think that means she twists the facts or makes it up as she goes.

I took my seat at the back of the class and opened my book to the current chapter we're studying. I'd read the pages twice in hopes of being prepared. Fat lot of good it ever does me.

The pulse of magik tickled my skin as Ms. Idlewilde transformed from her diminutive size as a pixie to the full size of a human woman, albeit a tiny one. She was quite beautiful, really.

Her oval face and almond shaped eyes had a look of perpetual wonder when not narrowed in disgust at me. Dark hair cascaded in loose waves over her shoulders. Her limbs were slender and willowy and in perfect proportion.

Like most pixies, her figure was very slim, almost void of all curves. The wings were the largest part of her body, stretching over her head and shoulders, framing her body down to the knees.

"Today, class, we will be discussing how the laws that govern para groups happened and why." Ms. Idlewilde's voice tinkled like ice cubes falling into a crystal chalice.

Cool, I knew this stuff. I learned it from Charlie before the fourth grade, but I dutifully listened.

"As you learned in Para-studies, all magik and paranormal activity stems from the wavelengths of color on the visible spectrum. From violet to red, magik exists to some degree in almost every living thing. Even Normals have a touch of it, though not much, thank the Powers." She giggled lightly as if she had just told an inside joke.

"Paranormal beings get their powers from these wavelengths of colored light. Most species tend to have powers within a limited color range. Can anyone give me an example of this?"

No one seemed excited to raise their hand. Hardly eager either, but class participation is supposed to count for some of our grade, so I reluctantly held my fingers high.

The pixie spied me willing to answer. Her features morphed into a malicious grin.

"Ms. Phillips? Color me surprised. Please, enlighten us."

My teacher gave another one of those silver bell giggles that grated on my nerves as she made fun of my visual disability. The phony Faery twit!

"Well, uh…" I cleared my throat. "For example, Elves have a tendency to fall into the green spectrum. They've got strong powers with things that are associated with that color in nature, and their magik has an earthy quality. An elf can have magik outside the green. But if so, it's a blue-green or yellow-green blend and usually not as strong as their natural green."

Ms. Idlewilde shrugged her shoulders dismissively. "Mostly correct."

My teeth ground together. I knew from Charlie I'd been more than 'mostly correct'.

"Could an elf be a sorcerer, Ms. Phillips?" Ms. Idlewilde pursued the subject.

I thought about it. From what I knew of Spectrum Magiks, para-genetics and our laws, I answered. "It's possible but unlikely."

"Can you explain?"

"Each magik on the spectrum wavelength has a talent or ability that is compatible with the light it reflects. Red light, closest to infrared, is a heat source. Heat changes things, like wood burning to ash or water boiling before it evaporates. The red wavelength governs shifters, alchemy, and other magiks of change."

"On the other end is violet or ultra violet. Ultra violet is just a step before x-ray and radiation that passes through things. Magiks in this wavelength are for those who pass themselves or items through time, space and supposedly, solid objects. Sorcerers and Djinn are in the violet spectrum and known for making things appear or disappear. That's not really what happens though. The items are brought from or sent to a place of magik."

"Green magik is more rooted, like trees, and changes gradually like seasons. It's called natural magik because it will mimic something that can occur in nature and because users can get power from living things."

"So why an elf can't be affiliated with a red spectrum or a violet, please?" Idlewilde's voice sounded disdainful.

"I suppose they could, but elves, as a rule, don't like change. Maybe because they're the longest living paranormals, but they've never mixed with other species either. Years and generations have kept their magik in the neutral wavelengths. It would be a genetic fluke for an elf to be a red or a violet practitioner. So again, it's possible, but I don't think it would happen."

My instructor smiled at me, looking like a sadistic cat playing with a mouse. "I can think of one very important instance when it did happen. Class, you may now turn to page three hundred and six in your books."

Much further ahead in the text than we'd been working, I turned to the page. There on the semi-gloss paper, a portrait drawn of a smug elf in clothing out of the Dark Ages.

"Ms. Phillips, would you please read the accompanying passage?"

I held back a sigh. Licking dry lips, I scanned the text and began.

"In 1042, Sancrenath Lyspladadas became leader of his elven tribe by treacherous means, combining a lethal mix of violet and green magik. Sancrenath murdered the High Elven King, Corlianessus, and his son, Kamandocius, by making them disappear, never to be seen again. His combination of spectrum magiks assisted him in subjugating a tribe of over 5000 elves into slavery for his own purposes."

"After more than 300 years of tyranny, Sancrenath met defeat at the hands of an outside, hired force of wizardry and an army of elves from neighboring tribes. This force subsequently executed the oppressor for crimes against his people."

"After his death, a personal journal revealed the Wizard-Elf King as the product of a union between former High King Corlianessus and a female jinni. Cross breeding of species and spectrums is the suspected cause of Sancrenath's unnatural ability to use the violet and green magiks."

"Other significant examples of inter-para breeding have led to devastating consequences for the supernatural community as well as the non-para world. Such mixing is believed responsible for the notable figures of Rowan the Raging Raven, Attila the Hun, Barthinius the Brute and Mordred, illegitimate son of King Arthur of the Pendragon line and his witch half-sister, Morgana, also thought to be a product of inter-para relations."

"Disastrous liaisons of different spectrums forced the Council to draft the Para-Sans Relation laws. These laws have been the backbone of a peaceful paranormal society for over 700 years. Penalties and sanctions for offenses are swift and severe."

The passage ended, and I sank into my seat, swallowing the lump in my throat. Yeah, no kidding they're severe. An instant death sentence could be considered a tad harsh.

I thought of Charlie and Sarah, my adoptive parents, a werelion and a witch. They are the only legal inter-para marriage I knew of in the last 700 years.

Charlie and Sarah met in college and fell in love. Being open and honest, they came to the Council up front. They petitioned for a special dispensation to marry. Their tactics of confessing all before being caught impressed the right people.

They'd been allowed to remain alive. They'd even been allowed to marry. But there was a catch. They had to agree to be sterilized. The Council considered them a test case.

Loving each other enough, they willingly submitted to both physical and magikal spaying and neutering. Neither could have children even if the other died or they divorced. Their families had severely protested the marriage before disowning them entirely.

Charlie and Sarah were warm and wonderful people who had a lot of love to share and wanted a family. They contented themselves with adoption. That's how I became Harmony Phillips.

Personally, I think they got the short end of the deal. All the time and effort put into finding a paranormal kid to adopt and I'm defective. Of course, they had no way of knowing when I was an infant that I would be colorblind.

Ms. Idlewilde's voice snapped me back to the classroom. "Thank you, Ms. Phillips, for proving yourself wrong again. Cross spectrum contamination has been responsible for some of the supernatural world's greatest villains and tragedies. And though quite possible, it's very much forbidden."

I scrunched down in my seat, arms folded, ticked off. So much for getting points for class participation; and I had *not* proven myself wrong.

I'd said possible but not probable. Which sounded pretty darn right to me from the information I'd read to the class.

The rest of the period droned on, but I tuned it out. Ms. Idlewilde did not call on me again, thank the stars. I might have said something really colorful. The more I thought about it, the madder I got, passing up disgruntled and moving on to furious.

That darn pixie could say what she liked, but she had shown me over and over her prejudice towards Normals and non-magikals like me. Her attitude could hurt my odds of getting into a good college in the human world. Bad grades on my transcript could leave me stuck in a place I didn't belong.

Yes, some paras mix in the normal world, but few leave our cloistered para communities.

But because we age differently than the Normals, we have to take four semesters of one grade. For those that want to go to college among humans, the school takes the standard, normal class grade and the para class grade and averages them for a transcript grade. An "A" and an "F" equaled a "C". Ms. Idlewilde's bigotry could stop me from getting out of here someday.

The bell rang none too soon. I tore from the classroom. I wanted out of there. Tesch was hot on my heels.

"Whoa, Trigger. Slow down. You can't tell me you are in that big of a hurry to get to Geometry." I felt his slightly webbed fingers on my shoulder.

I slowed my pace and turned. The muscles in my face were drawn tight in anger.

"She just makes me so mad sometimes, Tesch! At the beginning of the semester, I thought if I worked hard enough and tried my best, I could get a good grade in her class, but it isn't going to happen. I give up!"

Swallowing back another explosion of outrage, it felt hot going down, and like it might come back up. I tried to stuff my anger back in the box and get control. I didn't want the attention.

In school, I kept as low of a profile as possible. Being a shadow had helped me get through the years as a non-magikal in a very magikal world.

"You are really burnt about this, aren't you?" He drew back a bit from me. "It's like a force radiating off of you. Wow!"

Tesch held up his hands as if the air around me had substance. He reached forward slowly until a cool hand rested on my cheek.

"Harmony, you are burning up. I think you might be sick. Let's get you to the nurse."

"Don't be silly, I never get sick, ever."

The moment the words were out of my mouth, a rush of nausea overwhelmed me. A strange shuddering raced up my spine. My bones ached deep into the marrow, and my knees felt weak.

"On second thought, you might be right."

Tesch helped me to the nurse's office, conveniently located next to Mr. Bellfwigg's. I believe the room must be very white and very clean because there were hardly any differences in the bright shade I saw.

The nurse, Mrs. Tyck, blended with the room; her hair, face and clothes were all light shades. Only her quick, dark eyes broke the monotony.

She gave me a genuine smile. "Harmony Phillips, what a surprise! I don't think I have ever had the pleasure of treating you. What seems to be the problem?"

Mrs. Tyck appeared as a Normal woman in her mid to late fifties with close-cropped hair. The soft buzz of power emanating from her told me she practiced the healing arts and had to be around ninety to one hundred years old.

Witches age more slowly than humans but not as slowly as elves. She still had another forty to fifty years before she could retire from the school system with a pension.

I had seen her around plenty but never had the experience of her care. As I had told Tesch, I didn't get sick. I had the perfect attendance to prove it.

Tesch explained before I could open my mouth. "Mrs. Tyck, I think Harmony may be coming down with something. She's awfully hot."

"I thought I might throw up earlier, but it faded. My body aches like I've been shocked with electricity." I added.

I still felt awful yet strangely better. Maybe I should pitch a fit more often. The buzzing inside had become warm and tingly, but my bones continued to feel brittle and hollow.

"Come sit down and let me check you over, please." Mrs. Tyck gestured to a padded table covered in paper like on TV doctor shows.

I moved slowly, carefully. The world around me felt unreal. Tesch actually had to help me up onto the exam table, sitting slumped forward with my feet dangling.

The school nurse dragged out a wide array of tools to look me over with. She presented a thermometer, blood pressure cuff, one of those light things for looking in people's ears and eyes, and a stethoscope. She also brought out some crystals, herbs, an egg and matches.

Mrs. Tyck went through the mundane stuff first. She took my temperature and blood pressure and listened to my chest. Then she used the light to look into my ears and eyes. The eyes elicited a comment, they always did.

"Have you always been colorblind, Miss Phillips?"

"Yes, Ma'am. Since I can remember. It's a birth defect." I knew what she saw, or rather didn't see.

The ability to see color is the result of some part of the eye called cones. Most humans with basic color vision have three types of cones in their eyes. Some Normals, a rare few, have four types of cones. They have very good perception of color and usually some latent magikal abilities though they may not know it.

Paranormals have five and six cones in their eyes. They see color as an object and are able to touch shades of light metaphysically to do magik. At least that's what I'd been told.

I had no cones in my eyes. I saw only light and dark and the shadows in between. I was completely colorblind.

Mrs. Tyck took another look. I was sure she couldn't help her curiosity. I understood I was the only para ever to be so completely defective in the vision department. Lucky me.

"Hmm." She reached for the other tools of her trade; the herbs and a large quartz crystal.

In a small stoneware bowl, she measured out different dried plants before grinding them with a pestle. I could smell the rosemary, sage, thyme and Bella Donna.

Sarah, my adoptive mother, may not have been able to practice magik anymore, but she still kept a healthy herb stash for things like cooking and medicine. You could take the magik out of the witch, but you couldn't take the witch out of the woman.

Mrs. Tyck pulled a file from her pocket and gently rasped away some of the quartz into the powdery collection. She turned to me and Tesch, who stayed by my elbow.

"I am going to see if one of your more high-spirited classmates has decided to play a game with you."

"You mean you're going to check me for a curse or a spell?"

"Yes." Mrs. Tyck confirmed. "I don't think that is the case, but I would be remiss in my duties if I didn't. However, after breathing the vapors, you are going to be unfit for class for the rest of the day. I'll call your parents."

"Sarah and Charlie are both working in the city today. It'll be a while before they can come get me."

"I can take her home." Tesch volunteered. "My guardian is right here in town. He'll give us a ride."

Did I mention Tesch is adopted too? It's a common bonding point between us.

Mrs. Tyck eyed him as if trying to see inside his head. "You wouldn't be trying to get out of class yourself, Mr. Wight?"

Tesch gave a guilty shrug. "Well, yeah, but I'm all she's got right now."

The nurse smiled at the conspiracy. "All right, I'll excuse you as well with Mr. Bellfwigg, citing special circumstances. But you are to stay with her until her parents arrive home."

To me, she explained, "You'll sleep mostly; maybe have some strange dreams, but nothing of any harm."

Not that I minded Tesch getting out of class or taking me home, but I was curious about the need. "So why the babysitter?"

"It's the effect of the Bella Donna. Paras will do things they normally wouldn't, like try to fly or start a fire. A few under this spell will sleepwalk. Sometimes they just burst into fits of giggles or go about confessing their secrets, among other things. It's infrequent, but it happens."

"Oh." My stomach plummeted again, not so sure I wanted to be checked for maleficent magik, at least not in Tesch's company. There were one or two things I'd never told him. Like how I'd had a crush on him since grade school or how I had never kissed a boy. He's my best and only friend. I'd hate for that to change.

Panic set in. I could feel it coursing in my blood and setting the electric tingles humming again. It didn't hurt. Not much anyway. "Is this really necessary? I mean, I'm feeling much better."

"Yes, Miss Philips. I feel it is. Now just relax."

I gave Tesch an imploring stare. He patted my shoulder. A gesture meant to comfort. "It'll be okay, Harmony. You'll be fine."

Please, stars in the sky and powers that be, please don't let me turn into a babbling idiot! Please don't let me make a fool of myself with Tesch!

Mrs. Tyck struck a match. Sulfur assaulted my nose just before she dropped the flame into the cup of herbs. Her voice lowered as she whispered words of magik under her breath. The mixture became a sheer gauze trail in the air as she held it beneath my face.

"Breathe in deeply, dear."

With less than good grace, I took a deep whiff. I expected to cough but instead, I sneezed. The force of my reaction displaced the spell's components. They floated up in the air before me. I drew in for another good sneeze, sucking up the dust of herbs, getting a solid dose in my mouth and nose. I ended up coughing and sneezing, inhaling even more.

My vision swam. Bones that felt brittle turned soft and slippery. My head filled with angry bees. They buzzed so loud, my ears roared with the sound.

"Do you hear that?" I hacked out. "Is there a beehive around here?"

"Oh dear." The nurse said with concern.

"What?" Tesch asked, worried.

"Get her up and home now before you have to carry her all the way, Mr. Wight. She has inhaled too large of a dose. It won't hurt her, but she'll probably be unconscious soon."

"Well, can you tell if someone put a hex on her or something?"

The insects inside my head began choir practice. The last words on the subject before I heard no more, "I assure you, no one from *this school* has put a spell on Miss Phillips."

Chapter 2

I dreamed.

Each bee in the swarm turned into an idea, thought, or picture. They were random and had no pattern but were the most vivid things.

I heard songs sung by the sweetest voice. Lullabies that made me snuggle peacefully into the softness of my mother's breast. Her scent came to me as sunshine, spring grass and gentle rain. I could feel her arms, sense her presence, and then she faded. I wanted to cry. My eyes burned to cry.

My eyes were burning! I could feel flames licking at my cheeks!

Then…that faded, too.

Charlie swam before my face as I had never seen him before, in his lion form. I must have had a better imagination than I knew. Charlie had been magikally neutered before I came along. He couldn't shift anymore. Still, in my dream, I could see the real Charlie; half man and half great cat.

His eyes held more reflective surfaces than a Normal eye, like multiple shards of broken glass reflecting starbursts around slit pupils.

His soft, curling hair and beard had blossomed around his head and neck to make a thick mane over his chest and shoulders. The hands he reached out to me were tipped with sharp claws. They pulled back into his fingers as he took me into furry arms.

He cradled me to his chest as if I were the most precious gift. When he smiled down at me, his extended canines peeked through his lips. Seeing his face made me feel safe.

I drifted in the security of that smile.

The sun warmed my shoulders as I sat on the bank of the reservoir. Water lapped gently at my toes. I startled when a head surfaced a few yards beyond where I sat.

"Who are you?" I asked with a child's curiosity.

"I'm Tesch. What's your name?" The boy answered with an easy, open smile.

"Harmony."

"Do you want to come in for a swim?" He blinked large drops of glistening moisture from wide eyes.

"Sarah says the water is too cold."

"It won't be if you're with me."

"Why not?"

"I'm a Siren." He performed a flip in the water. His feet were like the flippers humans wore to swim deep under the surface.

The youthful memory swam away, and I was left with the still mirror of the deep. Mists rolled in, and sound and voices echoed off of the water.

I heard the witch doctor saying, "Mr. and Mrs. Phillips, Harmony is completely colorblind. As far as I can tell, it's a birth defect. She'll never do magik. Harmony will be helpless in our world. You should give her up to a human family where her defect won't matter as much."

Defect.

Helpless.

Colorblind.

Words cut me to the quick. I wanted to retreat from the hurtful truth. Other voices came to me with words that seemed more real but less clear.

"Do you think it's starting?"

"We won't know until she can tell us. I imagine it will be obvious when it does."

"I'm worried for her, afraid of what's to come. How will she be when she finds out? Angry? Hurt? Scared? I'm no longer sure you had the right to keep all this from her, to make me keep it from her."

"I know. But the Wizened thought it the best way, the only way. I don't think any of us expected to care this much, not about her as an individual."

"It's more than that. I love her."

I awoke.

Just like that, from being deep asleep to eyes wide open. I had a flash of disorientation before recognizing my room. Light shone through the lightweight curtains, illuminating the chaos.

My room was an explosion of design and textures and probably not the décor someone who could fully see would choose. Patterns, flowers, stripes, polka dots, furry rugs, a satin comforter, a velvet bean bag chair, I had a bit of everything. Because of my lack of color vision, I liked textile feel and bold prints.

Out of necessity, my wardrobe ran on the bland side. I had twenty pairs of the same white socks. Plain jeans were the most common thing in my wardrobe. They were easy to coordinate with. Most any casual shirt can be worn with jeans.

My other mainstays included solid colored T-shirts with the usual teenage messages like, *You Inspire My Inner Serial Killer, Contents Under Pressure, Be Nice To Kids, We'll Choose Your Nursing Home Someday.*

This sanctuary doubled as a sensory perception chamber. Here, I compensated for what I couldn't see with things I could. As my eyes took in all of my wild stuff, I relaxed into my pillow, ready to catch some more sleep.

Wait a minute. I recalled the events of… when?

I had no idea the day or the time. I rolled off of the bed and onto the floor to look for that stupid brass clock. Digital clocks didn't work so well for me. I had to have the old fashioned kind with a face and hands to tell time.

Feeling deep beneath the leopard print dust ruffle, I found some dirty socks, an old class notebook, a magazine, and a leftover cereal bowl; empty thank goodness. Searching farther, I came up with all kinds of goodies but no clock. I'm not a real neat freak, so the rest proved pretty horrid.

Crap. Okay. Fine. Not the end of the world.

Coming aware by stages, I began to notice the important things. One, my bladder felt a gallon too full, and two, shag carpet had been installed in my mouth while I slept.

Yuck! So, no matter the hour or the day, heading down the hall for the bathroom became priority. Still wearing the clothes I last dressed in meant I was good enough to stroll to the toilet, no problem.

When I tried to stand, my knees needed an extra minute to remember how to hold me up. My head got in on the act with my legs with a little dipsy-do moment. What the hell does Mrs. Tyck put in her spells?

Holding onto the walls and furniture, I crossed my room to the door. Opening it, the house sounded quiet, but I sensed it was not empty.

The distinct smell of bacon and coffee came wafting up the stairs. Charlie believed in breakfast being the most important meal of the day. We never skipped it. It made me feel better knowing it was morning and weird because I didn't know which morning.

The pressure in my groin reminded me to worry about it later. If I didn't pee soon, I'd wet my pants. I did the pee-pee waddle down the hall, holding my knees tightly together all the way.

After finishing my urgent business, I washed my hands and face and brushed my teeth and hair, starting to feel more like myself. In the mirror, I noted the puffiness in my face. I'd slept long and hard.

Studying my reflection, my eyes looked strange, different somehow. I rubbed at the glass, thinking it was dirty, though Sarah always kept things spotless. It's a witch thing.

The mirror was clean, but my eyes still looked weird to me. They seemed brighter, lighter, standing out more in the reflection. I decided it must be some kind of spell hangover.

Or the mirror itself.

An old fashioned medicine cabinet, the glass had age spotting on the surface. Charlie had restored the two-story, turn-of-the-century home himself. He kept the original fixtures. Our resident history professor liked authenticity.

Whatever.

I went back to my room to get out of my grungy, slept in clothes before heading downstairs. Now that my head had cleared and my knees were back to doing their job, I felt good, energized.

It didn't take but a few minutes to change and slap on some deodorant. I skipped down the steps, taking the last stairs two at a time, hopping down to the landing.

"Sarah? Charlie?" I called out as my feet planted firmly on the hardwood.

To my left, our living room stood empty. To the right, so did a formal dining room. To the back and right of the stairs was a hall that led to the kitchen and breakfast room.

"In the kitchen!" Sarah's alto voice echoed back to me.

In a big old home, sound carries. I hooked a hard right, using the banister for ballast, and followed the corridor past the stairs and guest bathroom to the back of the house.

Our kitchen felt very homey and antique while still having all the modern electric conveniences. Charlie had found an appliance company that specialized in contemporary stoves and such that looked like they came from the early 1900s.

Sarah had decorated in living garden. Big, tall windows let in lots of light, and there were plenty to go around. Window boxes were beneath each sill, bursting with fresh herbs.

Everything appeared bright like true white was. Our kitchen reminded me of those clouds that float across the sky in the summer that resemble cotton balls. Not in the fluffy sense, but comfortable and light.

The curtains, dish towels, and decorative tiles had an ivy pattern running along the edge. I just saw a dark vine; Sarah called the color deep green.

She always tried to help me out by identifying things that tended to be a specific color. Like red and strawberries. Anyway, it happened to be ivy, pretty and delicate. She'd painted the tiles herself.

Sarah had a love for growing things, anything planted in the dirt. She plotted gardens with the care and planning of a masterpiece. The kitchen reflected her passion.

A savvy businesswoman too, she owned a fresh produce trade. Sarah planted and cultivated fifty acres of fields and hot houses that provided tomatoes, strawberries, potatoes, corn, okra, carrots, cucumbers, melons, blackberries and mushrooms to local grocers and farmer's markets. The mushroom beds were her latest project.

Sarah had tried to teach me about plants and gardens and such, but it just didn't take. However, I deeply respected her talent for it.

Sometimes, I thought magik and talent was very close kin. I teased her about having a bit of elf in her veins. She just smiled and said, "You never know."

Bouncing into the kitchen, I saw Sarah bent at the waist, rummaging in the refrigerator. I waited for her to straighten before giving her an energetic hug from behind. Two years ago my arms went around her middle when I did this. Finally they went over her shoulders.

Not that I'm tall, Sarah stood very petite. Maybe five feet and a half inch in her shoes. I rested my cheek against the curve of her neck.

Her soft hair fell waist length and smelled like American Jasmine. She made her own soap and shampoo like any good witch would. Beneath the flowery scent, the more permanent smell of good earth and nature emanated. Her scent made me think of *home*.

"Goodness, Harmony, honey." She exclaimed over my impromptu gesture of affection. Patting one of my arms which rested around her shoulders while holding an egg carton with the other, she asked. "Are you hungry?"

"Starving." Total honesty, I felt ravenous after all that sleep.

When they didn't ask me a lot of questions about why I slept so long or so hard I knew Mrs. Tyck had called them. Tesch probably explained, too.

I knew my best buddy well enough to know he wouldn't leave me alone until my parental units were around to take care of me. I could see him hanging out on the sofa, flipping channels on the TV while I sawed logs, dead to the world.

"What about me, Kitten?" Charlie asked from the bench seat at the breakfast table.

He folded his paper down to give me a questioning look from behind wire-framed glasses. The teasing smile showed beneath a neatly trimmed moustache.

Kitten had been his pet name for me for as long as I could remember. I released Sarah to go scoot in next to him. Leaning in close, I put my arms around his middle for a solid hug. Charlie's cradled me to his side.

Remembering my dreams while under the influence of magik, I wondered. The image of Charlie in his man-lion form, holding me safe as a baby, filled my head. I knew it hadn't been real, but it had felt it.

"Have a good rest?" he asked above my head.

"Yeah." I agreed, letting go and rising from the embrace. "But I had some strange dreams."

"Really?" His voice was mildly curious.

"Yep. I had one of you holding me as a baby. But you were in lion form. It seemed like I saw the real you for the first time."

He paused with a coffee cup halfway to his lips. "You saw the real me in your dream? Are you sure you saw me? You have never seen me in my were-form."

"It was you. Just a dream, I know, but it felt right. I saw your eyes like the starbursts of a cat with the slit pupils. And your mane covered your shoulders and chest. You even had retractable claws, Charlie."

"Were you scared of me, Kitten? In the dream?"

"No way!" I laughed. "You were still you. Actually, I felt safe with you as a lion."

Some tension in his eyes eased, and he finished carrying the coffee to his lips for a sip then he smiled. "You're always safe with me, Harmony. But I wish you had dreamed me a little more ferocious. I mean, someday soon I'm going to need to be really fierce to keep all the boys off our doorstep when they figure out what a prize you are."

"I think we're safe from that happening any time soon." I mumbled.

Charlie and Sarah promised I'd be a great beauty someday, but I didn't see it. I didn't think I needed a bag over my head to go out in public or anything, but my face had distinct features. Strong jawline and sharp angles meant I could pass for a pretty boy or a handsome girl, but beautiful? No, I didn't think so.

"Here's your eggs, sweetie."

Sarah set my plate down. I reached for the bacon tray already on the table.

"Do you want milk or juice?"

"Juice, please." I answered before filling my mouth with a delicious slice of hickory smoked pig. Sarah made the bacon perfect; a little crispy but not dried out or burnt. I closed my eyes and savored the flavor.

Picking up my fork in one hand, I grabbed a piece of toast from the stack with the other. Cutting at my fried eggs with the utensil, glancing down at my plate, I screamed. It burst forth as a blood curdling, hair raising noise.

What had Sarah done to my eggs?! Something I'd never seen before ran from the yolk!

I jumped from my seat, pointing. Charlie came out of the nook beside me, trying to figure out what had gone wrong. Sarah turned from the fridge, a glass in hand. I screamed again.

What's in the glass, and why is it coming out of my eggs, too?

My breath came in hard, fast pants. My fingers went numb. Hyperventilation, but I had no power to stop it. I was scared to death of what I saw.

I opened my eyes for a second time that day. Lying on the kitchen floor, Sarah and Charlie hovered over me with worried frowns creasing their faces. Sarah had a cool cloth pressed to my forehead. Charlie rubbed my hand vigorously between his large warm ones.

"Harmony? Kitten? Are you okay?" His voice let me know his anxiety level.

"What's wrong? Why did you scream, honey?" Sarah sounded equally fearful.

My eyes wandered between them. Charlie's hair had changed. Paler streaks of goo from my plate appeared on his head! But it didn't look gooey, it just looked… weird. Something clicked, understanding dawned.

"Charlie?" My voice sounded hoarse and thick to my own ears.

"Yes, Harmony, I'm right here."

He tried to sooth me. Maybe he thought I'd gone all the way blind. My eyes did feel wide and too big for their sockets.

"Charlie…what color…is your hair?"

He stopped rubbing my hand. Sarah's eyes cut sharply from me to Charlie and back. I could see his Adam's apple bob hard in his throat.

"Dark blonde, Harmony, I have dark blonde hair." A hitch came in the last words as he spoke.

"I can see it."

"Oh my stars!" Sarah exclaimed. "Charlie! Do you think?"

Charlie gave a stern glance. One I don't think I had ever seen before. "Hush, Sarah. Let's get Harmony off of the floor before we speculate."

To me he asked, "Do you think you can sit up?"

I nodded. Both put supportive arms around my shoulders, raising me upright. Stunned, fascinated, I reached out to his locks.

They looked unreal but felt the same as always, soft and thick with unruly curls cut short. The hair on his head appeared vibrant, while his beard remained the same, void of color.

I looked around the room seeing things I'd never noticed. The glass on the kitchen island held juice, a bright shade unknown to me. Tiny little centers of this new color were in the plants that grew in the boxes beneath the windows.

I shook my head in wonder and got to my feet. Charlie and Sarah continued to hold onto me, in case I faltered. When sure I could stand alone, I moved forward to the glass Sarah had poured. They let me go.

My fingers wrapped around the cool, hard cup. There were droplets of condensation forming on the sides. It felt the same in my hand.

I lifted the contents to my nose and smelled oranges before taking a small sip. My other senses needed to confirm the revelation of my eyes. Touch, taste and smell hadn't changed with the glaring color.

"This is the color orange?" Wonder filled my voice.

"Yellow." Sarah explained in a soft sure voice. "It comes from oranges, but the color is really a deep yellow."

"Yellow." I repeated for myself.

Raising the glass, I took another drink. My senses said no real change had occurred, but magikally the juice seemed colder and sweeter. I drained the glass.

Once gone, I wiped away the liquid mustache with a shaky hand. A faint smear of *yellow* orange juice stained my fingers.

Charlie and Sarah watched me like proud parents would a baby's first steps. They knew those first awkward movements must be done alone but stood close by should I waver or fall.

"The eggs?"

"The yolks are yellow, another dark yellow." Sarah confirmed for me.

"I can see yellow."

The quiet statement slowly sunk in. Pressure built behind my eyes. The hot tears formed, but my lips split into a wide smile so big my cheeks ached.

"I can see yellow." The words come out as a harsh breath that could have been a whisper but instead carried. Tears began to spill. My next sound came as a shout of joy.

"Charlie! Sarah! I can see yellow! I can see it! I can see!"

I rushed forward to embrace them with all the pleasure and wonder bursting out of my chest. They met me halfway, enveloping me in their arms with tight, jubilant love. Half dancing, half jumping with excitement and marvel, laughter rang.

"Oh, baby," Sarah gushed with affection and warmth, "This is wonderful, so wonderful for you."

"Harmony! Harmony! This is terrific!" Charlie shouted. "I wonder what's happened. What's changed?"

"I don't know. I don't care. I can see yellow!"

Sobbing with happiness, we were swept away by the miracle.

Moments like this are remembered forever. The excitement didn't burn out; it settled itself into the center of my heart. No solstice, equinox or birthday gift would ever mean more to me than this moment in my life. The first time I ever saw a color.

Ever practical, Sarah chimed in. "We need to call Dr. Heckerman. He needs to examine your eyes right away!"

I groaned in protest. Dr. Heckerman first diagnosed my eyes colorblind. His voice was the one from my dreams, declaring me defective.

"Do we have to, Sarah?" I heard my voice whiney and complaining, but I'd rather eat spiders than see that old witch doctor.

She took my face in gentle hands, looking me square in the eye. No color appeared to me in her steady gaze, but a world of love and concern couldn't be missed. Tears of warmth and delight wetted tracks down her cheeks.

"Harmony, this is a blessing on you, and I am grateful. You don't know how often I have prayed to the Mother that there would be a way for you to see the world like the rest of us. I've felt helpless that I couldn't cast a spell or blessing to change it."

"Gaia has answered my prayers. This may not be Her first or only blessing upon you. I'd like Dr. Heckerman to look and see if your eyes are changing or growing or whatever this is. If it can happen once, it can happen again. I want to be prepared for this journey with you."

When she put it that way…

"Okay." I agreed without further protest, unable to remain churlish in the face of so much consideration.

I gave her a big smile. "But can I eat my eggs first?"

Charlie and Sarah laughed, gathering me in another warm, exuberant hug. We sat back down to eat.

I never knew there were so many yellow breakfast foods! Eggs, orange and apple juice, bananas, butter on toast, corn flakes cereal, I ate them all until stuffed. I tasted these things for the first time, again. Who would have thought that color had flavor? Yellow is delicious.

Chapter 3

"Well, let's have a look, young lady."

Dr. Heckerman had me on another padded table with another light scope in hand. My second exam in two days, some kind of record for me; the last time I'd been to see the doctor had been for my human inoculations twelve years ago.

Paranormal people age differently than other humanoids. For each human year, we only change maybe four to six months' worth. Some of the older races, like elves, even less.

That's why we double up on the grades in school. I am in my third semester of tenth grade. For a human, I am about sixteen.

Since it had always been assumed that someday I might want to join the "real" world permanently, Heckerman, Charlie and Sarah agreed to raise and treat me as if I would. I've had the same shots as a normal girl as well as a magikal one.

I've been vaccinated for measles, mumps, rubella, chicken pox, hepatitis and the human flu among others. I've also been given antidotes for Troll pox, Elf's disease, and Witchentary. Not that I'll ever need them.

Dr. Heckerman shone the light in my eyes. I stared forward. He took a good long look.

"Hmm, interesting, very interesting. I must say I have never seen anything like this."

His great, hulking form bent double at the waist to be at eye level with me. The large hands more suited for carrying a club, manipulating my eyes and the optical instrument, were gentle and sure. I would never have thought that they would have the healing touch. The good doctor came from a race of mythical Scandinavian giants, the Jotunn, making him a Jotnar.

Visually, he's the stuff of human nightmares; large hairy feet, a monstrous round head and great, ugly, sharp teeth. Gray mottled skin with sparse patches of coarse hair covered his body. He assured me he was the runt of his litter, but at seven and a half feet tall, I think he pulled my leg.

My prejudice against the doctor has nothing to do with his appearance or physical treatment of me. He had never been mean or rough. But sometimes people wound you with words and good intentions.

"What do you see, Doc?"

Charlie and Sarah hovered close, near the door of the exam room. Brave Charlie asked the question we all wanted to know the answer to.

"As near as I can tell, immature cones, at least three, possibly four types, are forming. Harmony's eyes are finally developing to perceive color. How did you say this all began?" His deep voice reverberated on my skin when speaking that close to my face.

"I looked down at my breakfast and there it was, in my eggs. Scared the crap out of me."

"Harmony!" Sarah exclaimed over my use of profanity.

If she knew the colorful and varied words I'd heard at school on a daily basis she'd have stroked out for sure. Not that I would ever swear like *that!* But crap, damn, and hell have been popping out of my mouth more often lately. High school had a bad influence on me.

"Sorry, Sarah."

"What about yesterday?" Dr. Heckerman interjected, putting us back on course. "Your parents told me you were ill yesterday? Tell me about that."

"Not ill really, my temper just got the better of me, and I had a kind of melt down. Tesch, my friend, said I felt hot. I got nauseous, and my bones ached. It had already started to pass, but Tesch made me go see Mrs. Tyck, the school nurse. She checked me for a jinx or a hex. Then the lights went out."

"You passed out?" Sarah interrupted, all concerned again.

"No." I corrected her. I didn't want my parents thinking I'd been swooning everywhere I went. "She said I breathed in too much Bella Donna. She had Tesch bring me home to wait for you."

"He only said you got sick at school and had to come home. None of the rest." Charlie scowled. "Going to have a talk with him about that."

"Mrs. Tyck said she would call you. Maybe he thought you already knew." I defended my friend.

I didn't need Charlie or Sarah being irritated with Tesch. He *was* my circle of friends. Though being the only one made him a spot instead of a circle. Tesch, my single dot on the radar of popularity. I sighed heavily.

"So, Dr. Heckerman, what does this mean for our Harmony? You said cones, three or four, are forming?"

There were many questions rolled into that one. I tasted the anticipation of an answer and what it could mean for me.

Don't misunderstand. Seeing yellow thrilled me more than I ever thought it would have. I could already imagine redoing my room in shades of banana and egg yolk. Cool, right?

"It's really hard to say at this point. It's too soon to tell."

Witch doctors were really no different from medical doctors of the Normal world. They covered their butts when they didn't know an answer.

"This could be a solitary occurrence. I can't even say if it's a permanent effect. I can see no medical or magikal malady that's causing the change, but then I could never find one that caused it in the first place either. Harmony is otherwise healthy in all respects."

"So, at this point my advice is simply, wait and see. When and if new developments occur, then we will re-evaluate."

Oh, yeah, Dr. Heckerman had med-speak down cold. Still, I felt no worse off than when I awoke that morning. Actually, I considered myself ahead. I had yellow. However long it lasted, I would relish the color in any form presented.

When we finished with the doc, I couldn't fight the urge to go and see the world anew. I could think of a lifetime of things I had been missing. I wanted to see them all.

For once, Charlie and Sarah were seeing things my way. We went into Oklahoma City for a rare Saturday off from chores, gardening and grading papers.

At the Botanical Gardens, they had a live butterfly exhibit. The roses, hibiscus, daffodils and tulips made my throat catch. But the Monarch butterfly… I couldn't stop the tears from raining again.

"God and Goddess, Sarah…" I choked as she held my hand. "They are so beautiful. I didn't realize."

Before, I had grasped the life cycle of a butterfly with the clinical detachment of a scientist. I understood the whole larva, caterpillar, pupae, and chrysalis to butterfly process.

Finally, I could see the significance and poetry of the change for myself. How remarkable that something nondescript and well, ugly, could transform into something beautiful, ideal. I wanted to be the Monarch butterfly.

She squeezed my hand in hers. "There are so many things you've lost out on sweetheart. So much I want to show you."

"Dr. Heckerman said it may not last."

She gave my hand another reassuring squeeze. "He couldn't say it's permanent. He couldn't say it isn't either, Harmony. We will have to trust the Gaia's wisdom in this."

I tried not to wish for more than I had already been given, tried not to crave more color in my life. A shutter on the window of my world had been cracked open to let in a little light. I prayed quietly to the

Goddess for a storm to come and fling it wide open.

Charlie and Sarah took me down to Bricktown, a high end entertainment district in Oklahoma City. There's a canal that people can take shuttle boat rides on. The boats are bright yellow. Only a trip to the Sooner Mall and a pair of screaming yellow, Converse high top sneakers would get me off the boat.

As the sun started sinking, and we headed home, I remembered the plans I had made with Tesch to go to Wes Watkins Reservoir and swim. I hadn't even called to tell him my good news! My cell still sat on my dresser at home.

Cussing silently so Sarah wouldn't hear, I felt awful. I'd been so wrapped up in myself I'd forgotten my best friend. I hoped my buddy would understand.

As soon as we made it into the house, I grabbed my phone and dialed. Tesch picked up on the second ring. I quickly explained, excitement rushing the words I spilled into the receiver.

"You're kidding! Harmony!" I heard my joy and exhilaration echoed in his voice. "That's great!"

Lying on my bed with the phone cradled against the side of my head, I shared everything I had seen and felt since I woke up. I stared absently at the large yellow polka dots that were a part of my wallpaper pattern and other bits of the color sprinkled throughout my room.

A poster of the hazardous waste symbol graced my door. I chose it long ago for the symbolism, now I liked it for a whole new reason.

"Sarah made me go see Dr. Heckerman. He said he doesn't know if it's permanent." I couldn't keep the dread from my voice.

I heard Tesch take a deep breath and blow it out over the phone connection. "Harmony, no one knows what tomorrow will bring except the Goddess, and sometimes I wonder about that. Don't worry about it until the sun comes up in the morning. If it's still golden, so are you."

"And if it's not?"

"Then you pick up and go on the same way you always have but with some beautiful memories."

I forget sometimes how much older Tesch is then me. Tesch is a fresh water Siren. He spent his first fifteen years as a guppy in a pond. It takes his kind that long to learn how to shape change and breathe air.

Tesch lost his family when a farmer drained their pond and filled it in. He barely survived. He'd been made an orphan.

How he ended up here in our para-community of McLoud, Oklahoma, I'm not sure. He wouldn't talk about it. I learned not to ask. He would say the past is only as important as tomorrow needs it to be. I believed it hurt him too much to remember.

"Thanks, Tesch, for reminding me that tomorrow I will wake up and be no worse off than I have ever been one way or the other. You're the best friend I could have. I don't know what I'd do without you. I mean that." I felt the heat of a blush in my cheeks, glad he couldn't see me through the phone.

"No problem, Princess. That's what friends are for."

"I've asked you not to call me that."

Tesch used to call me princess instead of Harmony when we were little. He would walk two steps behind me and act all formal about it. I finally got him to quit between third and fourth grade. Occasionally he still slipped it in.

"Sorry, I thought we were having a moment."

"We were, but it's over now." I chuckled with the good feelings I'd enjoyed all day. "Everything is back to normal."

"Cool."

I couldn't stifle a yawn. It echoed over the receiver.

"Sorry, Tesch, but I am so wiped. It feels like a week has passed since I woke up this morning."

"Understandable. You've had one of the biggest days of your life. I'm just happy you took a moment to share it with me."

From anyone else I would have thought the words a sarcastic, smart ass way of reminding me I had forgotten to call them sooner, but I knew Tesch to be sincere. Time spent on the phone filling him in on the details of the day made up for my lapse. He only wanted my happiness.

"Tomorrow I'm yours. We'll go swimming or whatever you want."

"Sounds like a plan. But Harmony…."

"Yeah?"

"Whatever tomorrow brings, yellow sunrise or shades of gray, I'll be there for you."

"I know. That's what makes you the best friend a girl could have."

"Just don't tell anyone. You'll ruin my considerable rep with the popular pack."

"Your secret is safe. I promise." I shook my head and smiled into the phone though I knew he couldn't see it. "Good night, Tesch."

Chapter 4

Dreaming again.

It's eighth grade natural sciences class. We are watching a time elapsed movie of a flower blooming.

The flower is a rose, and I am aware of the medium golden quality. I see the deeper tones in the middle where the true life of the bud rests. Pollination is reproduction and how the seed is made. The seed is the secret.

"You are the seed." A familiar voice whispers from behind me in the darkened classroom.

I turn, and I'm in a field of golden grain. It's almost time for the harvest. The seeds were planted. The plants took root in fertile soil and now have grown to maturity.

The wind picked up, moving the wheat softly beneath my outstretched hands. Stalks moving in the breeze make an eerie murmur, like soft voices speaking in the next room. I strain to hear what they say.

"The time…. Your time….. Time is soon…. Must find…. The time…"

A figure materializes across the field. I can't make out who they are, but they wave for me to come. I begin toward the mysterious someone, but the plants around my legs are thick. They pull at me, slowing my steps.

I realize that the stalks are clinging to me, pulling against me to slow my progress. The wind is growing, and the voice of the field grows to an urgent mumble.

Not yet…. Not time…. Soon.

The figure across the field waves impatiently, urging me to hurry, but I can't move. The yellow field has tied me down. I am rooted.

I know that soon the wheat will be gathered. The harvester will fire up and the wheat mowed down. I know that what is sown must also be reaped.

Don't Fear the Reaper.

Baby, Don't Fear the Reaper.

I'm Your Man.

Music from downstairs blasted its way up and over the balustrade and into my room. Groaning, I pulled a pillow tightly over my head. Sarah's oldies music station blared, the stereo cranked up. The butt crack of dawn on Sunday means one thing, house cleaning day.

I'd bet my iPod that she had the beeswax and lemon oil out. She would be polishing the banister or have some other equally monotonous and grueling chore underway. Did I mention witches are clean freaks?

No help for it. If I didn't present myself voluntarily I would be summoned for my share of the work detail. I might as well get it over with so Tesch and I could have the afternoon to swim and...

I pulled my head out from under the pillow quickly and looked around. Spying the hazmat poster, the breath I had been holding escaped with a sigh.

Still yellow.

I looked around the rest of my room. Nothing else had changed. Still my sanctuary of messy, textured, geometric chaos with splashes of my one color. But that color remained.

I offered the Goddess a prayer of gratitude. I could still see lemons and pineapple and butternut squash the way they were meant to be seen. My feet hit the floor, and my lips curved into a wide smile. Bring on the beeswax!

Several exhausting hours, one set of dishpan hands and two sore knees later, found me sitting on the bank of the water with Tesch. Fascinated with how the autumn sun glistened on the small waves and ripples, I would have never thought there would be color in the glare.

I had escaped the ginormous list of household tasks shortly after lunch. Sarah had given time off for good behavior and special circumstances.

We had only gotten about halfway through all the things Sarah wanted done around our home. Poor Charlie stayed behind, still at it, washing the windows inside and out. After that, he got to rake leaves.

Actually, I'd volunteered for that job and had the rake firmly in hand. Seeing some of the leaves had turned golden gave me inspiration to get out there and rake with the best of them. When Tesch showed up, I had separated the piles: yellow from the still-no-color leaves. I toyed with the idea of saving them.

Sarah vetoed that and sent me on my way to the reservoir. But not before I snuck a couple up to my room for safekeeping.

"So what do you think?" Tesch had a roundabout way of asking about my feelings.

"I don't know yet. Color, yellow, is new to me. I am still trying to see everything there is to see. Part of me is scared to death it won't last. That tomorrow, or the next day or in a week, maybe a month from now, I will wake up, and it will be gone again."

"And maybe in a hundred years you'll be sick of yellow and want to go back to the way things used to be." He offered as an alternative.

"What's that supposed to mean?" The thought irritated me.

"Just a comment on the condition of being. Humans and paras alike never seem satisfied with what they have. They're either wanting more or wishing for less. Everything is either too much or not enough."

I gaped at him with an eyebrow raised. "Well aren't you full of cheery-cheery-joy."

"Sorry." He gave a heavy shrug and sighed deeply. "I guess I'm feeling insecure. If you start seeing color, any or all of them, the whole world is going to open up for you. When that happens, I foresee a big change in the status quo at good ol' McLoud High. What will you need me for?"

"Do what?"

"You heard me. Challen Parks might look a lot better to you in full color. I think he only gives you crap because deep down he likes you. You know, like little boys will pull the braids of little girls they like 'cause they don't know what else to do. And what about when you get powers? What then? Hell, I'll need you to protect me, not the other way around."

Flabbergasted, I shook my head in disbelief. Tesch couldn't be serious. I wondered if he'd been using drugs or something.

"Are you high?"

"No. Why?"

"Tesch, what you just said is wrong on so many levels. First and foremost, Challen is an idiot, a first class jerk, an asshole in any color. As far as I am concerned, he is a waste of time and space. I would never have anything to do with him for any reason I can think of."

"Second, Tesch, I can see one color, one! There is no way to know if I will ever see any more. Powers? Magik? I haven't even thought about it. I don't even know if you can have powers with one color vision."

"And if I did, I can't see me pulling off a very good illusion or glamour with just one color. What am I going to do, make myself look like a giant pencil or blend in with the side of a bus? With my luck, it would be moving and run me over."

"And last, but hardly least, Tesch, you are my friend. I appreciate that you've always looked out for me even though I know it hasn't done you any popularity favors. Even if I didn't need you by my side, I will always want you there. I can't imagine my world without you in it, and I don't want to."

The last came out in a huff. I hadn't drawn a breath during my tirade. I hadn't needed one; I'd been talking too fast.

Tesch smiled at me like he'd just won the lottery. Weird since having me for his friend couldn't be a great prize. "An asshole in any color, huh?"

His beaming from ear to pointy ear infected me with good humor.

I'd been upset with his silly ideas; his mood always affected me too. Now, order had been restored. "Yep. And he's so full of it they should have named him Colon Parks."

Laughter erupted between us. Tesch fell back into the drying grass and sand holding his side. We made a dozen other unflattering jokes about Challen and his family tree. The world turned golden again.

"Want to go for a dip?"

"Isn't that why we came?"

For anyone else, the water would have been too cold. But with Tesch as my friend, swimming anytime of the year remained possible. I stripped down to a short wet suit and put on flippers. Tesch went down to a pair of trunks.

I noticed the trim build of his natural born swimmer's body. His abs were like a washboard. His skin was smooth and almost hairless. As my eyes traveled up to his familiar, handsome face I was startled to catch his eyes on me as well. A blush heated my face, and I turned away.

Thinking about his comments from earlier, I wondered. Could Tesch have been jealous? Could he be thinking about me as more than a friend? I shook my head and dismissed the thoughts.

Tesch wore handsome in an exotic way. Me, I managed ordinary, edging toward plain. He could have a pick of much prettier girls.

"You ready?" His voice beside me, I spun to find his large almond eyes inches from mine.

"If you're waiting on me, you're going the wrong way, water boy." I could get away with that comment. That's what friends were for.

He opened his mouth to sing. His Siren's song, or one version of it, wrapped and curled around me like a warm skin. Power caressed me.

In ancient times, sea Sirens would sit on the rocks of treacherous waters and sing songs to the sailors that passed by. The songs were so alluring that many jumped ship and swam to reach the magikal voices. The sailors drowned, and the Sirens feasted on their life force. Their young would eat the flesh from the bones of their victims.

The Siren's song could be deadly. It could coerce the soul into doing anything. It could put the listener into a deep sleep, make them forget or even see things that weren't real.

But a Siren's song could also be a powerful tool of magik. When I swam with Tesch, the water was always warm. I could be under the surface for a long time and not need a breath. My vision was as clear as it is on land. His voice gave me a very special gift.

The last of the melody died away. We waded into the water until it became deep enough to plunge in the rest of the way. Tesch's feet and hands transformed into their webbed counterparts. The gills in the side of his neck opened up.

Beneath the waves, he reveled in his element. He performed some water ballet and swirled so fast a small whirlpool formed above his head. I would have applauded, but below water sound isn't the same. He finished his Baryshnikov moves and pointed to the surface.

We surfaced for a breath he didn't need. "Take a deep breath. I want to show you something, but it is way down."

"Okay." I trusted Tesch.

I huffed air the way he taught me for best oxygenation, and we dove. This time he took my hand and pulled me along at a speed I couldn't achieve on my best day. Thanks to our frequent dips I was a very strong swimmer, but in the water, Tesch made even Michael Phipps look slow. My ears popped with the pressure as we went much deeper than usual. Tesch hadn't been kidding.

Light faded, and a small shiver raced down my spine. We were farther down than I could manage to get back up on my own, even with the magikal enhancements he'd given me. Any human or air breather would need scuba gear to get this far below.

We came to a rock formation barely distinguishable in the gloom. Tesch guided me to the rocks, motioning for me to hang on to an edge. Without weights to hold me down, I would have floated away.

He opened his mouth to sing again. Did I mention sound is different underwater? Oh yeah, I did.

His song on land is soft and full of melody. In the aquatic depths, it sounded an eerie chorus that haunted and threatened to overwhelm my mind. Imagine being caught in a reverberating cyclone of sound that whispers a thousand lyrics at once.

Instinctively, I covered my ears only to have to grab at the rock again to stay put. Self-preservation told me to grip the rock with my legs and use my hands to protect my mind. Thankfully, the song ended before I lost my sanity.

A glow filled the murky water. At first I thought it surrounded my friend, and then I realize it came *from* him. Tesch filled with an inner light that illuminated the deep around us.

He dug down into the thick mud of the reservoir bottom, unearthing an old fashioned, metal tackle box. He presented it to me. My legs were still clinging to the rock, so my hands were free to accept his prize.

Opening the box if I had had a breath it would have been stolen.

The radiance of his magik reflected a treasure trove. Necklaces, rings, earrings and coins glimmered at me. Tesch had a stash of wealth.

Understanding exploded! People swam here all through the summer, year after year. Often they forgot to remove jewelry or money from pockets only to lose it in the water. They accidentally knocked or dropped things overboard from boats.

It appeared as if Tesch had been finding and collecting those lost items for the years he had lived in McLoud. I held a small fortune!

I sifted through the cache of riches with water wrinkled fingers. The precious metals and stones were hard and cold and very real. What had he been saving this for?

I'd known Tesch to do without a lot of things he would really like to have, a new iPod, a laptop, a car or concert tickets. Things our parents either couldn't afford or thought we should work for to appreciate or flat out didn't need. Tesch could have had any or all of that if he wanted and had money to spare.

He took the box from my hands and sorted through the collection of valuables. Finding what he wanted before closing the lid, he returned the container to its watery grave.

Again he took my hand to pull me along in his wake. We moved like twin torpedoes, startling fish and turtles as we went. In less than a minute, we reached the surface. With Tesch's speed propelling us, we broke from the water like dolphins at Sea World.

I had sense enough to gasp some air before splashing back down into the lake. Tesch released my hand as we fell back into the embrace of the water. I swam up and got a deeper breath. We weren't far from shore.

Under my own steam, I propelled my body toward the bank. Much slower at it, I traveled at the speed of snail compared to Tesch's lightening. Making the beach in about five minutes, I hauled my suddenly heavy body onto land.

The great thing about swimming with Tesch, the water felt warm no matter the time of year. The not so great thing was getting out. In cool or cold weather, being wet made it feel worse. In October the world was sweater and sweatshirt ready. I began to shake from the chill of damp skin.

I snatched up my beach towel and wrapped it tightly around me. We had laid a campfire before going in but hadn't lit it. I couldn't help but wish we had, but we'd have been in bad form to leave a fire unattended in a state plagued by drought.

My hands were shaking too badly to work the long grill lighter we brought to get the blaze started. I didn't hear Tesch leave the water, but then he took the plastic from my hands, making it work.

The flame caught the tinder. Dry leaves and grass smoked and smoldered before flickering to life. In a moment that felt too long, a nice fire roared.

Tesch and I sat quietly watching sparks fly into the air as darkness seeped into the sky. The days were getting shorter. The feast of Samhain loomed, only weeks away. When I no longer shivered out of my skin, I got the nerve to ask.

"Tesch, what are you doing with all that stuff you've buried? I mean, why are you hiding it? Why haven't you cashed it in or used some of it?"

"What makes you think I haven't?" He grinned mischievously at me.

"Well, because you're always broke, like me."

"I spent it all on hair gel."

His usual spiky do lay in limp waves around his neck and shoulders. When it dried, the natural curls would consume his head.

I slapped at his shoulder lightly. "Come on Tesch. Be serious."

"Hey, just because I don't wear Abercrombie and Aeropostale or have a dozen pairs of Toms doesn't mean I have no style, babe. I prefer the understated look. Grunge-punk isn't cheap."

"Okay, fine, don't tell me." I crossed my arms over my chest and pouted.

Sighing, Tesch rolled his eyes at me. "Show you one little pile of treasure and you go all girly on me. I didn't know your bottom lip could stretch out that far. Do it again."

"I can't believe you are teasing me with this." I held my sulking posture and pivoted my face away from him.

"All right, you win."

I turned back to see his face. He'd leaned back on the heels of his hands, extending long legs out before him. "I'm saving for a rainy day."

I assumed he gave me crap again and resumed my defensive position of silent scowling. When his hand touched my shoulder, I shrugged it off.

"Really, Harmony, I'm saving the stuff for a really bad day. If a time should ever come when I need to make a quick exit, get the hell out of dodge or bail myself out of a no win situation, I want to have the means."

I felt stunned. Shocked. Appalled. And ashamed.

My first thought: without Tesch my life would be truly colorless.

No shades of gray, no tones of light or hues, just flat and empty of texture or pattern. I had been seeing the colors of the world for years through his eyes. The loss of my friend would devastate me.

My second thought: the security I felt with Charlie and Sarah. I'd never had to give a second thought about surviving on my own. I'd never been without a home or a place I belonged.

Tesch had. He had lost everything that mattered once before. How selfish of me to have forgotten that. I'd been taking a lot for granted. I didn't know how to respond to the revelation.

Maybe all the color drained from my face. Maybe my silence spoke for itself. I can't say. There must have been something because the next thing I knew, he had an arm across my shoulders giving me a gentle, supportive squeeze.

"Hey, Princess, calm down. It's okay. I'm not planning to go anywhere anytime soon. We still have five more years of para high school to get through. Think of the treasure as my college fund. You never know, I might actually want to be somebody someday."

"Tesch, I am so sorry. I never thought about… I've been really stupid. You don't ever talk about before you came to McLoud. I don't know why, but I've just never thought about you leaving. I thought you were happy. Well, as happy as can be in high school…." I babbled.

He brushed a soothing hand over my brow and down the side of my face to cup my cheek. "Hush, Harmony. I know, and it's okay. I didn't mean to freak you out by showing you my emergency stash."

I drew back for a good look at him. "Why did you show me?"

"*Mi casa es su casa.*"

"Say again?"

"Harmony, you *think* I'm your only friend. I *know* that you are my only friend. I know that you would give, do or say whatever you could if I needed it."

"Of course. And you are my only friend."

"Fine, have it your way. I'm your sole source of companionship and social support. Anyway, in the spirit of true friendship, I wanted to share my resources with you. Consider it *our* emergency fund now."

"Tesch, I can't accept that. It's a fortune. It's way too much. And how long have you collected all that stuff from the bottom of the lake? Twenty years? Besides, how on earth would I ever get to it without you? I just came along for the ride today, and I know it." I gave my best protests.

"This is how."

Tesch held a necklace up to my face. This must have been what he went fishing for in the tackle box. By the light of the fire, I saw a heavy gold chain and a deep yellow gem stone in the shape of a heart. "It's a topaz."

Holding the stone between two hands cupped together. I heard Tesch singing softly to the heart. Between his fingers a light glowed through. After a minute his voice died away, and the magikal illumination subsided.

Tesch moved to place the chain over my head, but I ducked away. He raised an eyebrow at me as if to say, *'Really?'* He waited for me to move back into the circle his arms and the chain created.

Embarrassed for flinching, I leaned forward. He placed the necklace over my head. "What did you do to it?"

"A simple enchantment of discovery for what is lost or hidden. If you think about what it is you need to find and are within a hundred yards of it, the stone will do the rest."

"That's a pretty neat trick you got there aqua man. You've been holding out on me." I told him with awe and surprise.

"I am a siren, Princess. That makes me a somewhat magikal being." His smiled unashamed and unapologetic for holding back the secret.

"Don't call me princess."

"Don't call me aqua man."

"Touché."

Chapter 5

I CHOSE NOT TO SHARE my new found color vision with the majority of people. Only Charlie, Sarah, Tesch and Dr. Heckerman were in on the change of circumstance. Until the new wore off and I could be sure the change permanent, I didn't want to tell.

I remembered well that first painful year of public education when my disability had been exposed during finger painting. Kids are cruel at best and downright vicious when inspired.

Everyone else's picture had the right colors; apples coming out red, trees and grass as green, the sun being yellow in the sky. My sun rose in the sky. My trees were the appropriate amount of fluffy on a stick. What had been the big deal? They had all looked the same to me.

Challen Parks had called me a stupid alien. He told the other kids I came from another planet where the sun shone purple and trees were black with blue trunks. He called my world ugly and me too. I got teased for months, the ugly alien from planet Yuck. I know, kids' stuff, but it stays with you.

If I revealed I could see yellow and then it didn't last, they'd think I lied or had tried to get attention or something. Nothing would have been further from the truth.

A week had passed with no new color developments. But I hadn't lost anything either. Maybe soon I'd share the news, then again, maybe not.

"How's it going, Gray? Any news from Area 51?"

Think of the devil, and he will appear. I glanced up from my locker, annoyed. I really didn't feel like playing these old games anymore.

"You know, Parks, you need some new material. That bit got old by fifth grade. Someone with your brains should be able to think of something better, like cooties."

Challen leaned down into my face, growling through gritted teeth. He'd missed a speck of cereal while brushing that morning.

"Are you trying to be cute, Gray? I would think a defect like you would know better. Or do you expect your weirdo, water boyfriend to swim to your rescue again? Is this a token of his love?"

Challen reached out for my topaz heart as if to snatch it from its chain. Oh no, not happening. I grabbed his wrist with a strength and speed I hadn't realized I had.

Gritting my own teeth, I seethed at him. "You know, Challen, picking on the weak may be a wolf pack thing, I don't know. But I think it's just an excuse for you to be a butthead. I may not be able to see much color, but even I can see you for the yellow dog, coward you are, and someday everyone else will too."

What happened next boggled my senses. A surge of energy, an electrical jolt, traveled from the center of my chest and through the arm that held Challen's wrist. He must have felt it too. His eyes got big and round. I think it surprised him even more than me, and I'd been very surprised.

"What did you do?" He hissed at me. I heard fear.

Not sure what I'd done, instinct kicked in. To admit I didn't know at this point would be a weakness. Challen pounced on those he saw as weaker than him.

I pulled my heart stone out of his grip. Looking into his eyes with what I hoped mirrored his menacing glare, I whispered. "Don't touch me or mine again, Challen."

I didn't see a point to adding 'or else'. It would have made the threat seem like a joke. I wasn't joking. Not in the least.

Mr. Bellfwigg strolled by and did a double take. He hurried over to where Challen and I faced off at the lockers. "Miss Phillips, where did that dog come from? Pets are not allowed on school property."

Looking at Challen as the words came out of his mouth, I looked at Challen. And Challen looked at me.

"Uh, what dog, Mr. Bellfwigg?"

The vice-principal gave a disappointed stare. "Miss Phillips, I know your visual deficits don't allow you to see color, but I also know that your vision is otherwise perfect. Aside from the dog being yellow, you can see it as plainly as I." He indicated my tormentor with his hand.

"I'm not a dog." Challen answered, offended.

"Great Gods and Goddesses!" Mr. Bellfwigg stepped back a pace. "Mr. Parks? Is that you?"

"Of course it's me."

"What has happened here?" Mr. Bellfwigg demanded.

"What do you see?" I wondered myself what I'd done.

"A big yellow dog with its tail between its legs." My vice-principal answered.

Challen growled. He declared loudly, "I am not a dog! My tail is *not* between my legs!"

Mr. Bellfwigg's expression appeared as startled horror. "Well, I'm sorry to say, you look like one. Did you do this, Harmony?"

A crowd gathered. People were confused and murmuring excitedly. I heard students speculating.

Challen Parks is a dog. Harmony Phillips changed him into a yellow dog. A dog. Yellow. Challen! Harmony did it. How did she do it? Is she a witch? Power? When? Yellow dog.

"I think we need to take this to my office and get to the bottom of things. Harmony, uh Challen, follow me, now."

That Mr. Bellfwigg used our given names and not Miss or Mister just showed how rattled he felt. Upset myself, I dutifully fell into step behind the Brownie. Challen brought up the rear. The crowd of para kids parted like the Red Sea to let us pass.

I could hear the rumor mill grinding into high gear. Gaia only knew what it would be saying by lunch. I felt a bitter groan building. I wished I could disappear on the spot then stopped myself.

I didn't know exactly what had happened to Challen. I did say that someday everyone would see him for a yellow dog coward and wished it would happen sooner than later. It might be safer to avoid wishing. If my words and wants had any power, then suddenly turning invisible would have thrown gas all over the fire of trouble I'd created. Burn baby, burn.

Later, much later, sitting in the vice-principal's office, I scooted down in a leather seat as far as I could go and not slip off the chair all together. That invisibility thing looked better and better all the time.

When we had gotten to the office, Challen and I explained what happened. Of course, our versions were widely different.

Challen's story painted him as an innocent choir boy simply wanting a look at the interesting piece of jewelry I wore. It reminded him of a piece his dear, sweet grandmother had. Then, for no reason at all, I had accused him of trying to steal it and cursed him.

Yeah, right.

My version came out less charitable to us both but much closer to the truth. I admitted to being angry and speaking in haste, but I couldn't honestly have expected what my words had done. Mrs. Tyck had been called to examine Challen.

The story had to be repeated for her benefit. This time, instead of pulling out the Bella Donna, she reached into her pocket for a peculiar pair of spectacles. I say spectacles because these babies were never made by Lens Crafters. The lenses were adjustable, like a jeweler's. Mrs. Tyck put them on, looking Challen up and down.

Finally, she pronounced. "It's an illusion, a very powerful one. Usually, only the personal illusion of an old and/or powerful Fae is this good." She looked at me with the glasses still in place. A small smile formed on her lips as if she was seeing more than I would ever know. "You really pack a wallop, young lady. Is this your first illusion?"

"Uh, yeah." Really the best answer I had, considering I didn't know what I'd done when I did it.

"You mean everyone sees me as a damn dog?" Challen demanded.

"Mind your mouth, Mr. Parks." Bellfwigg admonished him. "And yes, it appears so. Everyone sees the glamour effect, except Miss Phillips."

"Well make her undo it!" Challen barked.

All three of them turned to me in unison. I shrugged helplessly. "I can't. I don't know how. I didn't know I could do it in the first place."

That raised another round of questions about my ability to see color and exactly how extensive my powers were. They didn't believe me about my limitations at first. The school called Charlie and Sarah. They called Challen's parents as well.

His father raised holy hell in the school principal, Mr. Oliphant's office. Mr. Challen Parks Sr. could be heard threatening to sue my parents, the school, the city and anyone else he could think of.

Charlie and Sarah offered to pay for the witch doctor or Faery godmother to lift the glamour I had accidentally cast. The problem existed due to the illusion being so good, they weren't sure it would work. Terrific. Hence my slumping dejectedly in the vice principal's office.

"We'll just see about that!" Mr. Parks' voice echoed through the school offices and doors were heard slamming. The sudden quiet in the wake of his tirade hung eerily. I flinched when the door to Bellfwigg's office opened.

Charlie and Sarah entered, followed by the Brownie vice principal. Sarah took the seat next to me. Charlie stood at my back and placed a strong hand on my shoulder for support.

Mr. Bellfwigg took his seat behind the desk. He folded his hands in contemplation. "You've caused quite a stir today, young lady. It's been suggested that you should be expelled for what you did to Challen Parks."

That brought me to the edge of my seat. "Mr. Bellfwigg! I swear I never meant to do it! It was an accident. I got angry with Challen, and it just happened. Please don't expel me!"

Mr. Bellfwigg gestured at me with palms out while telling me, "Calm down, Miss Phillips. Calm down."

Charlie's comforting hand drew me back against the leather of the chair. I settled back, anxious to hear the verdict.

My vice principal continued. "Wiser and cooler heads have

prevailed. Mr. Parks is not physically harmed. While the world perceives him as a yellow, cowardly dog for a bit, he is in fact whole and able to continue in school. However…"

Here it came.

"Since you did indeed perform magik on a classmate, you will be required to serve the customary after school detention for the next two weeks."

"Detention?" I asked incredulously. "That's it?"

"Not quite."

"What?"

"Well, obviously when you were without any type of magikal ability, your course curriculum had a certain amount of leeway. You didn't have to take Witchcraft, Sorcery, Were-Abilities or Fae Studies. Now, that needs to change accordingly."

"Your adoptive parents are more than adequate teachers for Witchcraft and Were-Abilities. We will get you the text books, and you can take them home. If you can pass the curriculum tests at the end of the year, we will call those courses done."

Okay? I dreaded where this might be going. One of the first rules of the universe Sarah taught me had been: what you send out comes back to you threefold. I'd screwed up majorly, accident or not, and let anger get the best of me. I could feel that karmic wheel turning around to run over me.

"Professor Poff has agreed to teach you Sorcery every morning from 7:15 until 8:00.   Ms. Idlewilde, as our Faery expert, will instruct you in Fae Studies from 3:30 until 4:30 each afternoon once your detention has been served."

Karma sucks. Ms. Idlewilde? Really?

I sunk back into my seat. All the wind left my sails. I would have to spend an extra hour a day with that pixie… well, I thought of a word that rhymed with witch. This had to be what death row inmates felt like.

I'm sure the news spread through the entire McLoud Public School system before we even opened the door to Mr. Bellfwigg's office to leave. Harmony Phillips could see yellow and had power, Fae power.

One bright spot in this mess, people could stop suggesting I happened in the para world by accident, a human foundling. The question about my parentage had been answered. I'd been proven to be paranormal.

If the ability to see yellow, cast an illusion and the power of that illusion were any indication, odds were in favor of my being Fae. I felt

a nervous giggle building. Me, a Faery?
 Tesch would never let me live this down.

Chapter 6

"I'm never going to let you live this down, you know."

"Shut up, and quiz me."

"I can't believe you turned Challen into a dog. That is so priceless."

I gritted my teeth and heaved a deep calming breath. "I did not turn Challen Parks into a dog. He only appears that way, big difference. He's every bit as humanoid as when he came to school yesterday."

"Yeah, maybe, but yesterday he wasn't being asked to the carnival and Halloween dance by Pit Bulls and Yorkies. He actually had a shot at a girl going with him."

Trust Tesch to point out something new in my current dilemma. Tesch and I were comfortable on the sofa in the family room. All my new school books spread out around us.

On Saturdays, the living room provided a hangout spot. However, instead of vegetating in front of the flat screen with a movie or heading to the water to swim, he'd gone over some of the school stuff with me.

In school, I had taken classes like Home Economics, Wood Shop, Human Studies and Computer Basics. In the para-community, I took what amounted to the short bus classes. That sure helped my defective self-esteem.

I had nothing wrong with my ability to learn. The para-world just protected its core secrets. The powers that be parceled information on a need-to-know basis. The folks running the show hadn't thought I needed to know.

Tesch had already taken these classes, seventh grade Were-Abilities and Fae Studies, eighth grade Witchcraft and Sorcery. Assuming I would never need them, I hadn't been given these courses. Eventually I'd have been shipped off to the human world, never to share or tell a soul what I knew, especially any particulars learned in school. Seriously?

What they did teach in our school didn't cover everything anyway. The curriculum resembled a public school's sex education plan. They taught just enough that hopefully young paras wouldn't get into trouble. The school expected parents to teach the rest. We saw how well the theory worked when looking at the teenage pregnancy rate in Oklahoma.

Gratefully, Sarah and Charlie had more than explained the birds and bees, as well as the lions, and tigers and bears and wolves.

Ironically, shape shifting and sex education had a lot of similarities. Both revolved around hormones, changing bodies and what can happen in a parked car under a full moon. They equally spelled disaster if not controlled.

"Speaking of the carnival and dance…" Tesch began.

"Were we? I thought we were discussing Challen's new status, followed by the distant second of my extra school work."

He gave me a look that said either I was slower than I looked or was being deliberately thickheaded. "Well, I am speaking of the carnival and dance."

With emphasis on the word dance, I got a funny sensation in my chest, around my heart. Suddenly, I found my fingernails amazingly tasty. I nibbled first on the index, then the thumb.

Mumbling between finger food, "Yeah, what about it?"

"Do you want to go?"

"With you?" I squeaked.

Throwing his hands up in exasperation Tesch scowled. "No, you should go with Challen Parks, the dirty, yellow dog-boy. Of course with me, I think we could have a lot of fun."

Tesch had always been my best friend. I didn't want to lose the connection we had by confusing the issues. A small voice in my head, that sounded suspiciously like Sarah, chimed in that being friends first was the best start other relationships had.

Then again, maybe I read too much into it. Tesch and I had gone to the Halloween Harvest Carnival together since grade school. Being the first year we were eligible for the dance for high school students, it seemed logical to attend together. We did everything else as a team.

"Sure. I hadn't thought about going, but if I am, it would be more fun with you rather than Challen." I covered my nerves with a little humor. "I don't like my escorts to have fleas."

"I'll be sure to get dipped before I pick you up." He shot back at me.

"Okay, if we're going, what are we going to wear? Isn't it a costume thing with a contest?" That seemed redundant in a town full of paras.

"I think it should be obvious. I'm going as a siren."

"A siren?" See what I mean about overkill.

"Yes. I think you should go as a…" Tesch cocked his head to one side, tapped a finger against his chin as if thinking hard, "a Faery Princess."

"You are so going to pay for that one." I warned. My sorcery book launched itself at his head of its own accord, honest.

"Bring it, little girl, if you got the juice." He laughed as he dodged another free-flying school text.

Friends, you can't live with 'em and can't knock 'em upside the head with your *History and Anatomy of Were Beings* book either. But that didn't mean you shouldn't try.

My Coke can hit Tesch in the chest and bounced off. He looked surprised for all of two seconds and then smiled evilly. Suddenly on the defensive, I did what I do best. I ran.

Tesch chased me around the sofa and chair group. I shrieked as he launched himself over the back of the couch to tackle me. We rolled across the rug, coming to rest behind the furniture on the floor by Charlie's big desk. His long body spread over mine, dwarfing me by comparison.

"Get off me!" I groaned.

"No. Not until you say you're sorry for hitting me with the can."

"No. You called me princess."

"You threw a book at me." He answered back.

"Not until you called me princess."

"True. But you said I had fleas."

"I did not! Now get off!" I struggled beneath him, feeling smothered. "You're squishing me, you dumb jerk! I can't breathe."

"Well, we can't have that." Tesch pinned my arms to the floor with his hands and raised his body up to straddle my waist. "There, that better?"

He'd worn a bright yellow T-shirt with Scooby Doo on it. In my honor, he'd said when he arrived bright and peppy before lunch. The shirt fit snuggly and showed off the muscles in his arms and chest.

Though he'd ceased mashing me into the floor, it didn't feel any easier to breathe. "You're still too heavy, Tesch." I panted.

"No, I'm not."

He stared at my face in a way I didn't recognize. Tesch looked like I felt when I watched a Monarch butterfly emerge from its cocoon, as if he'd seen something miraculous and wonderful.

"Tesch?" My voice pleaded. For exactly what, I couldn't say. I felt confused. What was happening here?

Tesch, my safe harbor, the one I shared all the best and worst of my days with. Sarah and Charlie were wonderful parents, but they're parents, not my confidants. Some things were not the same telling them.

I'd have been a liar though if I said I hadn't noticed Tesch was a guy, a handsome guy. I'd seen the way girls in school stared at him. Like the way I stared at him from my position on the floor.

My heart beat fast. I felt short of breath as if I'd run miles without stopping. Did I want this? Did I want things to change? Was the decision even mine?

His lips lowered toward me. I closed my eyes. Here it came, my first kiss.

Starbursts exploded behind my lids before his mouth touched mine. A jolt of something I had no name for coursed through my body. Pain speared me.

"Tesch!" I screamed his name as my spine bowed, ready for an arrow. My eyes came open for a staggering minute.

A blast of power threw him back against the heavy oak desk, rattling the drawers and toppling the lamp. I heard the distinct pop of the bulb as my eyes sealed shut again in opposition to the tempest raging in my chest, threatening to crack it open.

I felt as if I'd swallowed an animal of some type. One with teeth and claws and fur, definitely fur because it rubbed in my throat, itchy and dry. The animal wanted out! It was set to come through my ribs and stomach!

Oh stars, it hurt. It burned! I was dying. I knew it. No one could survive this kind of torture. I fought just to breathe, to last another minute.

I heard Tesch calling my name, but I was unable to answer him. He shouted for help from Charlie.

Charlie came running. I heard the pounding footsteps against the hardwood. Sarah came too. Her tread lighter, but no less quick. My eyes were still tightly closed against the agony, but I felt their presence, smelled their scents.

"Oh my, Goddess!" Sarah's horrified whisper reached me. "Charlie, is she…?"

Am I what?

I wanted to shriek, but it came out a growl that grew to a scream. The kind of scream heard on a dark night in the middle of the wild, a screech to make small animals shiver and run for cover.

"I don't know, but I think so." Charlie agreed.

The stress in his voice reverberated down my back bone. I convulsed against the floor boards.

"But how is that possible?" Sarah's voice was etched with worry.

"Harmony! Harmony! Kitten? Can you hear me?"

Another wave of pain hit me, and a mournful cry escaped my throat. The best I could manage under the circumstances.

"Kitten, don't fight it. Fighting only makes it worse." Charlie coaxed me.

How the hell would he know? He couldn't know how badly I hurt? Couldn't he see I'd been poisoned or something. Call an ambulance for cripe's sakes!

As I writhed on the floor praying for an end to my existence, Charlie barked orders. "Tesch, close all the doors and windows. Seal up any way she could escape. Sarah, honey, I think it's time some of those chickens of yours served a higher purpose. Get a few and bring them in here."

"Should I wring their necks?"

"No. This first time we need to let instinct take its course."

The individual scents of water and rosemary drifted away as Tesch and Sarah went to follow Charlie's weird instructions. I might have understood under different circumstances, but I'd become a little preoccupied with getting ripped apart from the inside out.

My neck arched with another inhuman cry. My adoptive father knelt beside me. He took my hand in his. I gripped the lifeline to sanity.

"Kitten, listen to me. Listen to my voice. I don't know how, but you are shifting; shape changing."

He had to be mistaken or crazy! I couldn't be a Were-anything. I showed freaking Faery power. I saw yellow and accidentally cast illusions. That's it! That's all!

Charlie spoke to me again. "I know it hurts. The first time is hell. If you fight it, it hurts more and takes longer. When the next wave comes, don't try to get over it, ride it. Let the tide carry you where it wants to go."

His voice stayed calm and controlled, but I could smell his fear. The pain liked the scent. I rolled onto all fours, still gripping his hand in mine. My eyes opened to a new world.

Everything appeared sharper and more defined, at least up close. I saw shades of gold in Charlie's hair and a deeper color in his beard; like each individual strand had been outlined in light. I could have grabbed a single strand easily, getting the one I meant to snatch.

Dust motes in the air were vivid, a sunbeam coming through the window highlighting their dance. I'd like to pounce on them, but the idea was abruptly cut short as another spasm waylaid me.

I curled into a protective ball, still grasping Charlie's hand. When would this torment end?

"Breathe, Kitten. Don't fight. Take deep, even breaths."

I looked up at him from my misery. Tears leaked down my cheeks. It would have been a waste of energy to try to stop them.

I focused on Charlie. He took breaths with me, coaching me in some bizarre version of Lamaze. The ache in my center peaked again. I breathed.

Time split into short parcels of pain and breathing. My skin moved on its own, in ways I hadn't known it could. I breathed.

Sharp, lethal claws erupted from my fingertips with searing torture. I punctured Charlie's skin with my grip and breathed.

Life became reduced to nanoseconds of hell and sucking wind.

Sarah and Tesch returned together. She carried a couple of clucking hostages. They watched me with looks of wonder and dismay. I breathed.

Heat built in my core. I started panting. I couldn't help it. Something came, changed, and grew inside me! No human could achieve the shriek that tore from my throat as my body shivered violently and broke apart.

Some residual affection for the beings in the room had me slinking away from them. Instinct said hide. The predator observed for signs of weakness.

"She's beautiful." The young male's voice startled me. I hissed in his direction.

"Yes, she is." The older, bleeding man agreed.

"I've never seen a first shift." The female sniffed. Her eyes watered copiously. "I didn't realize it was so awful for you."

The one with the bloody hand put an arm around her, perhaps protecting her from me. He smelled familiar in a way the other two didn't, kindred to me. I didn't want to hurt him, but I would if I had to.

"Let's back out slowly, now. Let the birds out then leave. Her kind is a solitary hunter." The dominant male instructed them.

Good. I wanted them gone. I growled and shrieked again.

They backed away. The young one never took his eyes from me. That's okay. I watched him go too. One threatening move and I'd pounce on him and tear him to shreds.

"What kind of Were is she, Charlie?"

"A rare one; it seems Harmony is a Werelynx. I've heard of them, but she's the first I've ever seen."

The older male moved last, backing out of the room. He tossed two white birds at me as he closed the door. From then, I no longer cared or thought. The birds were squawking and running. The chase began.

Chapter 7

RECENTLY, MY LIFE HAD become a series of rude awakenings. That morning didn't break the trend.

I opened my eyes to find myself face down on the Oriental rug in the den. That would have been odd enough alone, but there were some other, more distressing, glaring peculiarities.

Why did it look like a cyclone had hit the room? Furniture had been turned over. The upholstery had been ripped to pieces. There were even claw marks scarring the walls. Unless I missed my guess, chicken feathers were mixed into the chaos.

My body felt like it'd been beaten. I noticed soreness in places I didn't even know I had. And certainly not the least of my concerns; how had I become buck naked except for a quilt spread over me?

Goddess, what had happened?

I rose up from the floor on my hands and knees to feel something mushy beneath my palm. Peering at the mess, what I saw didn't make a bit of sense. Nothing did just then.

My mind slowly grasped what my eyes saw. A dead chicken lay close to me; its entrails were the gushy stuff I had stuck my hand in.

Oh, how gross!

My stomach rebelled. I threw a hand over my mouth to hold back the tide. It took several swallows of saliva and bitter bile to save myself further misery. The stubborn nausea decided to wait just behind my breast bone.

With all the chaos and confusion and general nastiness around me, it took a bit to realize I saw something else new. Blood; I saw blood.

How could I know? Because of the chicken guts. The inside of the animal contains blood. The deep, dark color stained the rug. Brighter splashes were on the walls.

I scuttled back from the realization in disgust. Falling painfully back on something the size and shape of a large brick, I reached beneath my butt and drug it out from under me.

History and Anatomy of Were Beings had seen better days. Half the pages were torn to shreds. The cover hung loosely from the spine.

I wondered if there was anything on the Werelynx in the book, and it hit me. I remembered everything.

The nausea that had waited patiently for my brain to catch up to my stomach surged forward. I vomited all over the rug right next to the half-eaten chicken.

I didn't want to remember any more than that. Puking up the rest of the chicken would forever remain a low point in my life. Before I could finish regurgitating, Sarah came to my side. I didn't hear her.

She placed a cool cloth on the back of my neck and crooned nonsense sounds at me. Interspersed were comfort words like "There, there." And "It's okay." Or "It will be all right, Harmony."

We wound up with her sitting in the last chair standing, Charlie's dilapidated recliner, with my head in her lap while I sobbed. She allowed me to have at it.

When I had been reduced to nothing more than anguish and hiccups, Sarah raised my face, so I could see her properly. A long thick braid of hair, the color of blood, draped over her shoulder. I reached out to touch it and saw dried flakes of a deeper shade on my hand.

I snatched my fingers back and hid my face against her knees. This time she had to use two hands to make me look at her.

"It's red, Harmony; just another color and nothing to be ashamed of."

"Oh, Sarah!" I protested. "I was an animal. Look what I've done."

"Like you could help it?" She chided me. "You couldn't have changed it even if we had known. Charlie says the first time is always the worst. I'm only sorry for the pain you went through. I couldn't care less about the furniture."

She smoothed her hands over my cheeks, wiping away the last of my tears. "I told you Gaia might not be through honoring you. Sometimes her gifts are a mixed blessing."

"This is a curse."

"No, honey, it's not a curse. It could be a test. It might be something you need in the future. We never know what the Fates have in store for us. But I do know that they provide the tools needed to get the job done even if we can't see it that way at the time."

"What am I supposed to do?" The question loomed much bigger than the answer I got.

"For right now, I think you're supposed to pick yourself up off this floor, go upstairs and get in a hot shower. When you feel a bit more like yourself, I want you to come downstairs and talk with me and Charlie."

I can't say I had any better plan, so I went with hers. Nodding agreement, I pulled the quilt tight around me and climbed to my feet. Funny how a simple thing like standing up and walking forward on two legs instead of four can provide a small sense of normalcy.

As Sarah suggested, I went upstairs for a long, needed shower. Scrubbing away all the evidence of my evolution and its consequences made me feel much better. For a while I stood under the spray and tried not to think.

When allowed, my thoughts turned to Tesch. How could I ever look him in the face again? We were having a boy-girl moment then I went Were on him?

Perfect. Just freaking perfect. I couldn't even get my first kiss like a regular para girl. At least I thought I'd been about to have my first kiss. For all the romance I knew, Tesch had planned to blow a raspberry on my cheek.

Squeaky clean, dressed in my favorite comfort clothes and moodier than a stomped on cat, I showed my face downstairs. I felt extremely grateful that I either missed breakfast or my parents decided to skip it.

I didn't think I could have handled bacon and eggs that morning, especially eggs. I did know that anything that clucked, had feathers or laid eggs would be off my menu, indefinitely. I seriously considered becoming a vegan.

I stopped by the fridge on my way to the breakfast table for a can of Sprite and popped the top. On TV people were always given 7-up or something like it when they were nauseous. Plus, this morning's thirst nearly overwhelmed me. I swallowed half the can without a breath.

I plopped down in the breakfast nook in a sullen fashion. I *so* didn't want to do this.

Reminded of "The Talk" Sarah and I had when I started my periods, this felt almost as awkward and invasive of privacy, maybe worse. When I started having the curse, no one had to explain to me about eating live chickens. I avoided eye contact with either of them, too embarrassed.

Charlie had once told me that the first shifts for Weres were brought on by a powerful emotion and/or hormones, a chemical reaction. Natural Weres weren't tied to the moon the way movies portrayed.

Sure, there are human were-wolves that are affected by the moon, but that's a magikal malady or a curse. Born Weres shift only when they are deeply and emotionally affected by anger, grief, fear, lust or because they want to. Their hormones go all wonky, mimicking the fight or flight reaction, and they change.

I hadn't been mad when I shifted. I wasn't sad or grieving. I didn't think Tesch would hurt me. By process of elimination, any reasonably intelligent person could figure it out. Sarah and Charlie weren't stupid people.

Charlie broke the silence first. "I don't think we should tell anyone what happened here yesterday."

"Fine with me." Surprised at his attitude, I quickly agreed, no problem. "I'm all for it. We'll just clean up the mess, forget it ever happened and not mention it again."

Things were looking up. I thought I felt a smile coming on.

"That's not what we meant, Harmony." My adoptive father gave me a look that read half stern, half sorrow.

Dang it! My smile faded, defeated by the look on Charlie's face.

"Okay." I said, drawing out the sound, cautious now.

"After Tesch left, Charlie and I had a long discussion last night, Harmony. He explained why you might have, uh, what you might have been experiencing just before you shifted. Really, that's not our biggest concern."

My cheeks heated. I couldn't think of anything more embarrassing than the moment I lived in.

"Then what is? Honestly, I'm confused."

Charlie was a Werelion. He had always made changing sound like a very natural experience and nothing to be ashamed of. His voice would get sentimental telling about his glory days of shifting before the magikal castration occurred. I knew he missed it.

"Look at the bigger picture, Kitten."

Admittedly, I'd been blindsided. But what's the big deal, beyond that I have a thing for my best friend? My muddled thoughts must have read on my face. Charlie sighed with frustration.

"You're Fae, Harmony. The glamour you cast at school was a solid piece of yellow Fae magik. I can't do illusions. Even Sarah, before they took her powers, couldn't do that kind of illusion. Only a powerful Faery can."

"Now you're a Werelynx, too? Shifting is a red spectrum magik, Harmony; a very specific one. The strongest of the pure Fae cannot change their form. They can make the world see something else, but there's no actual physical difference."

That big picture came into focus, and it didn't look pretty. I reached for my can of Sprite. My mouth had gone bone dry. The name Sancrenath Lyspladadas rang a bell of terror. If the Council would execute people for marrying cross spectrum to prevent offspring, imagine what they would do to the actual offspring!

"Holy crap!" I blurted out. "The Council will kill me! Execute me!"

For once, Sarah didn't chastise me about bad language. The situation called for a bit of cursing. And I hadn't thought things could get worse.

I panicked. Trembling started inside my body. I shook so hard my teeth rattled. All my warmth leached away. Hyperventilating, my insides started to slide, and fur rubbed my throat again.

Charlie and Sarah were at my side in a wink. They wrapped their arms around me, holding my body together when it would have surely vibrated apart. Body heat from my parents soaked into my skin, keeping my blood liquid and flowing. Otherwise it would have frozen in my veins.

"What am I going to do? What if they find out?" I glanced from one worried face to the other.

"First thing, Kitten, you have to calm down. Sarah and I are here for you, always. We're going to protect you, help you get control. We're your parents, by fate or accident, and we love you."

"Charlie is right, sweetheart. We've been up all night thinking and talking about this. That we are a cross spectrum couple is probably the best situation you could be in. We can see your side and the challenges you're going to have. We'll help you through this."

"What about Tesch? He knows! What if he accidentally tells someone?"

I knew my friend. He would never hurt me on purpose, but everyone messed up sometimes. Look at what I'd done to Challen Parks by accident.

"Tesch heard a lot of our discussion before he left. He handled it surprisingly well. He's a very mature young man. He understood before we did what you're having cross spectrum powers could mean. He swore himself to secrecy." Charlie gave me a faint smile of encouragement.

"We just have to be cautious for now." Sarah chimed in. "Charlie is going to guide you through the shifting parts. Your animal, and his, are both feline. That's a plus. Finding out as much as you can about the lynx and its habits will be one thing to do. And I am going to start teaching you witchcraft at home."

"But I don't see green." Witchcraft magik is a natural power. The source behind the craft is green.

Sarah gave me a look I couldn't read. "You don't see green, *yet*."

"Yet!" I squeaked. I felt another round of rational panic coming on. It felt perfectly rational to be terrified as my problems multiplied.

"Calm down, Harmony. Get a breath and think. Don't let fear rule your mind and freeze your instincts. That's a big part of control for any kind of magik." Sarah recommended.

"Kitten, when you started seeing yellow, we didn't think about you having power with one color."

"We feel responsible." Sarah elaborated. "We were so happy for you that we didn't think about teaching you. You have to admit, it's all new to us too."

"You couldn't have known." I defended them to themselves.

"No, but we could have assumed the Fae power with yellow color vision. We didn't help the situation. A parent's job is to prepare their child for the curve balls life throws at them. We didn't think to even warn you. We're sorry for that." Charlie added.

"But now you have two colors and two powers. What if you see more and get the talents that come with them?" Sarah suggested.

"That's impossible." I argued.

She smiled in a way mother's have that makes the child feel she really does have all the answers, even when she doesn't. "If magik taught me anything, Harmony, it's that there's no such thing as impossible."

I absorbed at a snail's pace. I managed to swallow and nod, yes, yes, true. They were giving me good advice. I couldn't imagine the moving forward part. I didn't want to think about developing another color or talent.

Something Charlie said earlier stumbled around in my head like a drunk fumbling for his keys. I need that key, control. A certain resolve formed inside of me.

Cold iron will poison a Fae. Silver could kill a Were. I needed titanium control as my goal.

I sat up taller in my seat. "When do we start?"

They straightened away from me, no longer holding me together for my own sake. Charlie remained on the bench to my right. Sarah stood to my left.

"Today. I am taking you into the woods, and we are going to work on you changing at will and try your hand at partial shifting."

Charlie's face stretched into a warm, satisfied grin. Sarah smiled gently, if sadly around the edges, as if she could sense my childhood slipping away from me.

I looked into her eyes. They were still shades of nothing to me, but the tears she blinked away meant everything. They said she loved me, had chosen me and she would protect me with all she had. It's the look a woman has only for her child.

I got up and gave her what she deserved. Folding her into a strong hug, I kissed a cheek that smelled of rosemary and good earth. My voice came out in a choked whisper.

"I love you."

Chapter 8

CHARLIE SWORE I DID GREAT my first time in the woods. I felt it could have gone better. Patience may be a virtue, but it's not one of mine.

We started simple. He wanted me to call my beast.

This involved a lot of visualization of the red aura inside my head and shaping it into the form of the lynx then swallowing the image whole. Who would have thought just concentrating could cause me to break a sweat?

The hardest part was stopping my inner kitty cat from clawing its way back out of my throat. That's what Charlie meant by control. My throat became raw by the third try.

It didn't hurt as much as before. My new self-appointed coach said that once my body had made the change, a neural map and genetic code locked into place. My cells knew the form and didn't fight so hard against it. It compared to blowing up a balloon for the second time; the latex had already been stretched and expands into shape, making it easier the next time.

After the last near shift I found myself panting and needing a break. "Can we have a water break, Charlie? I'm feeling two quarts low."

"Sure, Kitten. Dehydration is a side effect." He pulled off his backpack and opened it. "Heads up."

He fired bottled water at my head, channeling Cal Ripken Jr. I caught it easily in the air before my nose. "Hey? What are you trying to do, kill me?"

"No, I was testing your reflexes. Cats, any cat, have good response times. But predatory cats have almost lightening quick reactions. You'll be able to climb, jump and land on your feet better than most."

"What about running?"

"Sorry, Kitten. With the exception of cheetahs, most cats aren't runners. We stalk and pounce. You're night vision will be better than a human. You're hearing too."

"Charlie, we've been out here a while and you haven't had me shift even once. Why?"

He remained quiet for a long time before answering. "Harmony, usually a young Were will shift with a parent the first few times for a reason. The mom or dad is the same type of animal. They can change with their child. They can keep up with them, communicate with them in Were form. I can't do that for you, sweetie."

I didn't quite understand. "You mean they can talk to them in their head?"

He chuckled wistfully. "I wish. No, it's not like that."

I could see him searching his own mind for a way to explain. "Do you remember how you thought and felt last night as a lynx?"

"Sort of. My thoughts were very basic. Safety. Threat. Food. Chase."

"Exactly. In a completely shifted body, we don't think like people. We are, for the time being, animals, with the simple animal needs to protect ourselves, our young if we have them and to hunt for food, shelter and water."

"But we can communicate with our own kind the way wild species do. It comes out as a series of growls, nips and necessary slaps. A parent lioness teaches her young how to hunt, stalk and survive like that, but instinct and nature have a lot to do with it."

"Okay. I'm with you so far."

"As a lion, if I could change with you, my communication skills with a lynx wouldn't work. You'd see me as a larger predator and a threat. We would either fight or you'd run and hide. I couldn't control you or the instincts."

"As a man, it's pretty much the same thing, except you could disappear, and I'd never find you until you shifted back and came home."

A light dawned. "And if I did that at the wrong place and time, the cat would be out of the bag for sure."

"Right." Charlie gave me a weak smile. "I'm sorry. I can help you with a lot, but not everything. I would if I could."

"I know. We are both doing our best here."

"And there's one other thing to think about."

I took a deep drink from my bottled water. "What now?"

"This is Oklahoma, Harmony."

"Yeah, so?"

"It's still legal here to shoot and kill bobcats."

"I thought I was immune to lead? Only silver shot can kill a Were."

"In Were form, that's true, but it still hurts like hell. Trust me. You don't want to test the theory."

Great! As if I didn't have enough stress on my plate. Now I had to worry about gun happy rednecks taking potshots at me if I shifted.

We practiced a long time. Once I had basic control of a transformation, Charlie wanted to add other factors to the mix like anger, fear and other things that might stress me into shifting accidentally.

I discovered Charlie had hidden talent for ticking people off. He would get me to thinking about things that made me mad or sad, then throw out blame on me or make some smart aleck comment that would get me seeing red in a bad way.

The last time, he made some particularly nasty comments about Tesch; I almost lost it and changed all the way. A warning scream that raised the hairs on both our necks echoed through the wooded area we stood in. Birds quieted, and nature paused in fear.

"I think that's enough for today. We are both tired, and I think the exhaustion is hurting your ability to hold it back." Charlie suggested wisely.

"Yeah, right." I growled, still on the edge.

"Enough, Harmony. Let it go. The lesson is over for today."

"That's easy for you to say when you've been provoking me for the past hour."

Charlie came over and took me by the shoulders, gently but firmly. He took in a deep breath and blew it out, trying to calm himself and me. He repeated the technique over and over until I breathed with him.

The red energy drained away. The lynx slipped into a deeper part of my consciousness. "I'm sorry, Charlie. I didn't mean to snap at you."

"No, it's my fault. I'm just not used to my Kitten having claws. I need to remember that from now on." He gave me a hug. We started walking out of the woods toward the car.

"Is it normal, I mean paranormal, for it to be this hard?"

He laughed for real that time. His arm slung over my shoulder comfortably.

"Oh yeah. The first time my father took me out, we almost killed each other in lion form. He called me a weakling cub not worthy of being king of the beasts. He didn't mean it, but it made me so mad I shifted and pounced on him."

"Remember what I said about lead bullets hurting? My mother ended up shooting us both in the butt to break up the fight."

"She didn't!"

"Yes, she did. She considered it as giving us both the spanking we deserved for acting like idiot children."

"Do you miss them?" Charlie had no trouble figuring out I meant his parents.

"Every day." He smiled, chagrined. "I love them, but I love Sarah more. I made a choice, Harmony, to be true to my own heart. I'm sorry they couldn't see that and be happy for me, but parents aren't perfect people any more than their children."

"Well, I think you're perfect. I want to be like you."

He stopped walking, turning me to face him, serious eyes searched mine. "No, I'm not perfect. Perfect people are only perfect because they are blind to their own mistakes. I make mistakes as a man and a parent. You will too. Try to learn from it when you do."

"Sure, Charlie, whatever you say." I agreed.

He didn't look entirely happy with my response. We were having a moment. He tried to share something important with me but wasn't sure I understood.

"Just do the best you can with what you've got. Okay?"

"Okay."

We headed home into the gloaming. The sun set and I could see more of it, shades of lemon and gold and now the pale reds. Where the colors touched there was a haziness I couldn't name. It wasn't a color but a void. Something should have been in-between. The sky remained an unfinished painting for me.

Charlie and I both jumped into eating the feast Sarah had made as soon as we came through the door. Corn on the cob, fried potatoes, beans and cornbread were on the table. She'd made a fresh garden salad, and the ripe cherry tomatoes were beautiful.

I couldn't say how appreciative I felt that she didn't put any meat on the table that night. I wasn't quite ready for that. When my belly felt about to rupture, I asked to be excused for the night, exhausted.

The next day I had my first early class with Professor Poff. I'd have been worried about what to expect, but I couldn't summon the energy. I sank into the mattress like a stone in a pond, down, down, down.

Dreaming again.

I went back to the wheat field, but this time as a lynx. I crawled through the stalks on wide paws made for spreading on the top of snow. They worked fine on dry earth too.

I kept low and silent. Another moved in the wheat. It made faint noises as it stepped on the dried shoots of grain. Was it prey or predator?

A voice whispered on the wind. So soft, I couldn't tell if male or female.

'Harmony, come to me, child. Come now. Find me, and I can answer your questions, daughter. I can protect you, Harmony. You will forever be safe with me.'

I wanted to believe that voice and its seductive promise. Not in the romantic way. But to be safe, to have all the mysteries solved and no more doubts.

I began to prowl through the tall blades in the direction the voice came from. I saw eyes reflecting at me an instant before the weight of another lynx pounced, larger than me. We rolled across the field.

My instinct to fight, to claw and bite surfaced, but as soon as the bigger cat threw me off course, it drew back. The other lynx crouched and waited, watching me with bright eyes.

'Harmony, child, I feel you. Come to me.' The voice on the wind called again. I turned to the direction of the sound. If the other cat didn't want to fight then I would move on.

I'd only gone a few paces when the bigger lynx pounced and rolled me again. The dance repeated as before.

I scented the other cat as female. This time she set herself between me and the direction I wished to go, blocking my path. I rose to my feet, making the decision to go around, but as I moved, she moved. She sent me a screaming hiss.

The voice had gone from the wind, and my desire to follow it left. I turned and slunk away into the wheat the way I had come. The other lynx let me go, giving a mournful cry as I walked away. The cat's call sounded sorrowful, so regretful. I would have cried if these eyes could form tears of emotion.

I awoke to tears on my pillow and the shrill clang of my brass bell alarm. The pitiful sound of the she-lynx still rang in my ears. I felt lost and lonely, and I knew they weren't my feelings but hers.

The sun barely breached the horizon. For a moment I wondered why I set my alarm so early, and then remembered. I had to get ready for my first class with McLoud Public's resident wizard.

Say the word wizard or sorcerer in the normal world and most people imagine the character Professor Dumbledore from *Harry Potter*, or maybe the actor Christopher Lloyd in the movie *Pagemaster*. They almost always thought of tall pointed hats with arcane symbols and flowing robes and wands.

Professor Poff must have missed the day they discussed dress code for sorcerers. He had the long hair and beard, but any similarities ended right there. Professor Poff had really enjoyed the sixties. I mean *really* enjoyed them.

He wore Bermuda shorts or bell bottom jeans with flower patterned shirts and Huarache sandals year-round, even in the snow. He had beaded necklaces hanging around his neck and a pair of round glasses permanently perched at the end of a long, hawkish nose. Think of John Lennon as a school teacher and you had Professor Poff.

Students rumored he never gave tests. His classroom demonstrations had a fifty percent chance of backfiring. Of course all the slacker students loved him.

When I arrived at his classroom, I found him kicked back behind the desk with his feet up. His head hung back and his mouth wide open with a snore.

"Professor Poff." I ventured in a normal voice. It didn't disturb his sleep at all. I added some volume. "Professor Poff!"

"What!" he yelled back.

"I'm Harmony Phillips. I'm here for some extra lessons, sir."

"I know. So?"

"So, you're supposed to teach me." I added perturbed.

"No, I'm supposed to be sleeping at this ungodly hour, but instead I am going to show you some stuff about sorcery." His head came up, while staring at me over the rim of his shades, his gaze assessing. I wanted to squirm under the weight of his stare.

"What have they sent me to work with, hmmm?" He sat up at the desk, eyes never leaving me. Finally he stood, walking around, sizing me up from all angles. "I sense a lot of latent talent in you, Harmony. The question is…a talent for what?"

"I don't know what you mean."

The Professor strode to a work table that resembled a science experiment in full swing. A small brass samovar heated over an open flame. I could see the yellows and reds as it burned.

"Yoko!" the sorcerer called. A raven flew to his shoulder. The bird had been on a perch in the corner, so still and quiet I had thought it stuffed.

My teacher whispered soft words to the bird I couldn't make out. It gave him a gentle caw in return before hopping to a shelf, retrieving a small cloth bag. The bird winged it back to its master, dropping the pouch into a waiting hand.

"Good girl." Professor Poff crooned and stroked her beak. With his back to me, he took ingredients from the pouch and mixed them into the urn over the burner.

Finally, he brought back two cups, handing one to me. "Here, drink this."

"What is it?" My tone suspicious at best.

"Turkish coffee, I can't abide the Arabica stuff they have in the teacher's lounge." He still held the mug out to me. "Did you think it a potion?"

My body language communicated my doubts.

"Really kid, I don't know you well enough to want to poison you yet. I usually save curses and jinxes for the kids in my second year class. Here, try it."

He offered me the mug again, and I took it. A small sip revealed the brew strong and bitter but not nasty. I tried a bigger swallow. He seemed satisfied and took a healthy swill from his own.

"Ahhhhhh. Okay, better. Give me a few more drinks and I'll be able to think straight."

Professor Poff resumed his seat behind the desk, gesturing for me to take one across from him in a standard student desk. Once planted with my coffee, he inquired. "Tell me a bit about you. Is it true you turned that dung heap Challen into a yellow dog? That's some pretty impressive casting."

"I didn't turn him into a dog." I explained. "It's an illusion. I just said that someday people would see him for the yellow, dog coward he is and now they do. But I didn't change his form."

I detected a smile behind Poff's bushy facial hair. "Awesome. Brilliant. So you're Fae then. You can do glamour and illusion."

"Yes. And no."

"Come again?"

"Yes, it seems I'm Fae. And no, I can't do glamour and illusion, at least not on purpose. It's a new power for me."

"New power? How old are you, kid? Did you just hatch or something?"

"I'm twenty-two, Professor. And no, I didn't hatch, just or at any time. But until recently, I was colorblind."

He dropped his mug as if I'd said a very dirty word, one he hadn't heard before. Coffee spread over a stack of papers. He didn't appear to notice or care.

"You're *that* kid?" His shock wore off. A weird jubilance extended across his features. He seemed genuinely tickled by the situation. "Oh, wow. Ain't that a kick in the pants?"

"I want you to know I voted for you. Some of the other teachers, the ones with sticks up their uh...hind parts, said you shouldn't be allowed in certain classes, but I was like, hey, the more the merrier. What's the big deal? The kid already lives in our world. It isn't like she won't know what's going on around her. What have we got to hide? And now, here you are anyway. Wow! That's freaking awesome."

Professor Poff's coffee kicked in. He acted as wired as an electrical socket.

"What vote?"

"Oh, when you started in the junior high, man. They had a powwow about you being, like, colorblind and not fit to go to school with other paranormals and shi...uh, stuff like that. I thought it all a crock, personally."

"Since we are a public school, they couldn't keep you out, I told them. But there was a vote to teach you the same as the other kids or modify your curriculum. I voted for you to get the same education as any other para brat. Separate but equal isn't equal at all. We learned that with Dr. King, baby."

"We lost the vote, but here you are at last. You made it anyway. That's cool."

"Who voted for me?" I wanted to know who I might count among friends, or at least supporters.

"Ah, man, that's ancient history for me now. Let me think. There was me, Bellfwigg, Tyck, Ursula Ashmore, the astronomy and calculus teacher, she's a Werebear. And there was Mr. Hemet, he used to be the shop teacher, but he retired last year."

I remembered Mr. Hemet. He'd always been kind and helpful. Mr. Hemet had been a selkie and had retired to go live by the sea with his family. I used to wonder how a selkie ended up so far away from the ocean and how he became so good with his hands.

"Anyone else?"

"Not that I can remember right now. But hey, it's all good now. They couldn't oppress you, little sister. They couldn't keep you down. Great! Let's get started."

I would have liked to ask more about that meeting, but once the professor decided to get down to business and teach he did it with rapid fire facts and practices.

"All due respect to witches and their harm ye none program, but they tie all their magik up with the natural aspect. Don't get me wrong, I object to human sacrifice too. But I don't consider toads, lizards, bats and birds a karma forbidden sacrifice."

The crow in the corner commenced to cawing and clicking in protest of his statement. Professor Poff sighed. "Not you, Yoko. I've told you that a hundred times." To me he whispered, "She gets so testy sometimes."

"A drop or two of blood from the right kind of donor ads kick to a spell. Move up the food chain and you amp up the power level."

I knew that was good information to have even if I never used it. I couldn't imagine any situation where I would willingly spill the blood of another living creature.

"Have you figured out the tie that binds us all yet?" Professor Poff asked as he showed me the proper way to grind snake tongue for a spell to find out a liar.

"Excuse me?" I had gotten used to him jumping from subject to subject in just the last forty minutes I'd known him.

"The tie that binds? The one thing all paras, no matter what their brand of power, have in common."

"Besides that we're all magikal?"

"Yes, besides the obvious." He shook his head at me. "That is your assignment to pass this course with me. You'll come in each day and learn something, yes, but your priority is to answer my question. What is the common thread of all paranormal species besides that we're all creatures of the mystical?"

In the distance, the first bell of the day rang, signaling 8:00 a.m. "Okay, We're done for now. Come back tomorrow and bring some doughnuts. I'll make the coffee."

I packed up my book and headed for my locker, thinking about the question. What did all paras have in common besides magik? I'd have to ask Charlie and Sarah what they thought. But one way or another, I'd have to answer the question to get a passing grade from Professor Poff.

Chapter 9

I'D SERVED A WEEK of detention and had a week of early morning classes with Professor Poff. Challen Parks returned to school. Everyone saw him as his usual butthead self again.

Dreading the moment when we would be face to face, I expected a tirade, an avalanche of scorn, maybe a few missing fingers from a well-timed locker slam. So it delivered an anticlimactic shock when Challen passed by with a curt nod. His eyes were wary. He kept his physical distance.

Tesch came up to my side on the way to my next class. He'd witnessed Challen's avoidance. "I see your number one fan is back in school. Just in time for the holiday break. Go figure."

Our school took Halloween off. With so many witches among the population that kept their sabots that night, half the school wouldn't show up anyway, so no school on Wednesday, Thursday or Friday.

From Wednesday through Saturday, a carnival would be in town. They came every year before heading for their winter camp. Thursday night we would have a dance.

"So do you have your costume ready yet?" Tesch asked with a lopsided grin.

I nudged him with my shoulder as we walked side by side. "Sarah and I have almost finished it, just some hems to baste and sequins to place. What about you?"

"I got it going on! I told you, I'm going as a siren." Tesch teased.

"Okay, fine, don't share."

He smiled in superior fashion. "By the way, I'll be picking you up in style for the dance."

"Oh really?"

"Yes. I cashed in some of our stash. Just a little and bought a truck."

"A truck?" I had a hard time seeing Tesch behind the wheel of anything with more horsepower than a skateboard. I mean, he occasionally drove Mr. Wight's ancient Ford to school, since the man had a city vehicle to drive for work, but only now and then. I didn't think he had a legal license and said so.

"Uh, I don't, yet. Old man Wight is taking me over to Shawnee tomorrow afternoon to get one. I've been studying the manual, getting ready for the test."

"Still, a truck? I would have thought you'd be more of a, I don't know, Honda or Nissan kind of guy."

He slapped a hand over his heart, acting as if mortally wounded. "Are you implying that I am not macho enough to drive a truck? That I don't have the, uh, gear shift and fuzzy dice to handle it?"

"Ew! I can't believe you just said that, Tesch! Don't be gross."

"You started it."

"Did not! I meant that you don't spit tobacco or know all the words to the latest Blake Shelton song."

"Oh, well. Then you're right. I'm not a truck guy by your standards. Be that as it may, I have bought one and I am getting a license and I will be picking you up in it Friday night for the dance.""You know, we live in a town that isn't even five miles wide. The biggest things we have are Dollar General and the farmer's market."

"Don't forget we have a Sonic and Mazzio's Pizza now too. We are moving up in the world."

"Yeah, I didn't think the town council would allow those to pass." The addition in the last ten years of recognized food chain restaurants had surprised a lot of people.

"It's only because town council members own the franchises and can profit from it while hiring locals. They went off to training centers to learn how to run the places rather than letting strangers come here. Plus, it looks good on paper. It keeps any new folks passing through from of the café. Don't want strangers messing around the regular para hangouts."

"I forget your guardian gets to sit in on town council meetings."

"Part of his job." Tesch shrugged broad shoulders.

"Anyway, point is, we can walk or ride a bike to most any place in McLoud without breaking too much of a sweat. So why the truck…or any vehicle?"

"Maybe I just wanted to be able to pick you up in style." A grin on his lips implied nothing, but something in his eyes told me that wasn't the truth, or at least not the whole truth.

"What are you not telling me?"

"Who me?" His look changed to one so innocent, butter wouldn't melt in his mouth.

"Tesch?" I gave him a questioning glare.

"Nope. Not telling you anymore."

"Tesch!" I wheedled a bit with big eyes and a pleading smile.

"Save it for Charlie." He laughed at my attempt to cajole him. "See you later. I've got to get to class."

As if summoned, the class bell rung. Tesch bounded off, leaving me to wonder exactly what kind of ride was in store for me the night of the dance. Did I even want to know? Hopefully I could find out more from him at the carnival. That I could hardly wait for. We always had a blast.

I'd get him drunk on the Tilt-A –Whirl turning around and around then ask him about his truck. He'd be so messed up from spinning he'd answer anything I wanted just to get off the darn thing. Tesch killed in the water, but I ruled the thrill rides.

Thursday morning after our exchange dawned chilly but fair. I got up and out of bed early with excitement.

I wanted clothes for the day not so much to make me look good, but to be comfortable for activity. I chose my favorite, well-worn jeans. The new banana yellow, Converse sneakers and a red hoodie clashed, but as far as anyone else knew, I didn't know that.

I dug out sixty dollars from my allowance stash. An armband for all the rides would be twenty dollars. I'd spend another twenty on junk food that tasted too good and the last twenty on the Midway. Awesome!

Thinking about it, wanting to have the best carnival day ever, I decided to take another twenty from my bank jar. I didn't plan to spend it, but I wanted to have it all the same.

Downstairs, Sarah fixed up a plate of pancakes for me. Charlie had already left for work. The University of Oklahoma didn't recognize Halloween as a religious holiday, so he'd be teaching his usual class schedule.

A bowl of fresh berries from her garden rested on the table. I had finally come to appreciate certain things that were red, like strawberries. Of course I had been eating them for years. Sarah's hot house plants yielded the sweet fruit year round, but just as yellow had given me a new thankfulness for lemons, orange juice and cornbread with butter, seeing red gave me a whole new closeness to the delicious treat.

I didn't mind the link sausages either. I found I craved protein more these days since my inner cat had shown up. However, since my first shift to a lynx, I avoided anything that had or once was a yolk.

"Do I need to even ask what's on your agenda today?" She teased me as she slid the stack my way.

"It's carnival day." The smile on my face felt a mile wide. "Tesch and I are going to get there early and ride all the rides over and over until we are sick from it."

"I will never understand what you get from spinning around in circles or going upside down at ninety miles an hour. Roller coasters make me feel like my stomach just fell out of the bottom of my shoes."

"That's the fun of it!"

"Poor Tesch, I think the only reason he goes on the rides is because you love them so. When you guys come home he looks positively green from it."

"I wouldn't know." I didn't add that I wasn't sure I wanted to either.

I had once thought being able to see in color would be the best thing that could ever happen to me. Seeing red and yellow had put my life in a precarious position. I thought I should quit while ahead... while I still had a head.

I refused to think about that. I intended for the day to be about fun and games, a last day of warmth the sun had to offer before winter's cold set in. I firmed my resolve to enjoy myself.

Before I had taken two bites of my breakfast, Tesch knocked on the back door then let himself in. I laughed when I spied his outfit. He'd worn a yellow hoodie and red sneakers, opposite of me.

"You stole my color scheme!" I accused in good humor.

"I just wanted you to be able to see me if we got separated."

"Like anyone else in town has spiked hair like yours."

"I think you two look cute together." Sarah chimed in as she pushed another plate of pancakes across the table to Tesch.

"Thank you." Tesch replied. Whether he meant the compliment or the food, I didn't know.

After my comrade in hi-jinx and mayhem polished off two helpings of buttermilk flapjacks, we climbed on our bikes and pedaled toward the center of town. The carnival sat in the same spot each time. There was a park and ball fields behind the grade schools. These were practice fields, so if the rides and games and people walking around trampled the grass, it wouldn't be the end the world.

Arriving, I noticed the carnival had grown. They had added more circus-type attractions. Beyond the standard Ferris wheel, bumper cars and my other favorites, they had elephant and camel rides. A big top now dominated one entire ball field. Canvas posters advertised three different show times. The first show would be at one p.m., the second at five, and the last at eight.

"This looks interesting."

I inspected the cloth poster of a motorcyclist. There were several depictions of the rider, one going through flaming hoops, another showing an aerial flip backwards and finally, the rider going around the inside of a sphere shaped cage.

"Yeah." Tesch agreed. "I wonder if it's included in the armband price or if we have to pay extra for it?"

I gave him one of my, *are you kidding me*, looks. All the years we had been coming here, surely he'd figured out nothing at the carnival came included. The idea was to make as much money as possible, not give it away.

"My bet is its extra. You know how the carnival is, anything and everything to make a buck." Looking at the poster again, I added, "But this just might be worth the ticket."

"Okay, we can do the five o'clock show. By then we'll be ready to sit down and eat and rest a bit."

"Sounds like a plan."

The Midway had grown larger too, with new lures of a fire eater, sword swallower and fortune teller. We bypassed the rigged games and hawkers, saving them for later. It became more exciting when the sun went down and the lights came on.

Getting there early meant shorter waits for the rides. Tesch and I went to the ticket booth for our all day passes. The yellow band stood out against the sleeve of my red sweatshirt and blended with Tesch's.

As soon as the bands were snapped in place, we headed for the Spider, one of my favorite rides. I could almost guarantee making Tesch throw up at least once because of that ride. We'd ride it several times.

For the uneducated, the Spider is just that. The ride has eight arms that move up and down on a pivoting arm while the center spins. On top of that, two to three people can sit in the bucket at the end of the arm and spin around as fast as the wheel can be turned.

We were one of three groups of riders waiting in line. Some older kids from school were in the first group, two girls and two boys, then a father with two young boys. We had a nice balance. The operator knew how to seat the ride for best results. As soon as we were in the bucket, I grabbed the center wheel and started spinning us around. I loved centrifugal force.

"Will you stop that?" Tesch griped. "The ride hasn't even started yet, and I'm already feeling sick."

I didn't stop but slowed it down. "Why do you do this with me year after year if you don't like it?"

"'Cause I like the way your eyes light up and the rosy color your cheeks get when you're this happy. Something about the carnival makes you freer than any other time."

I just about forgot to give the wheel another twist. I knew there was a blush on my cheeks that had nothing to do with feeling free and everything to do with Tesch. He caught me off guard with his candid words. I wasn't sure how to respond.

Thankfully, I didn't have to. The bucket gave a buck as the center wheel began to turn. The ride's arms started their up and down motion. I resumed spinning our seat as fast and as hard as I could. Since becoming a Werelynx I noticed an increase in my speed, strength and stamina.

I laugh aloud as the wind buffeted my face and hair. Tesch understood about how the rides made me feel unrestricted and alive. He gripped the safety rail for dear life.

"Harmony, slow it down or I'm going to hurl!"

I gave a maniacal chuckle and spun us that much harder. When it came to carnival rides, I had no mercy.

By the end, Tesch looked positively ill. Climbing out of the bucket, he needed a moment to get his knees steady again before I dragged him along toward my next instrument of torture, the Tilt-A-Whirl.

The lines grew longer as the crowds picked up. Tesch got longer spans between being spun, whipped and zipped. The tone of the flesh on his face evened out, and he even managed a few hearty laughs.

"It's four thirty."

"So?" I asked as we waited for our turn on the Avalanche.

"So, if you want to make it to the big top on time, I suggest we go get in that line after this ride."

"Oh, yeah, right. I almost forgot."

Fifteen minutes later we had been spun, rumbled and dropped weightlessly before coming to a stop. We ran to the red striped tent. They asked for ten dollars at the flap. I smiled glad I had grabbed the extra twenty before I left my room this morning.

A single ring as big as a baseball diamond, made with hay bales, had been formed in the center of the tent. Bunting had been strung around the outer edge of the bales to provide a festive atmosphere. From the patterns of stars and red stripes I assumed it to be an American flag motif.

Bleachers were positioned at what would be third base to home and home plate to first base in a half circle. Two poles, so large I wouldn't be able to reach around them, supported the center of the tent to its peak of about sixty feet. From one pole to another, a thick rope stretched tautly.

We were able to get the last two seats near the front. Everyone coming in behind us would have to sit up higher on the bleachers.

A clown strolled around the ring offering balloon animals to the smaller kids and occasionally teenagers, too. He offered poodles, giraffes and bears, even making one young witch a crown.

"I think I might get one of those for you, Princess."

"Don't you dare."

"Aw, come on. If you can spin me inside out until I puke, you should at least have a Carnival Queen crown on while you do it."

"Tesch, I mean it. I will kill you if you do."

"You're no fun."

Before I could protest further, the house lights dropped. A spotlight focused, and the Ringmaster entered from the other side of the tent. A hush fell over the crowd the way they talked about in stories but never happened in real life.

She had dressed in the customary skin tight trousers, knee boots and ruffled shirt. Her deep red coat glimmered with sequins. A traditional top hat perched at an angle on her head. Whether for dramatic intent or not, she also had the traditional handle bar moustache.

The Ringmaster curved in all the right places like a fabulous pinup girl, and the clothes showed off her figure very well. Even under the heavy stage makeup, the perfect symmetry of her lovely face showed.

I heard Tesch give a low wolf whistle as she strode across the ring. I bet I wasn't the only female in the tent that hoped the mustache was real and not part of the show. Sadly, it didn't detract one bit from her beauty.

When she spoke into the microphone she carried, her voice came out as a husky contralto, sexy and breathless with a faint eastern European accent. To me, she sounded Russian.

"Ladies and gentleman, thank you for joining us today for our show. I am Katarina, and I will be your Ringmaster. Our goal today is to entertain and amaze you. Please feel free to laugh, scream and hold your breath as needed. I know I will." She chuckled in a throaty way that implied intimacy.

I'm no expert in seduction. I couldn't flirt if I had to. But I knew instantly that Katarina would be skillful at it. I'd wager my entire allowance stash she could lead any guy around by the nose inside of ten minutes.

Tesch seemed mesmerized. I dug my elbow into his ribs just for spite.

"Ow!" he cried in a loud whisper. "What was that for?"

"Gawking."

A female that gorgeous inspired teeth gnashing jealousy on the spot. I couldn't help it. It was a matter of principle.

The spotlight swiveled away from Katarina and came to rest on the tent flap. She melted into the shadows as a small group of clowns and poodles emerged. One poodle had been dyed bright yellow. The others probably were too, though I couldn't be sure.

With the voluptuous Ringmaster out of sight, concentration on the show before us became easier. The dogs pranced and danced and performed tricks only when their master's back turned. It seemed that they were determined to make the heavyset clown look like a fool. Laughter rang freely.

All too soon the poodles were over, and Katarina returned. Even though she only encouraged applause and introduced each new act, she stole the spotlight easily.

Next were a group of tumblers who were very skilled and compact. I didn't think any one of them were over five foot two. They twisted, bent and flipped in ways I had never seen a human body move.

At one point, a man held a chair elevated on a pole on his shoulders with the seat ten feet above his head. Another man ran, hitting a springboard to jump and land on the velvet cushion. The team quickly handed up another chair of the same height.

The next tumbler, a small female, took a longer run, followed by a series of back handsprings. She hit the same board and landed securely in the seat above the second man's head. The timing and skill captivated me.

Tesch seemed equally amazed. He never took his eyes away as he whispered to me. "I never thought I would see someone as graceful on land as I am in the water. That takes skill."

The tumblers were followed by the elephants and their slow but graceful dance. They performed tricks and a bit of play for everyone's enjoyment. The trainer allowed a child to hand-feed one elephant peanuts.

Another act included tightrope walkers. They were so high up and yet never showed an ounce of fear. One young man rode a unicycle across while a lady sat on his shoulders. I held my breath and swallowed hard.

Katarina returned to announce the final act while the ring cleared and the tightrope was taken down. A series of hoops and ramps were brought out as she spoke.

"I would like you all please to join me in welcoming our fearless and talented Ferro," she said, rolling the 'r's in his name heavily. "He will risk his life today for your entertainment as he defies flames and gravity with his motorcycle feats."

On cue, the cyclist burst through the far side of the tent, riding in on one wheel. All in red leather, the rider alone caught the eye. He continued to do the wheelie around the entire ring. I watched, fascinated.

He made a small series of jumps and flips using the ramps that had been placed at each end of the staging area. I held my breath with each backflip or demonstration of precision.

The Ringmaster's voice broke in as assistants brought out a huge round cage that had its own ramp. "The next trick Ferro will perform for you is one of concentration and skill. We ask that you please refrain from applause until our rider is safely finished."

The audience watched in silence as Ferro rode his motorcycle up the ramp and into the ball. Once the door to the ball had been closed and secured, the biker began to rock his cycle back and forth before giving it gas.

At first he rode the bike in the small tight circle of the bottom of the ball. As he gained speed and momentum, he climbed the sides, using the centrifugal force to keep him from falling.

As he made laps inside the ball, his bike climbed higher and higher until he made a full circle from top to bottom. When the ball began to move I realized it was attached to a mechanical swing arm.

As Ferro went round and round inside the ball, the ball went round and round the ring. The audience gasped and awed quietly so as not to break the concentration of the rider.

Tesch grudgingly offered. "He's really good."

The spinning ball slowed and came to a stop. The rider slowly wound himself down from the inside walls of his round cage. When the door opened again and Ferro was safely outside once more, the spectators offered up the clapping and praise his performance deserved.

Katarina came back. "If you will indulge us but a moment while Ferro prepares for his last stunt."

Large rings were moved into place between the ramps, three in a row, the center ring slightly higher than the others. Katarina herself carried the torch that set them ablaze.

"I don't see how he'll make that jump if he doesn't back up." Tesch commented.

The rider had positioned himself as far back as the troupe tent flap would allow and still be inside. I noticed his trajectory would take him right out of the other flap where the customers entered. I hoped someone had thought to clear the path outside.

My fingers found Tesch's hand, and I gripped them. "I hope he makes it."

As if my words were the go signal, the rider hit the gas and tore across the ring toward the ramp. My breath caught in my throat. I squeezed Tesch's fingers so hard he winced but didn't make me let go.

The rider hit the ramp full throttle and went airborne. Time stilled as he sailed through the burning rings, one... two... three! He'd made it!

The bike cleared the edge of the bales and as I thought, he went right out of the public entrance. I didn't hear any screams or noises of a crash. In fact, the definitive buzz of the engine returned as the helmeted Ferro rode, peeling back into the tent.

He bunny hopped the bike back into the ring, and the crowd broke into an enthusiastic round of applause and whistles. I stood on my feet showing my appreciation for his bravery and skill. Tesch stood with me, giving a fair amount of approval.

Finally, the rider parked and dismounted his bike. He tugged the helmet off and flashed the world a wide, satisfied smile.

He was beautiful. There were no other words for it. Stunned, I forgot to clap.

The young man's face had been shaped in a portrait textbook oval. The cheekbones were high and perfectly prominent. The nose presented as noble without being hawkish or large. His lips were full even when pulled into a wide grin. Long hair in a dark shade had been pulled back in a tight ponytail, revealing a widow's peak.

I felt a sharp elbow digging into my side.

"Ouch!" I cried. My eyes were drawn back to Tesch who now frowned seriously in my direction. "What was that for?"

"Gawking," he replied sourly.

Chapter 10

WE LEFT THE BIG TOP out of sorts with each other for the same reasons.

"Well, you were staring at Katarina like she was the last female on the planet!" My voice came out half teasing and half petulant. "So I stared at Ferro. He was very handsome."

"What am I, chopped liver? And I did not stare like she was the last girl on earth. Though I will admit she was very attractive, mustache and all." His voice reflected mine in its tone.

"All right, I declare a ceasefire. You thought she was pretty. I thought he was cute. It's okay for friends to admit that to each other, right?"

"Right." Tesch agreed sourly. "Now let's go hit the Midway. The lights are up."

He turned his body away from me. I heard disgruntled muttering that sounded like *"Freaking friend zone again."*

I stood immobilized. Tesch and I had come close to having a more-than-friends moment once or twice, but each time something came up, like shifting to a Werelynx for one.

Since he had never brought it up again, I'd assumed he had changed his mind or whatever. My inner voice reminded me, *you never brought it up either, cupcake. Maybe he wants you to bridge the gap.*

That scared me. I depended on Tesch to be the brave one. If he waited for me to make a move on him, well…

Tesch's long legs had carried him far enough I had to run to catch up. When I reached his side once more, I tentatively reached to hold hands with him. I swallowed the metaphysical rock in my throat when his hand returned my grip.

He gave me a small smile that I returned shyly. It was a start.

Tesch and I had a system for visiting the Midway, or maybe more of a tradition. We would start at the end by the entrance and work our way down one side, picking the games or treats that most interested us.

Then we would go for more rides, the ones that were most brilliant after dark. After the night lit rides, we'd stroll back down the other side of the Midway and home.

This night I got caught up at the coin dozer booth. A rolled up twenty dollar bill hung on the edge, and I intended to get it.

"You know you'll spend more than you'll make getting that."

"Maybe, maybe not." I replied. "It's a matter of honor now."

"Or coming up broke, whichever happens first."

"Killjoy." I remark to his negative vibe. I dropped another quarter through the slot as the metal plate pushed forward. Six responding quarters dropped out of the bottom, but the twenty only teetered on the precipice.

"Told you so."

"If you can't be any more helpful than that, just shut up." I replied in a teasing tone. I scooped up the six quarters to spend once again in the machine. "Watch and be amazed by my powers."

Tesch stood back a bit and made a sweeping gesture with his arms open wide as if to say '*Be my guest*'. I turned back to the game; Tesch stepped up to my side.

His closeness mildly disturbed me, in a good kind of way. I could smell his scent of water and male and sandalwood cologne that were all just right together. I released my next quarter all wrong. It did me no good at all. Shaking my head to clear it and concentrate, I waited and angled my next drop to go more to the left of my last.

"Do you know that you bite your lower lip when you're thinking really hard?"

I released my lip from between my teeth. "No, I didn't. Thanks for noticing. Not."

"No, it's cute. Like now when you are trying so hard to win this impossible game. It's a scam, Harmony."

"Shut up, Tesch. I am trying to focus here."

"Yes, Princess, as you wish."

I knew that last comment had been for my benefit. Just to mess me up. It worked. My next quarter landed on top of two others.

I threw Tesch my sternest glare. "You are so asking for a beat down."

"Promises, promises."

Turning back to the coin drop, I meant to block Tesch and his smart mouth out of my head. I did something I'd never tried before without Charlie at my side.

I reached down into the red power within my core and pulled out just a flare, a taste of the lynx. In response, my vision sharpened. My depth perception and reflexes were much better as a Were.

Coin dozer is just another approach to lying in wait for the right moment before springing. Kitty cats are very good at pouncing games. I dropped another coin a split second before the metal push plate moved forward. My quarter went right into the line I planned to build to push the twenty over. Tesch didn't comment, but I heard his breath catch in his lungs, anticipating.

I positioned my last quarter in the slot, holding on gingerly. I saw my moment, exhaled and let go. The quarter fell exactly as I wanted. The wide silver wall slid forward. The whole coin and money structure wobbled like a house of cards.

Nothing went over the edge. I couldn't believe it!

"Sorry, Harmony, I really thought you had it there for a minute." Tesch commiserated for me.

I shook my head in denial. "I really thought I would win it. I just had this feeling."

A deep sigh escaped my lips and fogged the glass for a second. I let go of the red power I held inside my head.

I don't know if my breath against the window did it. I can't say if the needed push came from releasing the power in my head. But the pile of coins with the twenty toppled over the edge.

"Oh!" I squealed with delight. "Tesch, look it fell! It fell!"

I did a little happy dance. My shoulders shimmied from side to side while I fist pumped and wiggled my butt.

Tesch laughed at me so hard tears formed in his eyes. His arms crossed over his middle, holding his belly. "I don't know what you spent or what you did for that money to fall, but it's worth it to see those moves."

I stuck out my tongue at him and scooped up my winnings, the twenty first and then the quarters. I ended up with $23.75, doubling my money, plus change.

"You're just jealous 'cause I got skills, boy."

"If you say so, but remind me to wear my steel-toed dance shoes tomorrow night."

I stared at him aghast, mouth agape. My glare returned, and Tesch took the warning. He sprinted for the rides, and I chased. He led me a merry path until we reached the Ferris wheel, out of breath and laughing.

The Ferris wheel was always a great ride, day or night. By day you could see for miles around our small town. By night, it brought you closer to the stars.

Taking seats on the wheel, Tesch moved in close and put an arm across my shoulders. I liked it. It felt right.

The roll moved slowly as more passengers loaded. We swung lazily in silence for a few moments.

"Today has been a great day. I'm glad you took the time off to come out with me." Tesch broke the silence.

"We always go to the carnival, every fall and spring. It's like our thing. I wouldn't miss it."

"I know. But you've been so busy lately with the extra studies and new talents." His voice contained an ironic chuckle. "I've missed you."

We moved up and over and back, the wheel stopping a third of the way from the top. I turned to him in the seat. "I'm sorry, Tesch. I've just been so busy trying to catch up with everyone else. I didn't realize I was leaving you out. Why didn't you say something?"

"Harmony, I get it. I'm trying to be understanding of what you are going through. I know you have a lot to learn, and you have to learn it all at once it seems. Your powers coming on suddenly, seeing some colors for the first time, finding out that you could end up *numero uno* on the Council's hit list for something you can't even control. That's all a lot to deal with."

The wheel jerked, and we moved to the peak. "Tesch, I couldn't deal with it half as well if I didn't have you."

That tell-tale heat spread across my cheeks again. I looked away, out over the town and surrounding countryside to hide the flush. From there I could see the lights from the big casino on the highway.

"Isn't it gorgeous?" I gasped. "I see the Grand Firelake. It's the prettiest thing to see up here."

"I disagree. I'm looking at the prettiest thing to see up here."

"What?" I turned back to him eager to see what he thought was better. Instead of looking out over the town and county, Tesch looked right at me.

"Oh."

I didn't know what to say. My heart did a flip-flop. I licked lips that were suddenly dry.

"Tesch, I…" My breathing stuttered, and my heart switched to an irregular beat.

"Shhh, Harmony. I'm not going to hurt you, but I want to kiss you. Don't go Werelynx on me. Just relax."

Easy for him to say, it's not his first kiss.

As if he heard me, "This is the first time I've ever kissed a girl, Harmony. You're the only one I've ever wanted to try it with."

No pressure there.

He touched my face softly with warm fingertips, drawing my lips closer to his. I watched every move he made until we were so close I could see the darkness of his pupils clearly against the lighter shade of his irises. Each long dark lash stood out against the paleness of his eyelids.

"Close your eyes."

Oh, yeah, forgot about that.

I dutifully closed my eyes. Lacking sight brought so many other sensations into focus.

There was an easy breeze blowing in on us. The Ferris wheel bucket creaked softly as we swayed. Below, the carnival music played as screams of riders and the buzz of voices were muted. I could smell popcorn and funnel cakes.

When his lips brushed mine gently for the first time, I almost missed it, the touch was so light. The warmth of his breath gave it away. My own mouth parted in surprise, and Tesch pressed his firmly against mine.

He didn't try for more than a kiss. Nor did he try to invade me with his tongue like I've read about in some steamy romance novels. But the sensation felt sweet and powerful nonetheless for it.

The fluttering that had been in my heart dropped to my stomach. My arms snaked up and around his shoulders as if they knew what they were doing even if I didn't.

His arms followed my lead. We were cuddling tightly into one another. I'd always known Tesch had strength, but in an embrace, I appreciated the muscled width of his shoulders in a whole new way. I clung to him, craving closeness I wasn't sure was possible to achieve.

His lips moved from mine and over my cheek to come to the hollow just below my right ear. Tesch planted a feather light kiss on that spot. In my ear he breathed my name like a prayer. "Harmony."

Goosebumps spread down the back of my neck and spine. An adrenaline rush better than any thrill ride had given filled me. I held him tight as a trembling passed through me.

The ride lurched forward, forcing us apart. I open my eyes to stare into his and saw... a new color. The irises of his gaze had a new brilliance I couldn't name; I could only think 'beautiful'.

Tears choked me. Their warmth brimmed.

"Harmony, are you okay?" He asked, worried. "I'm sorry. What did I do wrong?"

I smiled through the tears and touched his cheek. "Nothing. It's just that for so long I've wanted to know what color your eyes are."

Confusion crossed his features. "You could have asked me. They're green."

Green, I can see green.

"You could have said it, but I didn't know what it was. Green was just a word to me until I opened my eyes now."

Understanding dawned in his light green eyes. "You mean…? Just now?"

I shook my head, unable to express my feelings with words.

Tesch threw back his head and laughed to the world. Pulling me tight, he gave me another kiss, full of joy. I returned his caress enthusiastically.

We kissed for as long as the wheel revolved, oblivious to the carnival below or the stars above. When our seat landed at the bottom and the ride ended, our lips were still planted firmly together.

The carney operator opened the guard rail from our bucket. Tesch whispered to me alone. "If I had known kissing you would help you see colors I wouldn't have waited so long."

Give a guy a kiss and it goes straight to his head. I had to remind him. "The last time you almost kissed me I turned furry."

"Yeah, but you saw red for the first time too."

"Fine then, you win. Let's go check out the rest of the Midway."

"Be nice to me or I won't bring anymore color into your life." Tesch teased.

I tugged his hand, guiding us toward the bright lights and music. Crowds meandered from one game to another, trying their luck. The lane bulged with strolling people.

Tesch decided to spend ten dollars on dart throwing trying to win me a huge stuffed dolphin. Instead, we walked away with a parrot four inches tall. I assured him it was just what I wanted. Its colors were red, yellow and green, all my favorites.

"It's adorable. Gil is my new best friend."

"Gil?" He gave me a doubtful look. "You're naming the parrot, Gil?"

"Yeah, why not?"

"I don't know. It just seems that, out of all the exotic or cute names you could pick from, you wound up with Gil? Why?"

"I like that old TV show, *Gilligan's Island*. The guy on the show is goofy, awkward and always in a jam, just my speed."

"Okay—if you say so." I could tell he was laughing at me without actually busting out with it.

Almost to the end of the Midway, I spied a dark green tent with yellow-gold stars and moons on it. The tent seemed small, maybe six by six feet square compared to the attractions surrounding it.

A sign read, '*Madame Osza, Fortunes Told and Palms Read. Come inside and see what fate awaits you.*' A pay scale below the advertisement reported palm readings as five dollars, tarot card readings as ten.

"Oh, let's go in here. I would love to have my future told. What about you?"

"I'm fine with my present. The past is gone, and I say let the future take care of itself, Harmony."

"Come on, Tesch, it's just for fun. I've got the twenty I won from the coin dozer."

He seemed reluctant to go inside. The smile he'd worn since we got off the Ferris wheel dwindled.

"There's nothing to be afraid of."

"I'm not afraid." He remarked quickly. "I just don't put a lot of faith in such things. I think sometimes they do more harm than good. Like a curse of expectation, you can believe things into coming true."

"You mean like Charlie says? If you expect to find the bad in someone, you will."

"Something like that." He agreed.

I couldn't help but laugh. "Tesch, my biggest dreams and worst fears have already been happening. I don't see how things could ever be better or worse than they already are."

"What's that supposed to mean?"

"It means I am seeing color, but the price for it is I have to hide my powers because the Council could declare me an outlaw. It means I finally stood up to my nemesis, Challen Parks and ended up in hot water for it. It means I finally have a boyfriend, but my new best friend is a stuffed parrot."

"I'm your boyfriend?" His eyes lit up with the question.

"Do you want to be?"

Taking my hands, Tesch pulled me close for a hug. "Of course I want the job. But I'll always be your best friend too."

"Promise?"

"As long as I'm breathing, Harmony, I'm here for you."

I smiled up into his green eyes, startled again by the light, vibrant color. "Good to know. Now let's go see what the fortune teller has to say."

Chapter 11

"Come in, children, I've been expecting you."

The statement escaped from the mouth of an ancient woman in a wheelchair, sitting behind a cheesy round table with a glowing crystal ball on top. This promised to be fun.

I had a hard time not laughing out loud. The whole set up reeked of the stereotypical. It could have been a scene from a bad B movie horror flick or a satire about one.

The only light came from three dozen or so candles, spiked into place on large, freestanding candelabra. The wax had authentically melted down and spilled onto the grass floor of the fortune teller's tent.

Once upon a time, the old woman must have been beautiful, but time had erased the looks if not the presence of beauty. Her very light hair, probably silver, had been pulled back and worked into a heavy braid. The braid had been secured around her head like a crown.

She sat straight and proud in her chair, a deep red shawl across her shoulders. The shawl appeared shot with gold thread that glittered in the candle's soft glow.

Her withered face appeared soft and translucent, folds hung gently at her jawline. Madame Osza's right eye pierced darkly, so dark I couldn't see a pupil. I'm sure she had one, but it wasn't easily made out. I don't think I'd ever seen someone with eyes, um, an eye so dark. Her left eye she concealed with a pirate's patch of silk.

At my back, Tesch snorted loudly with disbelief at Madame Osza's greeting. The old woman chuckled as well.

"I see you doubter. I see you very well. No matter, it is she who called forth my vision. Come in girl, and sit down. Let me have a better look at what there is to see." Her voice sounded lightly accented, like a person who started life somewhere in Southern Europe long ago.

A nervous chill patterned my arms and shoulders with goose bumps despite my hoodie's warmth. Why did I feel like she spoke about more than my appearance?

Tesch and I moved forward in tandem. There were two less than stable looking wicker chairs available. We sat down together.

I put my palm forward to be read. Madam Osza looked at my hand as if there should be something more.

What? Oh yeah.

I fished out the money from the coin dozer game, handing the bill forward. "Do you have change for a twenty?"

"This will do." She snatched the paper currency from my fingers where it disappeared beneath the table. Somehow, I knew I wasn't getting any change back from her. I felt a wry smirk coming from Tesch; I didn't even have to look to see it.

Instead of taking my hand, Madame Osza pulled out a deck of cards from her lap and passed them to me. "Shuffle the cards three times. Cut them once. I will deal."

The cards were a thing of beauty themselves. Ancient as their owner, the paper a thick, yellowed board, vellum maybe. They were hand painted, not printed with ink, the pictures incredibly detailed. Whoever made them had possessed astounding skill.

When I picked them up, a sizzle traveled up my arms. It reminded me of the jolt that had passed between me and Challen when the illusion had been cast but on a much smaller scale.

Intuition had me believing Madame Osza was no fraud. I became afraid. Not of the old woman herself, but of what she might have to say. Silly but true.

Tesch, in tune with my inner self, moved closer. He put a protective arm around my shoulders and let it rest. Comforted, I relaxed a bit.

I shuffled, once, twice, three times and then cut the deck. Cautiously, I pushed the cards back to the fortune teller.

Careful not to actually touch her, I tried to recall if she had touched me when she took my money. No, she had not. I wanted to keep it that way.

"Now let's have a look." Madame Osza began to lay the cards out on the table. As she did, she told what each meant to the pattern.

"The first card is your present."

She turned over 'the Fool' card. A lovely card with a man in a jangled three cornered cap smiled up at me. His clothing had been bisected with the colors red and green. He stood on one leg; the other rose, crossing his knee, making his legs into the number four. A yellow dog barked at his foot.

I'm no expert, but that didn't sound encouraging. The symbolism wasn't lost on me. So at present, I'm an idiot. Great.

As if reading my inner thought, Madame Osza murmured. "Don't think that this is necessarily bad. The Fool can mean change as well as ignorance."

Okay. I'd buy that. I had been going through *a lot* of change recently.

"The next card is an immediate challenge you must face." She turned the card over across my present Fool. "The Queen of Swords."

A queen sat on her throne. Long red hair flowed from beneath her crown and down her shoulders. A single sword in her hand held point up. She had landed across the Fool, head down, looking at his feet.

"A sly, deceitful person. Be careful what they observe from you. They will do you cruelly with their gossip.

I knew a few of those types. It wouldn't be the first time people had talked about me behind my back, or for that matter, right in front of me like I wasn't there. That didn't faze me much.

The next card, Madame Osza claimed as my distant past. "The Five of Cups. The card upright like this means a loved one lost, sorrow, disillusionment. Either you lost someone you loved or someone who loves you lost you and is sorrowful."

Since I had never lost anyone that I loved, I wondered about her accuracy. Then, a small stirring in my head, a half remembered dream of a voice singing and being secure in the arms of the voice had me rethinking my opinion.

Could the distant past represent my birth mother? I guess I'd never know, but it felt good to believe for a moment that she regretted giving me up for adoption. That it had been a hard choice to make, whoever she had been.

"Your recent past." Madame Osza turned a card that had a bride and groom facing each other. Their arms were twisted together in a toast. The two cups showed prominently, golden and large in comparison to the rest of the picture. "This is a well-balanced friendship or new romance in your life."

I blushed. Tesch's hand gently squeezed my shoulder. Madame had hit that nail squarely on the head.

"The first, third and fourth cards influence the best possible outcome of the second card." the old woman told us. She smiled, full of knowledge and irony. "The fifth card tells us where the others are leading or dragging you, reluctant of your fate."

She turned this card with anticipation. The card held a gondola-type boat steered by a young man, his face away from the viewer, looking off to the horizon. The boat's helm had been pierced with six swords.

"A journey, safe passage away from sorrow. Your adventure is only beginning, I think, young lady."

Madame Osza gave me a piercing look as if she tried to see

something more in me that no mirror could ever reflect. I wanted to squirm beneath her scrutiny but held myself still and met her one eyed, dark gaze. Satisfied with what she saw, I guess, she gave me a short nod.

Tesch remained still and quiet through our stare down. When the woman's gaze broke, he leaned over and whispered into my ear, the slightest of air passing his lips. "She's good. I almost believe her myself. Great stage presence."

Madame gave my friend, my new boyfriend, a scowl but made no comment about his hushed words. Personally, I bought it. I couldn't be sure how this card-reading, fortune-telling, future-seeing business worked, but my blood could feel the power of the truth.

"The sixth card is immediate future. The past influences but is not the only factor. Many influences can shape what will happen soon."

This card was no less beautiful. The woman on the card wore a headdress and carried a staff; similar to what I had seen the Pope wear on TV, except the upper part of her robes had fallen off the shoulder revealing the figure as definitely female.

"This card, the High Priestess, can represent wisdom, a teacher. There is much learning to be done by you. Knowledge and wisdom are not the same; you will need both in life. Do not be impatient with yourself for what you don't yet know. It will come."

"Your seventh card is inner feelings and factors you can control that are affecting the choices you make, what road your journey will take."

I first thought of how lonely he looked when I saw the card. A man holding a staff and a single lantern to light his way walked through dark barren trees. The golden beams from his light made the card seem even more desolate.

"The Hermit is withdrawing from the situation. But it also implies inner strength and courage to go forward alone. It is prudence and caution. You alone will reap the consequences of your situation." Madame Osza told me.

She turned the next card. The card rested upside down from the rest. A knight, sword raised, charged into battle on a pale horse. It gave me a chill.

Madame Osza's face agreed with me.

"The Knight of Swords reversed. He is a tyrant and a trouble maker. I cannot see who this person is in your life, or how he influences you child, but he is there nonetheless. Be wary of him and be brave within."

She shook herself before my eyes and hurriedly turned the next card. She seemed as eager as I to get past this dark spot in my future.

"The ninth card is your hopes and fears. Bear in mind, hopes and fears are closely intertwined. Often what we secretly wish for is also what we dread most."

On the card were three five-pointed stars within circles. I knew pentagrams when I saw them. I lived with a witch. Even if she couldn't cast spells anymore, Sarah still had a lifetime of experience.

"This is your desire for approval, recognition of your growing talents, of what you have learned. You're fear of shining and showing your gifts doesn't change that you want to be accepted for what you are."

I blushed again and didn't try to deny it. I understood the need to not let the world know I could see more colors and had gained powers. There were so many possible repercussions from it, I couldn't list them all.

Still, part of me hoped for, wanted, that very thing.

"Now we reach the final outcome. What will be the results of the learning, the journey, the gossip? What does the Fool become? Let us see."

She turned my last card.

I, the Empress, sat in the wheat field again. This time perched on a stone bench in a flowing green gown. A crown of stars rested on my head. I held a golden scepter in my right hand. In the distance a waterfall cascaded, becoming a flowing river of life.

Magik moved in the air, and I could almost see it shimmering in the atmosphere. Power covered me so heavy and thick, I might have choked but for the solidness of Tesch at my side. He tied me to the real world, not as an anchor, but as a safety line, lest I float away on the mystic breeze. I felt this card reflected me, or would someday.

"The Empress is a symbol of new life, new beginnings, of nurturing and diplomacy. This is a card of evolution. She can also be just what is seen, a benevolent ruler of all." Madame Osza's voice came in a hushed whisper.

I tore my eyes from the card to meet her single dark stare. "Who are you?"

"Me, I am no one of import to a queen, but to a fool, a wanderer...maybe I am a messenger. The question is, young woman, who are you?"

I felt the weight of the question. Did I really want it answered?

I believed. I believed that she did have insight to my future. There were many things about what she's said and the cards that rang true.

Some I thought I could handle, no problem. Gossip, getting some powers finally, the change of the status quo between Tesch and me seemed more in line with normal, para development.

But a journey, becoming a recluse, the pale horseman? The Empress?

Those cards gave me ideas about a future I wasn't sure I wanted. But whose future is ever theirs alone to decide or take credit for? No man is truly the master of his own fate. Not so long as his life includes other living beings capable of mucking up the best plans and intentions.

"Come on, Harmony. Let's go home."

Tesch, forever at my side, always there to make the best of any situation or to protect me from it, put a firm but gentle hand around my upper arm and pulled me to my feet. I felt dazed, only nodding my assent. So many thoughts swirled in my head.

Tesch guided me to the tent flap and lifted the heavy burlap. Abruptly, I turned back to Madame Osza, a new thought in my head.

"You're like me aren't you? You are mixed blood."

She gave me a sad but open look and sighed. "My lady, there is no one like you."

Madame Osza paused while I pondered her meaning before she added. "But if I answered the question as you intended it, I would jeopardize much and many. I can only advise you to let your eyes see and your heart feel the truth."

. I understood perfectly. The carnival was a traveling paranormal community, a mixed-breed community. Charlie and Sarah were the only legal mixed couple I knew of, anywhere. They were accepted only because no children could ever come from their union.

To admit that there were mixed breed paranormals of any nature loose in the world, much less in our tiny town, would open an ugly can of worms. I had visions of a mob-like situation similar to the Salem Witch Trials, which ironically, no real witches were involved in.

Tesch pulled on my arm, urging me to follow his lead out of the tent. I looked at him sternly. His shoulders tensed and then sagged. He knew me well enough to know that when I dug my heels in, I could not be moved.

I turned back to Madame Osza. "Why come to McLoud then? You visit twice a year, Samhain and Beltane. Aren't you more likely to be exposed by coming to a para community than a human one?"

"We all have our reasons for doing what we do."

Her answer sounded so fatalistic, as if there were no choice. She looked at Tesch when she said the words. She had me looking to him again; to be sure he hadn't grown a second head or sprouted wings.

He hardly met my eyes when he repeated his earlier plea to leave. "Really, Harmony, it's getting late. We need to get home."

"Do not feel you will never have the chance to ask your questions again my young Fool. I know we will meet again. Just as I knew you would come tonight, I know you will return when the time is right and your need is great." Her wise and knowing smile gave me the willies.

Suddenly, I wanted to be out of there as much as Tesch wanted me to go. He no longer had to pull me. I ducked under his arm where he held the tent entrance open, out into the cool October air. The chill came as a shock to my fevered imagination.

Neither of us had much to say as we collected our bikes from the school and began pedaling home. We had made the ride here in record time, full of anticipation and energy. Now we went slowly, like a funeral procession, mourning the last days of warmth and childhood.

"Harmony," Tesch broke the silence as we rode smoothly side by side at an easy pace. "You shouldn't take what that old witch said too seriously. She's a carney. Their job is to give a good show. Don't be a sucker for riff raff like that."

I hit the brakes and stopped dead in the center of the street. "Teschandarian Monroe Wight!" Using his full name, I exclaimed, hurt. "I can't believe you!"

He'd stopped his bike a few feet beyond mine and walked it backwards to face me. "What?"

"I'm thinking that most of those carney people, if not all of them, are mixed breed paras, like me."

Tesch gave me a 'duh' look. "You are just now figuring that out after all these years we've been going?"

I'd become used to being teased and tormented for being colorblind. People were often prejudiced to me as being different from them. But hearing it from Tesch's lips? That mixed breeds were riff raff. It hurt my soul.

"And they are nothing like you, Harmony. You haven't got a deceitful bone in your body."

"Oh." The wind of offense diffused, leaving my sails empty. I stood straddling my bike. "I thought you were talking bad about them because they are mixed blood paranormals."

Now he looked at me, angry. "Really, Harmony?"

Tesch gave a disgusted snort and started pumping his bike away from me, leaving me in the dark behind him. I hurried into motion to catch up. "Tesch, wait! Please. I'm sorry."

I caught up to him, panting a bit. We stopped again on the side of the road.

"I can't believe that you would think me as shallow and prejudice as jerks like Challen Parks and Ms. Idlewilde." He accused. "Do you really think I care if someone has pure Fae blood or pure Were blood or pure anything for that matter? How long have we been friends?"

"I said I'm sorry." I wiped a drop of sweat from my brow made in the effort to catch up. I no longer felt the cold of the night air. I defended myself. "But it's kind of become a sensitive issue for me."

"You think I don't know that?" He practically screeched. "I'm the one that brought it to Sarah and Charlie's attention the night you first shifted to a Werelynx that we needed to keep it quiet. I've been scared to death ever since."

The hurt those words caused. He saw it in my face and answered the unspoken thought. "Not because I'm afraid of you, idiot; I'm afraid *for* you."

He dismounted his bike, letting it fall to the ground before coming to stand beside me. He took my face in his hands forcing me to look up into his green eyes.

"I could never be afraid of you, Harmony. I'm crazy about you. I have been ever since first grade when you punched Challen Parks in the nose and called him a bully."

Surprised and scared by his words, I answered back. "I never did that."

"You sure did. You don't remember?"

"No."

His touch left my face, arms wrapped around my shoulders, enfolding me to his chest. "We were outside. Challen strutted around being all alpha, trying to impress you. You were hunkered down watching a cocoon that was trying to open. You were fascinated by that butterfly and not giving him any attention. I think that's what made him come over and stomp on the pod. You were about to cry, and he teased you for it."

"That's when you doubled up your tiny little fist and let him have it, right in the nose. He fell on his butt and started wailing and bleeding. Everyone just stood around stunned."

"Then you told him, I remember, *'pick on someone your own size next time, you big bully baby.'*" Tesch made the last words a high pitched imitation of my voice. "That's when I fell in love. I didn't know how or why, but I knew I had to be your friend, had to get you to like me."

His telling it made me remember. I'd always had a soft spot for butterflies. They were such fragile creatures. Sarah called them flowers with wings. Tesch kept on talking, filling in details I hadn't even noticed then.

"After that, Challen always gave you a hard time. He'd pick on you for everything. I think you broke his heart when you broke his nose. Up to that point, he'd told all the other boys you were his girlfriend."

"Yuck! No way!"

"Yes. That's what he had bragged about. How the prettiest girl in class was his girlfriend, and she liked him better than any one of us."

"Oh, well, then he wasn't talking about me."

Tesch *tsked* his tongue at me behind his teeth. "Harmony, when are you going to realize how beautiful you are? Your eyes are like starbursts of lavender, blue and green, so bright and amazing. Your hair reminds me of living wood that's been polished to shine. I want to kiss you every time you smile; your lips are so full and soft. They remind me of cotton candy, and they are just as sweet."

He lowered his face. His lips hovered above mine, waiting. I bridged the gap, rising up on my toes a bit.

The kiss came sweet and soft but grew urgent. A tingling grew where my chest pressed against his and spread to other parts of me. My arms tangled around his shoulders, pulling us closer together. Tesch responded enthusiastically.

Quite a few years ago, Sarah had "the Talk" with me. Since then, she had added, revised and offered a lot of information to go with the basics. I had discovered that the talk never ends.

Thanks to Sarah, I recognized what I experienced now as desire. Intimate parts of me sizzled and buzzed as Tesch's body imprinted against mine. I could have no doubts about him responding to me as well.

Moments passed, and he pushed back, stepping away from me. His breathing came in quiet, ragged pants. He swallowed heavily before he spoke. "Harmony, um, we need to back up a step here. Don't get me wrong, I think about you like this sometimes. I'm a guy…"

A flush spread over his cheeks. Wait a minute? Was that pink, a softer shade of red?

I started to say something about it but held my tongue. We were having a different kind of moment here.

"I just want you to know I care more about you than to be standing in the middle of a black top road making out."

"I know that, Tesch. We've been friends for more years of my life then we haven't. I don't think us being, uh…. more involved is going to change who you are overnight."

"Yeah, but I've been thinking about it for a *long* time." He chuckled out loud. "Seeing me as a boyfriend is new to you."

My turn to laugh. "You think I've never thought about kissing you before tonight?"

"You have?"

The surprise on his face gave me a fit of giggles. When I sobered, I gave *him* the 'duh' look. "I am twenty-two, Tesch. I'll be twenty-three next Beltane. I know I'm a little young by paranormal standards, but I'm not *that* young. We've watched enough movies and TV for me to have been curious a long time ago. Charlie and Sarah aren't exactly in the closet when it comes to sex either. I can hear just fine. I know what goes on."

"Oh, don't tell me any more about them." He raised a hand against the images that were coming to mind. His body shuddered with revulsion. "I so don't want to know about that."

"Then don't offer to hang out at my house on a full moon. It's positively gagging." I warned.

"My point is, Tesch, I've thought about kissing you before tonight, even before the Werelynx thing. You're not the only one with these feelings going on."

"I'm not?"

"No, you're not."

He came closer to me, wrapping loose arms around my waist. "I'm so glad I'm not."

He gave me a light kiss on the tip of my nose and a hug that made me feel so content and safe. I breathed in his unique scent of male and clean water.

My butt buzzed.

I fished out the cell phone from the hip pocket of my jeans. Charlie had sent a reminder text that midnight approached, and I wasn't home yet. I quickly texted back that we were minutes away.

"I got to get home."

"I know."

His arms left me, and we climbed back on our bikes, pedaling in peace the rest of the way to my house. A companionable silence had settled between us, nothing heavy or awkward about it.

Pulling into the yard, Tesch asked. "Do you want me to walk you in?"

"Yes and no."

"Say again?" Tesch looked confused.

I got off my bicycle and walked to him, giving him an ironic smile. "This has been the best night. We had fun, we uh, kissed, and we like each other more for it. Even Madame Osza's reading was interesting, creepy-weird, but interesting. I can see green and pink."

"Pink? When did that happen?"

"Out on the black top."

"I told you, my kisses can do wonders!" Tesch crowed.

"I've been thinking about it, especially as we rode home. I think it's got something to do with my emotions, new emotions maybe. But I want to discuss it with Charlie and Sarah. And you of course."

Tesch nodded in agreement, his face in serious mode. "I get that. And you might be right about the emotions. You started seeing yellow after you got really hacked with Idlewilde. So not like you. Most of the time you just ignore it or bottle it up for later. Maybe your bottle is full?"

"I was scared too." I added.

"Scared? Of what?"

I felt another blush rise. "Of Mrs. Tyck's spell. Well, more nervous than scared I guess. But I felt very concerned that I would start babbling while under the influence about my secret crush on you."

Tesch laughed lightly. "No way."

"Yes way." I confirmed, shaking my head. "I just knew I would start running off at the mouth about how I'd never kissed anyone, and I wanted you to be my first."

He brushed a stray lock of hair from my face before lightly taking my hands in his. "I guess that's one less worry for you now, then."

"I guess." Another kiss: soft, sweet and slow. Boy we sure seemed to be making up for lost time.

"Hhrmphm!"

We startled apart to find Charlie standing under the porch light, hands on hips, arms akimbo. "I guess I don't need to ask what's been taking you two so long."

He appeared every bit the outraged father. Blushing furiously, my eyes darted to Tesch and then to the dried October grass. I couldn't bring myself to look at Charlie right then.

Tesch is made of sterner stuff than me. He looked directly at Charlie and gave a manly nod. "Hello, Charlie."

"Good night, Tesch." My father growled; his meaning clear.

Tesch squeezed my hand and pecked my cheek. "I'll see you tomorrow night. I can't wait."

I had to smile. "Me either."

Charlie growled again. Tesch let go of my hand and sauntered back to his ten speed. I watched him fade into the darkness before turning back to the angry lion at the door.

"Get in this house, young lady. We need to talk." He opened the screen door and strode into the foyer. The screen door slammed behind him.

"Sarah!" he paced around. "Sarah! Come here! We need to talk with Harmony! Something happened!"

I reluctantly went up the steps. By the time I opened the door for myself, Sarah hustled down from upstairs, worried.

"What's wrong? What's happened?" She demanded in fear. Her eyes roved up and down me, probably looking for bodily injury. We converged at the bottom of the stairs.

Charlie's voice echoed loud and upset. "I just found Harmony kissing Tesch out on the front lawn!"

Sarah looked at me stunned then back to Charlie. He nodded confirmation. She looked back to me again. I felt my shoulders drooping with dread.

Her face broke into a radiant smile. She gave me an exuberant hug. "Oh, sweetheart! I'm so happy for you! You've finally had your first kiss."

"You're what?" Charlie's voice raised a few decibels. "You're not upset by this? Shocked?! Outraged!? How dare that young man that we've welcomed into our home take advantage of our daughter!"

Sarah pulled away from me to face our ticked off Werelion. "Charlie, be serious. You just said *she* kissed *him*. No time ago, Harmony shifted to a Werelynx when she and Tesch were fooling around. It didn't happen because she was laughing too hard."

"I...uh, I assumed that happened because she felt trapped or scared." He stammered.

An unladylike snort came from Sarah. "Really, Charlie? Think about it."

I saw the gears in his mind working to argue, rejecting thoughts. It showed on his face as plain as his nose. "Still, she's too young...."

Sarah turned to me. "Harmony, honey, why don't you go on upstairs, take a shower and get ready for bed? Charlie and I need to have a talk. I'll come check on you later."

"Sure," I nodded and beat feet up those polished wood steps. I did not want to hang around for Charlie's first paranormal parent's birds and bees lecture. If Sarah proved half as thorough with him as she had been with me, it would take a while.

I heard the opener as I made the landing. Below me, Sarah started in, "Charles Dwayne Phillips, how could you embarrass Harmony like that! She is not a child..."

Chapter 12

I WOKE EARLY, stretching my arms above my head, content. Sarah had not made it to my room the night before to catch up on my current events. I assumed that her talk with Charlie had been much longer than the one she and I had years ago.

I turned to my right side to watch the sun rise and the wash of colors I'd never seen before. I lay in awe and wonder as darkness lifted slowly with vivid pinks, oranges, gold and yellow over the tops of mixed evergreens and brown barren limbs. Obviously, I gained quite a bit from my trip to the carnival.

Blue skies eluded me still. At least I assumed blue. Blues and purples were the only colors I had yet to identify with my own eyes. Quiet happy tears were shed hotly onto my pillow case. I continued to watch for a long time after the Technicolor display resolved into nothingness for me. Only the tree tops retained their colored depth.

If my theory proved true and emotions were the trigger to my color sight, I wondered what emotions blue and purple would come from. Despite the emotional roller coaster of the previous night, I arose, eager to get started on this day. I wanted to talk to Charlie and Sarah about a lot of things.

I spent extra time in the bathroom, at first startled, and then caught up in my own reflection. My hair was indeed a mixed shading of browns; light, medium and dark. When I turned my head this way and that, different highlights gleamed.

I practiced flipping my hair and turning my head the way I'd seen other girls do. For the first time I understood the obsession with the condition of their hairdo. I needed a haircut. I'd ask Sarah to take me to a beautician. She'd probably short circuit with glee.

She'd wanted to take me many times, but I hadn't seen the point. I trimmed my bangs myself; let her straight trim the back for split ends.

My skin remained pale but different. A touchable warmness that I'd been unaware of existed in my cheeks.

My eyes were pure strangeness to me. I could see the hints of green and gold Tesch had mentioned; the starbursts that reminded me of Charlie's eyes. But pieces of the puzzle were still missing. To me, the eyes were alien and unreal inside the rest of my colorized version face.

Spending an unheard of hour and fifteen minutes in the bathroom, I finally went downstairs to breakfast. I came into the room cautiously, but everything seemed normal, casual. Charlie had his accustomed seat at the table. Sarah bustled about the kitchen.

When she noticed me, Sarah offered a cherry, "Good morning, sweetie. How did you sleep?"

"Fine." I replied, wary of her effervescent smile. "How are you?"

"We're fine. Charlie and I had a long talk last night after you went to bed. He's been waiting to tell you something."

I glanced across the room to where Charlie hid behind the *Daily Oklahoman*. The paper rustled crisply in his grasp. I eased into the breakfast nook across from him, not sure what to expect.

"Charles Dw…" Sarah began.

"Oh, all right!" Charlie huffed and folded the periodical. A tell-tale red flush crept up the exposed areas of his neck only to be hidden by the deeper strawberry blonde whiskers of his neat beard. It must have been a humdinger of a talk with his wife if he blushed this much about it.

Distracted by my own thoughts, I neglected what he started saying. "I'm sorry?"

"Yes, I'm sorry. That's what I meant."

"No, I meant, I'm sorry. I missed what you said first."

"I said I'm sorry."

"I know. But what did you say first?"

"I'm sorry." Charlie enunciated. "That's what I said, or what I'm trying to say anyway."

"Oh." *Light bulb*. I finally got it, he had apologized to me. "For what?"

The blush crept back up the skin of his neck. His glance slid over to Sarah as she continued to fuss around the kitchen, in her element of mixing and making.

"For overreacting when you and *that boy* finally showed up last night." Charlie grumbled, on the verge of another growl.

"Tesch, dear." Sarah chimed in calmly. "He's been Tesch for fifteen years in this house. Remember our talk last night. He's not 'that boy' or 'that interloper' or 'that scheming little pervert' either."

I actually blushed about that one. What all had they discussed out of my hearing? Charlie looked none too pleased with the reminder.

"Anyway," he heaved an annoyed sigh. "Sarah reminded me that you are in fact becoming a young woman and not my kitten for much longer. And I guess, when all options are considered, if you must be involved with a young man, then *Tesch*…" My best friend and boyfriend's name slipped past his lips through gritted teeth. "Is indeed the young man I am most comfortable about you being with."

I wasn't sure how to respond back. Thank you?

"Uh, no problem. Can we still go to the dance tonight?" Hopeful, I pushed my luck.

"Of course you can." Sarah responded as she set a plate of French toast in front of her husband's scowling face. "As I pointed out to Charlie last night, you haven't done anything wrong." The last, she spoke toward my adoptive father with a meaningful stare.

"Yes." He agreed tightly. "Nothing wrong at all."

"Besides," Sarah beamed. "All that work on your costume shouldn't go to waste just because someone is feeling unreasonably stubborn about his little girl growing up."

"I'm going to work." Charlie started to stand.

"Wait." I pleaded. "There's something I need to tell you guys."

Charlie hesitated. He gave me an apologetic smile. "Really, Kitten, if this is boy stuff, I don't think I can take more right now."

"No, it's not. Well, I mean, Tesch is a part of it, but it's not like… romantic stuff." My cheeks heated. I so did not want to go there with him either.

Charlie sat back down and then scooted over farther around the table to allow Sarah to squeeze in at his side. They wore matching looks of concerned interest.

It took me a moment to frame my thoughts. "The day before I saw yellow for the first time, I had been really angry and frustrated with Ms. Idlewilde. Before I saw red, well, Tesch and I had been close to having, uh, well, our first kiss."

I couldn't believe I had brought that up, but it had become part and parcel of what continued to happen with me. "Last night, well, last night was wonderful. We had so much fun. So much excitement, and well, a lot went on."

"What kind of 'went on'?" Charlie demanded.

"I don't think that's the point, Charlie." Sarah admonished him.

"Well, I think it's a helluva important point."

"Not like that, Charlie!" I gasped, a little shocked he'd think it, but Sarah had been right. I did have another, more important, point to make.

"Charlie, your tie is a very light brown with dark brown stripes. Sarah, the flowers on your skirt are orange and pink with green leaves."

In unison they gasped and visually inspected the clothing I had mentioned. They looked up at me in awed wonder.

"It happened last night, after, after a lot of mixed but intense emotions. I've been thinking about it. I think there's some connection between what I feel and what I see. Does that make any sense at all?"

Charlie and Sarah looked uneasily from each other to me and back. They seemed very uncomfortable with the idea.

"We're not sure, Harmony." Sarah answered me.

"Not sure?"

"Well, we've done a lot of speculation ourselves recently. You were also very upset with Challen Parks when you manifested that illusion as well." Charlie spoke. "We may have dropped the ball with your whole 'yellow' experience, but since you changed to a Werelynx, we've been doing a lot of research on our own."

"As you can imagine, the subject of mixed breed heritage, powers and history beyond the propaganda the Council approves is sketchy at best." Sarah offered.

"And digging too deep is frowned upon. Nervous, bigoted bastards actually asked me to leave the Council archives when I asked for certain 'restricted' text." Charlie used his fingers for quotations for the word restricted, accenting the idea.

I don't know why their efforts on my behalf surprised me. I might not have been the child of their bodies, but they loved me. They were my parents. Afraid to ask, but I had to know. "So, what did you find out?"

"Not as much as we would have liked, but we're still looking, asking, trying to find resources." This came from Charlie.

I started to speak then caught myself. I knew where there happened to be a large group of living breathing resources that we could ask; the carnival. But, no, I couldn't say that.

For one thing, suspecting it and confirming it were two very different things. Second, just because I or Charlie or Sarah asked didn't mean we would get any answers.

For the third and most important reason, I didn't speak up. Knowing my own precarious position, the mortal danger I could be in if someone outside my small world were to discover my secrets, would I dare possibly expose someone else to that?

No. I would not.

I certainly wouldn't appreciate someone I didn't know speculating on my parentage and power in a way that might leave me open to Council justice. So the carnies, whatever or whoever they might be would have to remain their own secret. And I would keep mine for a while longer.

Neither of my parental units noticed my hesitation. Sarah continued to explain what they had discovered.

"As you may have guessed, children of a mixed parentage have mixed abilities. Sometimes the child will have either or both parent's gifts, but usually one more than the other. Based on that, we assume that one of your parents was Fae and the other Were."

"But, that is when the parents are both pure bloods themselves." Charlie chimed in.

"Yes." Sarah confirmed. "What we discovered, before we were cut off from the archives, is that when the parents are mixed blood also, the mixture can get a little volatile."

"Volatile?" I squeaked.

I thought about everything I had been going through recently. How much more volatile could it get? I already felt like a walking, talking time bomb. "Do you think I'm like that?"

Charlie looked to Sarah. "We honestly don't know. Everything that we did find, the information we were allowed to see, described the average paranormal maturing process. The children had some indication of their natural abilities in infancy, toddlerhood, childhood and adolescence, all the way through. And none I read about or that Sarah read about had ever been colorblind."

Sarah nodded sadly at the relayed information. "I took another track while looking for answers."

"What do you mean?"

"Well, sweetie, when you were little and they told us you couldn't see color or do magik, we hated it for you. But we accepted what Heckerman and the other witch doctors told us. That your problem was a birth defect. We didn't question that assumption. Even then I asked over and over what we could do to fix it. I feel stupid that I never thought to ask what caused it."

"Now you do?" I wondered what they were leading up to and what would be the consequences.

"In all the reading I did, even in human children, no one is ever completely colorblind. Sometimes two colors look the same to them, like red and green, but they see something."

Sarah took a breath and held it as if deciding whether or not to go on. She reached across the table and took my hot hands into her cool ones. The elevated temperature of the Were in me bled into her slim fingers.

"As long as we weren't asking about mix breed paranormals, the archive librarian didn't seem to mind what I poked around into. The only reference I found to complete colorblindness came from a very old spell. I mean a really ancient spell. I didn't see the spell itself. The Grimoire it's written in is so old it's in a magically protected case so it doesn't fall apart. You have to have a special spell just to read the spell.

I only saw a scroll of spell descriptions and uses."

I leaned in closer, afraid to know but unable to not know what Sarah had found. "And?"

Her soft brown eyes stared into mine with worry and fear for me. "It's a binding spell, a very powerful binding spell."

"Excuse me? A what?"

I knew what a binding spell did of course, but I had a hard time swallowing that in reference to myself. I could be bound with a simple Teflon cord. I'd always been a magikal nil. No spell needed of any kind for me, much less a powerful one.

Sarah shook her head at me as if she understood where my confusion rested. "You are missing the big picture, Harmony. This spell is used to bind the powers of an extremely powerful being. It takes an unbelievably strong coven or powerful magik users to even get past the first phase. It's designed to suspend the creature's powers until the requirements of the spell are fulfilled. The spell not only takes away their powers, its masks their power signature, making them almost human. It's unbreakable. I'd never read anything like it before."

A sliver of foreboding unlike any other slid down my spine. I pulled my hands away because they had begun to tremble. Sitting up straight, I wrapped my arms around my own body to suppress a shudder.

"You keep saying words like creature and being. What are you not telling, Sarah?"

Moments can brush by like the flit of a hummingbird's wings, so fast you can't see them, or agonizingly slow. This moment didn't pass on colorful feathers.

To give her credit, Sarah never flinched. "The spell, Harmony, is used to bind the powers of a dragon."

Okay, this had to be a joke. Some asinine practical jest that my parents had decided to play on me for Halloween that had seemed hilarious when the thought occurred, but now in retrospect probably wasn't such a good idea. Any minute now they would laugh in that way parents did when they realized their kids didn't think they were funny and then they'd tell me about their prank.

Any minute now.

Any minute.

Now.

Now, dammit!

Okay, if they wouldn't take the lead then I would. "Very funny, ha, ha, ha. Is this your guy's way of showing me that things are never as bad as they seem? I get it. Boy, I really walked into that one." I chuckled. They didn't.

"The joke's over. I'm not buying it. A dragon? Pul-leeze. No one has heard of or seen a dragon in what, eight or nine hundred years? They're extinct. Like dinosaurs." I shook my head with scornful disbelief.

"I said it was a very old spell." Sarah replied.

"They say the alligator and the Komodo dragon are prehistoric relics, close cousins of the dinosaurs." Charlie supplied.

"I am not part dragon." There, I said it, a statement of fact.

"Dragons were white magik personified. They could do it all, shape shift, sorcery, illusion, enchantments." Sarah didn't help.

"I am *not* part dragon. I can only do two of those things and not very well, I might add."

"You don't do them *yet*." Still not helping, Sarah.

"I am not part dragon!" I bellowed, practically breathing fire in my aggravation with them.

Charlie pursed his lips. "I've heard that dragons were extremely stubborn and set in their ways too."

Okay, he had me there. I crossed my arms over my chest and refused to look at them.

I felt them move around me. Sarah scooting into the seat on my left, Charlie moved around the u-shaped bench to come to my right. Their arms came around me together.

"Kitten," he coaxed. "We are not saying you are anything other than what we can see and know for the moment, our daughter. But our daughter is experiencing some things that neither we nor she, have ever been through before. Like any good parents, we are going to look at all options and keep our minds open for ways to help you."

"Help me?" I almost choked on the words. "How is suggesting that I am... that I might even have a drop of... that kind of blood in me, helpful?"

"To be forewarned is to be forearmed." He quoted at me.

"For what? Against whom? A knight, errant, riding up on a white charger with his ten foot lance?" Okay, that had been smart-assed and disrespectful, but I operated in panic-slash-denial, leaning toward denial. It worked better for me than full on panic.

Both Charlie and Sarah gave me reproachful glares. Their arms fell away from my shoulders.

"You'll not take that tone, Harmony Leigh, not in my house." Sarah warned me. I instantly felt bad about it, contrite.

"I'm sorry." I mumbled then whined. "But it's just too much. Too far out there to be real. I just can't, I mean, I just can't…"

I felt overwhelmed. My eyes prickled with tears. Blood pounded in my ears, giving me a roaring headache. My chest heaved against what felt like the weight of an ocean.

"Don't you understand? It's too much. I just can't take anymore." I lay my arms on the table, dropped my head and sobbed bitter tears.

Outside the window of the breakfast nook, ominous dark clouds gathered over our quaint home. A deep rumble of thunder shook the house once before the skies opened with a deluge.

Over my head I heard the soft whispers of Charlie and Sarah as they exchanged thoughts.

"Youth." Sarah sighed.

"Hormones." Charlie's deep voice countered.

"Control of the elements." Sarah proposed as the rain kept pace with my crying. I buried my head and cried harder at the thought. The rain poured.

Ten, twenty, possibly thirty minutes later, I finally cried myself out, mostly. I had it down to painful hiccups, snotty nose and a few stray drops of sorrow juice. Sometimes you just had to have a pity party before you could move on.

Charlie had left after the first five minutes of hopeless wailing. Men aren't the best at dealing with tearful tirades. It's their nature to want to fix things. To make it all better. To slay the mythical drago.., uh, beast for us.

When they discovered that sometimes women just want to have a good cry before we did our own fixing or slaying of the beast, they were useless. So, instead of waiting on the rain to stop, both literally and figuratively, he went to work.

I sat up in the bench seat, wrapped my arms around legs I'd drawn close to my chest and watched the rain dissipate as my tears dried. Sarah had continued to bustle around her kitchen, cleaning away the breakfast remains that had gone uneaten.

"Do you really think I caused that?" I asked quietly. "The rain?"

Sarah faced me with a speculative look, frying pan in one hand, dish towel in the other. "I don't know. Do you want me to make you cry some more and see if it happens again?"

She looked so benign, but a twinkle in her eye belied the dry casualness of the question. I couldn't help the sheepish grin that spread.

"Thanks, but I'd rather not."

"Then what would you like to do today? There's no school, and the Halloween festivities won't start until evening."

"Well, when I came down this morning, I'd planned on asking you for a trip to the beauty shop. I wanted to get my hair cut and styled, maybe. I thought about letting you buy me some makeup like you've always wanted to."

"Oh, really?" she asked, the hand with the dish towel going to her hip to strike a saucy pose. "You were going to let *me* get *your* hair done and buy *you* some makeup, maybe for the dance tonight."

I shook my head in agreement with the proposal; like she had the great idea and I would go for a ride along. "Yeah, that sounds like a good plan."

The corner of Sarah's mouth quirked in a half smile. She placed the clean pan on the stove, thinking it over. "Nothing like a little girl's day out to lighten the load, I guess."

My own long face had perked up into a wide smile. "Really?"

"Really." She agreed. "Go get your coat. I'll finish in here and meet you in the foyer."

I raced up the steps to my room to snatch up the hoodie from last night. Pulling it over my head, I caught a whiff of Tesch's scent. Being held in his arms, his unique fragrance had rubbed off onto the fabric. I felt better by the second. Sunbeams poked through the last of the clouds and shone brightly.

Nothing like a good cry, shopping and first love to chase away the blues. I bounced back down the steps to meet Sarah, ready for the rest of the day. I would think happy thoughts, sing and dance my way through my troubles and enjoy being a girl. Eat my dust, Walt Disney.

Chapter 13

AT THE TOP OF THE STAIRS I stood hesitant and nervous. I felt dizzy, my head swimming. Blood pounded at the pulse points of my wrists and neck. My stomach churned with butterflies. Ha, butterflies, how ironic.

I glanced over my shoulder at the gold and black gossamer wings Sarah and I, mostly Sarah, had made for the Halloween dance tonight. The filmy material had been stretched over a wire frame to form a graceful replica of the Monarch's glory. Sequins and golden glitter accented the patterns of the delicate creature's beauty.

For the dress, we had chosen black velvet. The soft nap of the material reminded me of the subtle hair of the butterfly's body. The dress itself had been fashioned into a simple, clinging sheath with long sleeves and a high collar, the style almost oriental. Modest slits ran from my knees down to the floor, allowing walking room.

The neckline fastened with a single jet bead beneath my hair before opening in a slim keyhole fashion to allow for the wing apparatus. My spine, from neck to waist, lay exposed.

Though I found nothing shocking about the dress, fabric modestly covered my flesh, I felt exposed. The way the velvet hugged me like second skin made me feel uneasy. My small waist and hips were outlined by the material. I wished my bust were less prominent. Usually I hid the fact that I had more than most upstairs with baggy T-shirts. I'd never been more aware of my figure.

Sarah had taken me to an upscale Fae salon where I'd been pampered and plucked, shampooed and styled. The hairdresser had oohed and aahed over the virgin quality and thickness of my hair.

She had applied a conditioning rinse to moisturize and bring out the natural highlights of ash, oak, cherry wood and mahogany. I'd never had my hair towel dried with a length of raw silk, but the sidhe stylist swore by it as the only way. She had trimmed the length and added some long layers from shoulder to waist, revealing a natural curl that had been weighed down by my previous cut.

Finally, she had piled the heavy mass on top of my head in a loose up do and left a few deliberate strands of curl hanging down my back and over my shoulders. The hair artiste had then secured the black antennae amid the curls on top of my head.

I didn't know if by skill or magik, but the style promised stayed in place for the rest of the day. Not a single curl had slipped. Before leaving, she had made me promise to come back and see her soon and to never, ever allow anyone to talk me into coloring my hair.

"Your hair has the most wonderful collection of natural colors and highlights I've seen in two hundred years. I know women in this city who'd pay a fortune to have this very combination chemically."

After that, Sarah had taken me to a cosmetics boutique. There, a very human lady had exclaimed over my flawless complexion and the peaches and cream nature of my face. She had shown me the art of applying makeup that looked like I wasn't wearing any at all. I wondered aloud: if the goal meant to look like I wore no makeup then why put it on at all?

She explained kindly, "Makeup is to accentuate the beauty that is already there, not make a mockery of it; small contrasts and enhancements to bring out the best of you. It's the difference between painting a barn bright red and Da Vinci painting the Mona Lisa. Both get noticed and get talked about, but the barn eventually fades, while the Mona Lisa is beautiful always."

Sarah helped me decide that a mask would be hot and uncomfortable at the dance, so after cosmetic basics 101, the nice Merle Norman lady helped paint my face in a domino style of ambers, gold and bronze with black curlicues.

She added false topaz gems and glued them to my cheeks with a special adhesive. She swore my eyelashes were so thick and long I needed only a touch of sable brown mascara, and not a pair of false eyelashes.

Simple black pumps and the beloved golden heart Tesch had given completed the look. The giver and keeper of my heart now waited downstairs for me.

I could hear Tesch and Charlie's voices murmuring but couldn't make out more than an occasional "Yes, sir." and "No, Charlie, I won't." from Tesch. I prayed quickly to Gaia that my parent wouldn't embarrass me.

So why did I feel so nervous? It wasn't like Tesch had never seen me before. We'd been friends since first grade. Maybe because he had never seen me like *this*.

Heck, I'd never seen me like this, all dressed up, decked out and well, pretty. I wanted him to like the new look.

Too late to back out, I took a deep breath and started my decent of the stairs. The voices halted mid conversation. I had one hand on the bannister and my other holding the hem of my dress slightly up so I wouldn't trip. I watched each step carefully since heels were not my favorite footwear.

Reaching the bottom step, silence greeted me. I looked up to see surprised faces on the men in my life. I heard the soft feminine steps of Sarah as she came in from the kitchen behind me to join us.

"Well?" My voice shaky to my own ears.

"Doesn't she look…" Sarah began.

"Amazing." Charlie interrupted.

"Beautiful." Tesch finished.

Warmth spread in my cheeks, my lashes dipped and a shy smile spread across my lip glossed mouth.

"Thanks, you look…um," I raised my eyes to take in Tesch and his costume. I used the only appropriate word. "Loud."

He wore a fire engine red suit. His curls had been forced into their usual spiky crown but amid the points, slightly off center, cocked to the right, a rotating light flashed red and another color I had yet to name in my growing repertoire. On a heavy chain around his neck a red, miniature, air raid siren dangled.

I giggled as I got the joke.

Tesch had dressed as a siren; redundancy at its best. My amusement seemed to break the spell I held on the two males. Simultaneously, their mouths finally closed.

"Well, Kitten." Charlie smiled. "You are going to knock 'em dead tonight. You look absolutely gorgeous."

"I couldn't agree more. I'll be the envy of every guy there. Wow, Harmony. I don't know if anyone would recognize you if you weren't going with me. I'll have to keep you close so no one tries to steal you away." With that, he leaned over, and in front of my parents, planted a soft kiss on my flushed cheek.

"See that you do." Charlie warned. "But not too close." He gave Tesch the hairy eyeball.

A look passed between them. Tesch gave Charlie another of those manly nods of understanding. It made me wonder exactly what they had been talking about at the bottom of the stairs before I arrived.

"Men." Sarah sighed with exasperation. She stepped forward between the two and handed me something luxuriously warm and furry. "Here, wearing a coat is out with those wings, and I don't want you to get cold."

I gasped. "Your sphinx stole?"

The length of black fur had been a gift from Sarah's grandmother long ago, before Sarah had been disowned by her family. The pelt had come from one of the magikal winged lions and had been enchanted to keep the wearer perfectly comfortable no matter how cold the temperature. It had always been one of Sarah's most prized possessions.

"I want you to wear it. In fact, I want you to have it." Her eyes misted. "It's been passed down for generations in my family. It's only right that my daughter have it."

I didn't know what to say. Thank you seemed lame.

"Oh, Sarah, you are the best mom anyone could have. I love you. I'll take care of it, I swear."

She took the stole from my hands to drape it across my shoulders in the correct fashion. "I love you too." She replied before enveloping me in a fierce maternal hug, chuckling as she released me. "And you better."

"Ready, Princess?"

For once, I felt the part, dressed in velvet and enchanted fur and jewels. I didn't tell him to stuff the nickname up his nose. "Ready, my prince."

Tesch smiled widely and offered me his arm with a courtly bow. "Your carriage waits."

Of course, leaving didn't prove quite that simple. Sarah and Charlie wanted pictures to commemorate the occasion. We dutifully posed on the stairs and the porch and the lawn as directed. Two rolls of film later, Tesch led me away to his newly purchased truck.

I don't know what I expected, but the faded, dark green seventies model Chevy hadn't been it. The back had steps on the side just behind both doors and didn't seem as long as other trucks. The fenders on the truck bed rounded out and were knobby with small dents here and there.

"Well? What do you think?" I could hear the male pride in his voice, and I had no desire to crush it.

"It's great!" I enthused.

"Really? You like it?"

"Of course. It's got a lot of potential. I can see that."

Tesch beamed. "Yeah, it does. I want to paint it and fix it up and all that. But what sold me is what's under the hood. The body is old, but the engine and transmission and stuff are all new. The guy I bought it from intended on fixing it up for his kid, but the kid didn't want it. He wanted a brand new truck. Spoiled brat if you ask me."

Tesch walked me to the passenger door which he had to open from the inside through the window, all the while expounding the virtues of his new ride. His voice rushed, enthusiastic as a kid with a new toy.

"It's got a four hundred and fifty five cubic inch engine block the guy ordered from the factory and a modified, five speed stick transmission. The thing will run like a scalded dog."

"Is that good?" I tested the springs of the bench seat he helped me climb up on. It looked clean and wouldn't ruin my dress but was lumpy.

Tesch rolled his eyes. His expression clearly shouted, *girls!* "Yes, that's good. In fact, it's great if you need to get somewhere in a hurry."

"Great, then show me. Let's get to the dance in a hurry." I felt the mischievous twinkle in my eyes as I smiled.

"Oh, you are so gonna get it, little miss carnival queen." He promised as he closed the door on my side. "For years you've been scaring the crap out of me with your thrill rides, now it's my turn."

As Tesch came around to his side, I rolled the ancient crank on the window glass till it closed. Only then did I notice a small modification to the truck that could have only been his doing.

Etched in the glass by the door lock on my side, the word Princess showed pale in the moonlight. I glanced over my shoulder to the window on his side before he got in. There, he'd engraved Aqua Man. Special warmth spread through my chest that had nothing to do with the magik of the sphinx stole.

I realized that I never strayed far from Tesch's thoughts. He loved me. He'd given me his heart in more ways than one.

I loved him too, but it had come as a much newer idea for me than him, I believed. These feelings we had were yet to be tested outside the small world we circled in. I'd recently discovered that any kind of power comes with a price. Love exists as power unto itself. With a shudder of apprehension, I hoped to be up to the job of keeping his heart whole.

We sped off through town, taking a longer route to double back on highway 102, which ran into McLoud. It gave Tesch the chance to show off his truck's abilities. I have to admit he had me reaching for the dashboard as a hand hold, hitting a burst of straightaway and pegging the speedometer out at 110 miles per hour. But I loved it.

Someday I'd like to fly. I'd never been on a plane. His old truck didn't look like much, but it could definitely fly over land. The ride exhilarated me.

We arrived at the school gymnasium. Already, the music could be heard from outside. From the pulsing rock and roll beat, I could imagine the dance in full swing. Good, we could go in without much fuss.

Still nervous about my new look, and unready to come out of my shell, I hesitated. The stars twinkled overhead as Tesch again offered me his arm to escort me inside.

"Don't worry." He told me as if reading my thoughts. "You look incredible. I'm just jealous everyone will see what I've known all these years. That you're one in a million." He placed a hand over the fingers that rested on his other arm and gave me a gentle squeeze of assurance.

The gym had been transformed with black and neon green and orange crepe paper into a Halloween gala. Though All Hallow's Eve was a recognized holiday among the witch community and treated with the sanctity of the Christian Christmas. For a high school dance, the human conceptions were hard to get away from.

There were grinning jack-o-lanterns with candles inside as center pieces on black draped tables. Yellow and black witch cutouts dangled from the ceiling with black cats and white, bony skeletons. Collecting tickets at the door were Mr. Poff, dressed as a ghost, and our computer science teacher, Ms. Hensley, dressed as a ghoul.

"My, my, my, I think the egg is hatching. Or is it a cocoon?" Mr. Poff teased, recognizing me.

I teased back. "The ghost of John Lennon called, Mr. Poff. He wants his sandals back." I glanced meaningfully down at the well-wore Huaraches that were his trademark.

"Good one, Phillips." He glanced at the tickets Tesch held out, not bothering to tear them the way he should. "Been giving any more thought to my question? About the ties that bind?"

"Some." I answered, though truthfully with everything that had been recently going on, it had been only a passing thought.

"And?"

I knew he wanted some kind of answer. Process of elimination can be a handy tool. If wrong, I'd be no worse off than when I started. I stood there and gave it some serious pondering.

An idea wormed into my brain that felt right. "Fear." I said. "High or low, male or female, doesn't matter. We are all afraid of something."

Poff smiled. "Good guess, a really good guess, but no. That's not the answer I'm thinking of. Keep working it out."

Tesch slid the tickets into the breast pocket of his suit, and we turned to face one of my fears, my peers. I smiled humorlessly at the thought.

Until very recently, I hadn't considered any of them as peers. You have to be on equal footing with a group for them to be considered peerage. They had been the Lords and Ladies of the high school. I had been the magikless peon, everyone above me. Now, I came as a card carrying member of the club. I had done magik.

More than a few heads turned and looked our way as Tesch led me by the arm to an unoccupied table. "You okay?" he asked.

My body tense, I knew Tesch could feel the stiffness in me. "Yeah, I think so. But my mouth feels as dry as one of those skeletons they have hanging from the ceiling."

He held out a chair. I removed the stole and draped it over the back. Glad to sit, my knees felt a little wobbly.

"I'll go and get us something to drink." He offered. Before I could protest not to leave me, he began weaving his way through the throng of students over to the other side of the dance floor.

I heaved a sigh and tried to smile. Mentally I coached myself to relax. This wasn't a fate worse than death, just a dance.

"Is that real sphinx fur?" A female voice invaded my internal, self-calming, pep talk.

I turned to find a cheerleader. Not one of our schools actual cheerleaders but close enough. She wore a maroon and white uniform emblazoned with the Oklahoma University, OU Sooners logo. Her midnight hair had been pulled up in twin dog ears that hung past her hips. She had the dark skin and exotic beauty of the Arab people. I knew her heritage to be older than Persia.

Joliet Coombs, a senior and reigning high school everything stood just behind my right shoulder. Joliet's father presided as our mayor, her mother head of the school board. They were both respected Djinns. It had been predicted Joliet would be valedictorian this year, as well as prom queen.

I dry swallowed at my tongue to make it work. People like Joliet never spoke to me.

"Uh, yes, yes it is."

"Oh wow! I've always wanted something made of sphinx fur. It's so rare. Give you three wishes for it." She offered brightly.

Shocked. No other word for it, I gaped at her totally shocked. "Excuse me?"

"Three wishes. You know, you say I wish for and poof... it's yours."

I hesitated. Not because I would ever part with the fur, but surprised by the offer on so many levels. "Um, no thank you. It's special. My mom gave it to me."

"No? You sure?"

I shook my head no. The look on my face must have been resolute.

"Oh well, can't blame a jinni for trying. You're Harmony Phillips, right?"

"Yes."

"Mind if I sit?"

She didn't wait for a reply. Joliet sat down at my table in a 'most natural thing in the world' way. Thankfully, I didn't have to say a lot. Joliet had the reputation of being a talkative girl and didn't disappoint.

"I've been hearing a lot about you lately. I mean, people have always talked about the colorblind kid. How you couldn't do magik and all. My mom's on the school board and well, I remember when they considered not letting you into school. Some people wanted your parents to send you to Dale or Harrah with the human kids. But some felt that since you did know about magik and stuff, even if you couldn't do it, that you could be a blabber mouth and bring the whole works down on our heads, so they let you stay."

"Really?" I asked tightly. It's supposed to be nice to be the topic of discussion among the proud and powerful. Not.

Joliet continued to babble on. "But now, the rumor is you can do magik, that you're not colorblind anymore. I heard you pulled of a really good illusion on that over-stuffed jerk, Challen Parks. You know his dad ran against mine for mayor once. Can you believe it? As if." She curled her cherry red lips in disgust.

"Anyway, so now that you can do magik, are you going to keep doing it or are you planning on getting out of here and away from the whole paranormal world like me?"

"Uh, I hadn't thought about it."

True. Magik remained very new to me as far as my having powers went. And what I had I couldn't control. They didn't seem very useful right now, more of a pain really.

"Well, I have. Of course, my parents want me to go to a Djinn university back in the home country. They feel it would be good for me to spend a century in a bottle. Please! Me? Trapped in a moldy bottle or tired lamp for a hundred years, making everyone else's dreams come true while mine rot? No, thank you. I want to go to a real college, like OU or LSU."

"My dad teaches American History at OU."

A look of surprise came over her striking face. Instinct in me denied the sincerity of her look.

"That's right. I think my mom mentioned that a long time ago about you. Your parents gave up their magik and live like humans. I think that would be awesome. To not have to deal with magikal parents that can blink you to your room anytime they don't like what you have to say."

"Well, they may not blink me there, or whatever, but trust me, they can still send me there when I mess up."

"But they can't magically seal the room and keep you there until they see fit." She countered. "You could still sneak out a window or something if you wanted to, I don't know, go see a boy, right?"

"I guess I could. I never have though."

She seemed disappointed in my answer. "At least you could if you wanted."

"I suppose."

"Is that your boyfriend heading this way?"

I looked up and smiled to see Tesch moving carefully in our direction, trying not to spill the punch cups on himself or anyone else. I blushed as I answered. "Yes, he is."

"He's cute. You are so lucky. My parents would never let me date anyone who wasn't pure Djinn. They are too afraid it might get serious and well, you know the laws on mixed breeding. But your parents did it and gave up their powers for love, didn't they? Are they happy they did?" For the first time since she started talking, I felt like the question had some weight.

I thought about Charlie and Sarah and their sacrifice for true love. Did they regret it? Maybe, sometimes, but not enough for it to matter. "Yes, they're happy. At least I'm pretty sure they are. They seem to be."

Joliet sighed wistfully. "You are so lucky."

I didn't disagree. I had been very lucky in many ways and knew it.

"Well, your boyfriend is almost back, so I am going to get out of the way. See you around sometime." Joliet quickly got up and flounced away, much like she had sat down.

Tesch arrived and set the cups down on the table. "Was that Joliet Coombs?"

"Yep, it was."

"What did she want?" His face as confused I felt.

"I'm not really sure. Maybe my sphinx fur, maybe not." I answered with a shrug.

Reaching for the cup he had brought me, I took a sip. Ginger ale and pineapple sherbet mixed for punch wasn't bad. I liked yellow as a color and taste I recognized.

"Okay." He drew out the vowel sounds making the word much longer. A thing guys did when they didn't understand a girl thing we did. "So, you want to dance?"

"Sure."

Now, I might have been insecure about a lot of things, but dancing wasn't one of them. Tesch had made fun of my carnival happy dance when I won that twenty, but give me something with a beat and I got rhythm, baby.

He took my hand and led me to the floor. I recognized the first song as the latest by Bruno Mars, which I liked, followed by an 80's pop tune by Modern English.

The music eventually slowed. Some song that invited couples to put their arms around each other began. The dance floor thinned a bit. Tesch pulled me a little closer, and then I heard a deep voice rumble from behind.

"May I cut in?"

Tesch's face darkened, and his eyes narrowed. "What's do you want, Parks?"

I turned quickly, astonished. Challen Parks stood tall and wide. He'd come to the party dressed as a gangster. Not the modern bling-bling, baggy pants 'gangsta', but as an Al Capone, roaring '20's, spats and suit wearing, Tommy gun toting type.

Being honest, I had to admit the cut of the clothes emphasized the better aspects of his physique. The broad shoulders, tapered waist and narrow hips were all flattered by the black and charcoal gray pin stripes.

The tall boy had the grace to flush. "Just a dance."

I felt the tension gathering in Tesch as he took a deep breath to blast Challen verbally with something I knew wouldn't be polite or politically correct. I squeezed his hand before he could get started.

"Tesch, it's okay." He gave wide eyes of surprise. "It's just a dance. The whole school is watching, so I don't think he'll try anything."

"If I do, Harmony can always make me look like a dog again, right?" He smiled lopsided, half grimace, half apologetic. His eyebrow elevated with the question.

Tesch's gaze quickly took in me, Challen and the student body several times. His lips tightened with a decision. "All right. One dance, but you keep your paws to yourself Parks, or you and *I* are going to dance."

Challen held his hands up in surrender. Tesch backed off the dance floor reluctantly. I turned to Challen. "Well, you wanted to dance."

He held out his hand and took me stiffly into the dancer's pose. I held my body erect and away from him. It made our moves awkward and stilted.

Our feet shuffling, his voice came low near my right ear, "You look really nice tonight, Gray."

My feet stopped moving at the old taunt. I looked up at him with loathing.

"I'm sorry. I'm sorry. Old habits, old *bad* habits die hard." He apologized.

"Tesch had the right idea. What do you want, Challen? I know you hate me. You've made it painfully clear for years."

"I don't hate you." He began. "Well, I thought I did, but… well, now I don't know."

"Excuse me? Could you run that by me again, in English?"

"Your spell started it." He accused with hesitation. "My parents had to send me to a witch doctor, a strange woman, to get it lifted. She said to break the glamour I had to break the idea behind it. You called me a coward when you cast it, a yellow dog coward. And I *was* afraid of people seeing me as scared of anything."

"Yeah, so?" I felt uncomfortable with this conversation but true to his word, he wasn't being deliberately nasty. We scuffed our feet some more, turning slowly in time to the music.

"This doctor, she said I had to look at my fears and get over them or past them or some crap like that, but it started making some sense after a while. I realized there were some things I felt frightened about. One of them was you."

"Me?" I couldn't keep the astonishment from my voice. I stopped moving and looked up into his hazel stare. "Challen, I am five feet nothing and one hundred and twelve pounds completely dressed. You have at least a foot of height and a hundred pounds on me any day. Until very recently, I couldn't cast anything, not even a dirty look, that you didn't give me grief for. How on Gaia's green earth could you be afraid of me?"

His face turned scarlet beneath his tanned good looks. I watched his brown and green eyes look anywhere but my face. "Not scared like that, more scared of well, uh, how I feel about you. I'm so confused."

I couldn't help but admit in a disbelieving tone, "That makes two of us."

"Really?" He brightened.

"Yes. I mean no. I am not confused about how I feel about you, but I am sure confused about what you're saying. Could you just spit it out?"

The color came again to his cheeks before bleaching away. His lips tightened in a grim line.

"Harmony, there's something about you that makes me want to be around you. It's weird, like a pack feeling. Weres are drawn to each other because pack is family. Weres move in groups as a rule, a pack, a pard, a flock or whatever. I'm drawn to you like that, but I shouldn't be."

"Oh."

I thought about my recent discovery of being a Were and wondered if other Weres could sense it on an instinctive level. But my lynx and Challen's wolf didn't mix. There's that old enmity between cats and dogs. Challen's next comments made my suspicions stronger.

"But when I do get around you, suddenly I'm thinking about ways to take a bite out of you. And well, you're pretty, and I shouldn't think that about anyone who's not a Were. It gets me very frustrated, and I get mad and well, I've acted like a jerk."

The song wound down. Soon we would part ways. Challen rushed through the next part of his speech.

"So, anyway, my witch doctor says I should stop trying to make my feelings make sense because feelings don't always make sense. She says I should stop taking it out on you and just accept it. I'm saying I'm sorry. Even if you don't forgive me, I've said it, so there. Truce?"

His posture became defensive, haughty. I understood it now as a way to protect him, a shield against feelings he didn't want and didn't understand. Boy did I ever sympathize with confusion these days. If he could be big enough and brave enough to call a ceasefire, I would accept the white flag he offered.

"Sure, Challen, truce, I accept your apology. I never wanted to fight with you."

He smiled sadly. "I know. My bad."

The music died, and we stepped away from each other. I turned to leave the floor to find Tesch, but his fingers held onto mine a moment more. I turned back toward the pull of his hand.

I didn't see it coming. Challen leaned in and planted a soft kiss on my cheek. I felt my eyes go wide with surprise. My mouth curved into an 'oh' of disbelief.

Before I could utter a sound, Challen smiled widely. "You really do look crazy hot tonight. I just wanted to be able to say I kissed the prettiest girl at the dance even if I didn't get to take her home."

He let go of my hand and moved off into the crowd that filled the floor for an upbeat song. I stood in the middle of the mass of kids too stunned to move.

Challen Parks had kissed my cheek. I didn't know if I should be flattered or get a rabies shot. The unkind thought belittled the gesture.

Old habits and bitter conflict die a hard death.

Shock wore off and I stumbled off the dance floor to find Tesch. I found him sitting at the table where we'd left our glasses earlier. He knocked back a cup of punch like a redneck would a brew.

"Did you check that before you chugged it to make sure it's not spiked?"

"I was rather hoping it was."

"And why is that?"

"'Cause it would explain what I just saw a lot easier. Tell me I did not see Challen Parks lay his mongrel lips on your face?"

I picked up on the dangerous edge in his voice, realizing we weren't just bantering. Tesch seemed genuinely angry, jealous of an innocent, unsolicited kiss.

"Tesch! You're jealous!"

"I am not!" he denied hotly. "I'm just afraid of you coming down with some strange dog disease, like Parvo. There's no telling what kind of germs that fool is carrying around in his mouth. He probably licks his own butt when he's in wolf form."

I sat down in the chair next to him and slid my arms around his shoulders. This awkward maneuver had me leaning in close to his handsome face, chest to chest. His arms loosened their rigid posture to slip under my wings and around my waist.

"I didn't ask him to kiss me, Tesch. It surprised me too."

He rested his forehead against mine. His eyes lowered toward my chin. "I know. Still, I don't like it. We just started being more than friends and it's new and when I saw him sneak in like that on you, I wanted to flip out."

"Harmony, I've known for forever how awesome you are. I can see other guys figuring it out too, especially after tonight. The competition is going to get stiff. I want to make sure I'm way ahead of them before they start putting the moves on."

I couldn't help but laugh. "Oh, come on, Tesch. You can't be serious."

"Very serious. Look around, open your eyes, sweetie. Half the males in the room haven't been able to take their eyes off of you."

"Doesn't matter." I replied with a shrug.

"Why not?"

"Two reasons. One, cross species dating is frowned upon. For all anyone knows, I am strictly in the Fae category. Only Fae boys would ever actually ask me out. Of course, a yellow-green elf or a warlock is a possibility, Gaia forbid."

"Definitely, Gaia forbid." He agreed with me, some of his natural good humor leaking through. "And reason two?"

"It's the more important reason. No matter who is looking at me, Tesch, I only looking at you. You are the only one I have ever seen that way." I tried to reassure him.

He gave me a smile, half grateful, half longing. "And I pray every day it's always going to be like that."

Our lips met in a soft cling of passion. The urge to take the kiss deeper hung between us, but I held back. Public displays of affection at school functions were frowned upon.

As if conjured by the thought, an angry buzz of ethereal wings hovered above us. "That will be enough of that, Ms. Phillips or you'll be right back in detention."

We pulled back from each other reluctantly. Ms. Idlewilde floated above us in her true pixie form. Even with the new color vision I had been experiencing, she appeared to me as a lovely slate of gray.

"Hello, Ms. Idlewilde. How are you this evening?" I inquired politely.

She ignored me completely.

"Mr. Wight? Does your guardian know that you are consorting with this... person? I think he would be very disappointed to learn about your low taste in companionship."

I felt the air leave my chest in a gasp. Ms. Idlewilde had often regarded me with hostility, but she usually stopped short of insulting. I didn't think teachers were supposed to talk to students that way, under any circumstance. Then again, she wasn't actually talking to me; she talked around me to Tesch.

Tesch stiffened also. He released me and stood to come eye to eye with the winged female. I reached out for his hand to give it a gentle squeeze, a reminder to keep his cool. He returned the gesture.

"Ms. Idlewilde, my guardian is well aware of who I spend time with. He's a rare breed of paranormal with an open mind and liberal spirit. He judges people by how they act, not who or where they come from. He's not at all like a lot of prejudice bigots we have in our town and in our school."

Tesch's voice remained controlled but hard. His pale green eyes had narrowed to a dirty look of disgust. There could be no doubt as to which prejudice bigot he meant as he raked the pixie with his cold gaze.

Idlewilde's cheeks pinked with two angry dots of color. The only color I could see in her, but not the only indication she seethed with anger. Her wings whined with the speed of their livid beating. Tiny fists clenched and her face contorted with hate.

"I really expected better of a city employee and his family. I may have to speak to someone at the next town council meeting about our lack of standards and mongrel acceptance issues. We can't have just anyone working for this community." Even I understood the veiled threat to Mr. Wight's job.

"I'm sure my guardian would welcome the chance to share his views as well. He seems to think that people working in public service should work for the good of everyone in the town, not just those they think are worthy, especially when *all* the public are paying their salary. Maybe Harmony's parents would like to be at that meeting too."

Ms. Idlewilde's small form shook with fury. Without another word she turned and flew off, away from our table.

Tesch stood tense, watching her go. I had to pull on his arm to shake him from the concentrated wrath I felt pulsing off of him. "Tesch, please sit down and relax."

He came to himself with a deep breath before sitting next to me again. "Fae and other paras like her just make me so mad! Can't they see what's becoming of us?"

I wasn't sure what he meant. "What do you mean, becoming of us?"

Tesch gave me a look of wonder. "Look around you, Harmony. Look at us, this community. Do you ever wonder how we came to be like this?"

"I still don't get what you are talking about."

Tesch sighed heavily. "Mr. Wight and I talk about this a lot. I think it's one of the reasons he agreed to take me in all those years ago."

I sat still and listened, sensing he had something serious to say.

"Think about it like this, Harmony. McLoud is one of two paranormal towns in this state. It's the same all around the country, around the world; small groups coming together because there just aren't enough of us anymore to live outside the protection of groups. We have about ten thousand people here, but only about six hundred kids in school for the whole system, grade school through seniors."

"Yeah, okay."

"So that's barely a five percent ratio of kids to grown-ups. The other paranormal towns aren't any better. We're the largest by far in the central area of the country. And this cross spectrum breeding law the Para-Council imposed nine hundred years ago doesn't help."

"What about..." I looked around to see if anyone close listened, and lowered my voice. "What about the carnival people?" I whispered.

"An isolated traveling group." He whispered back. "There are only a hundred, maybe less."

"The paranormals of the world have never been heavy on the child bearing side of the equation. Some people think its nature's way of balancing the books since we do live so much longer than pure humans. But in the last few hundred years, all paranormal populations are falling off."

"People are so afraid, no strike that, the Para-Council is so afraid of another Sancrenath Lyspladadas coming into being that they would rather see us die out than risk it. But I say, with the advancement of human technologies, it couldn't happen. Humans wouldn't let something like that happen."

"But then you get into the whole humans finding out that the paranormal world really does exist, and that's another can of worms no one wants opened."

"Wow, Tesch, I never realized you were so…" I searched for the right word, "political."

A grim smile twisted his lips. "There's still a thing or two about me that you don't know. I don't share every secret I have."

Absently, I reached for the topaz heart that hung below my breasts. "I'm starting to realize that."

He seemed to give himself a mental shake, and his smile grew into that lopsided, endearing grin I knew so well. "What am I doing? This is a dance, our big night out on the town of McLoud. We can talk politics and paranormal extinction anytime. I want to see some of those boogie down moves of yours again. Can you show me those steps you did at the coin drop last night? Those were some signature moves."

I slapped his arm half-heartedly, glad to let go of the seriousness and sour mood. "Just for that, I will *not* teach you how to dance."

"You, teach me how to dance? I don't think so, Princess. I got moves that you haven't even dreamed about." His eyes twinkled with humor and challenge.

I raised my eyebrow. "You think so, huh?"

"Oh, I know so."

"Put up or shut up, Aqua Man."

"Just waiting on you to get off your butt and hit the floor."

I laughed, took his hand and led the way. The rest of the evening blurred into dance after dance, interrupted by the occasional punch break. I had kicked off the pumps by nine o'clock, choosing comfort and fun over style.

I enjoyed a surprise by the number of students that stopped to make idle conversation during those times when Tesch and I did take a break from dancing. I got several compliments on my costume. Tesch teased me about having passed some bench mark of para-accceptance now that I'd been determined a Fae.

Like any good Cinderella story, midnight came and the dance broke up. I felt so tired, my feet aching; I curled up on the seat beside Tesch. My head resting on his shoulder, I fell asleep on the ride home.

I barely remembered him walking me to the door, except that the porch light shone, and Charlie remained up. I absolutely remember the good night kiss Tesch gave me and how it curled my toes and put a fire in the pit of my belly. Suddenly wide awake and craving his lips like a diver craving air, I returned his kiss.

After what seemed like only moments, the porch light winked on and off letting me know Charlie felt we had said enough goodbyes and good nights for the time being. Tesch gave me one last clinging peck on my swollen lips. "Sweet dreams, Princess. I'll talk to you tomorrow."

He opened the door for me, and I slipped into the house, closing the heavy wood behind me. I saw him walk away through the oval stained glass and watched his blurred image until it disappeared. Waiting until I heard his truck start and drive away, I turned and leaned against the door frame. A satisfied sigh escaped my lips.

"I take it you had a good time?" Charlie stood at the entry between the foyer and the formal living room, his smile indulgent and knowing.

"We had a great time. We danced so much my feet are numb and tingling."

Charlie chuckled. "You'll probably be sore tomorrow."

"Probably." I agreed. "Is Sarah back? I wanted to tell her everything."

"Not yet, Kitten. You know how these Samhain things go. Sarah may not be able to practice the craft, but she still likes to keep the sabots, and her old coven will keep her for hours just catching up and trading recipes. Many of the witches still respect her spell craft and ask advice on tricky bits of magik."

I thought about that for a minute. "You know, Charlie, before yellow and the illusion thing happened with Challen, I would have done almost anything to have a bit of magik of my own. I wondered how you two could give it up like that, for each other, for love."

"And now?"

"Well, now, I have magik, some anyway, and I have love."

"And if you had to choose?"

"I'd choose Tesch."

He shook his head at my answer the way adults will do when their children say something that is particularly naïve. "You can never know how the future is going to play out, Harmony. Sometimes, even if you have a clue, fate can make a liar out of you. I sincerely hope you never have to choose, but if you do, I know you'll make a good choice."

I moved forward to give him a big hug, but stopped mid-step and groaned. My feet felt like I had stepped on a bed of nails. "Oh Stars! My feet are killing me. I don't know if I can get up the stairs."

Charlie's laughter tumbled from his chest. He came forward and hooked a strong arm around my waist to help. "Come on, little dancing queen. I'll help you get to your room, and then you are on your own."

We laughed and traded teasing remarks as he half carried me to my room. Once there, I did manage to wiggle out of my dress and wings before collapsing onto the bed. I fell asleep before my head touched the pillow.

Chapter 14

I dreamed.

I stood in the wheat field once again. I felt the dimensions of the grain around me shift. Where before the crops had been vast, as far as my eyes could see in any direction, now the rows had narrowed on either side, yet forward and back stretched endlessly.

The wind moved through the stalks, whispering my name in many voices I recognized and some I did not. With the swaying of the wheat heads, I saw faces form and change and reform, Tesch, Charlie, Sarah, Mr. Poff, Madame Osza, Ms. Idlewilde, Mr. Bellfwigg, Doctor Heckerman and a hundred, no, a thousand others from our community.

"The seeds have been planted, and the harvest is at hand. Will you allow the grain to spoil in the field and the land to lie fallow?" A feminine voice echoed huskily inside my head.

The words spoken felt warm and comforting; the cadence reminded me of Sarah reading bedtime stories about the Little Red Hen when I'd been small.

"Who are you? Are you my real mother?"

The breeze ruffled my hair and caressed my face. "Yes…and no. I am Mother of all who walk in my fields and gardens."

"Gaia." I sighed. The gentle embrace of the breeze on my face came as answer enough.

"I ask again, daughter, will you harvest my fields and gather the seeds I have sown for you or allow it all to go to waste and ruin?"

"I don't know anything about farming. You need a witch or an elf or someone good with growing things."

If the air could laugh I felt it chuckle against my skin. "I have those. I need a harvester, a leader. It's true you have much to learn, but there are those who can help, if you are willing."

I scanned the endless stretch of grain and realized I stood in the center of a road of wheat, a wheat path. So much bounty to be gathered and I had no tools, no scythe or basket. I had no idea where or how to start. It seemed an impossible task.

The Goddess flowed around me, reading my thoughts as easily as Sarah and the storybook from long ago. "No, it is not an easy thing I ask of you, little one. The way will be long and hard, but I will provide you with what you need. Though some tools will be sharp and reap a bitter fruit."

Overhead, dark clouds gathered and lightning flashed in the distance. A storm brewed on the horizon.

Gaia spoke to me once more. "If the storm breaks before the wheat is harvested, the crop will be lost. There will be no more seeds to sew. Are you willing?"

I thought again of the story. 'Not I' had said the cat. 'Not I' had said the duck. 'Not I' had said the pig. I thought of losing the faces in the wheat forever. Gaia asked if I was willing, the choice mine.

"I am."

The wind rustled through the field with a sigh of relief.

I woke to an overcast morning with the images of the dream fading. Dreams that seemed so vivid in the night could fade quickly with the light of day.

Sore from head to foot, I groaned deeply as I rolled over to search for my clock on the floor. I had no idea of the time and with the cloudy sky, the sunlight couldn't help me gauge how late I'd slept.

As the saying goes, I'd danced to the music, now the time had come to pay the piper. Apparently he charged a hefty rate. I pulled my legs out from under the covers and put feet to the floor. My groan grew to a moan. Remembering what an awesome time Tesch and I had with a smile, I felt the bill due had been worth it.

It took me longer, moving slower, to get dressed and downstairs. I'd taken the time to hang my lovely dress and precious sphinx stole in a garment bag Sarah had given me a few days before. I'd wondered at the time why she wanted me to hang the thing in my closet but now understood. Sneaky, loveable witch.

Reaching the kitchen, a rare wonder met me. Charlie stood at the stove, Sarah's apron over his sweater and slacks, scrambling eggs and Spam in a big skillet. Sarah sat in the breakfast nook, looking pale and bleary eyed, while nursing a large mug of coffee.

"Good morning, Kitten." Charlie beamed. "I was just about to call you downstairs. You're right on time for eggs a la Charlie."

I waved sleepily and mumbled good morning, plopping down on the breakfast bench next to Sarah. She groaned, using the hand that wasn't holding the coffee to cradle her forehead.

"What's wrong, Sarah? Are you sick?" Stupid question since the answer appeared obvious.

"Witch's Brew." Charlie called cheerfully over his shoulder from the stove as he scraped portions of eggs onto plates. He reached for a bowl of grated cheese and began to sprinkle it liberally over the steaming food. "It gets her every time."

I glanced at Sarah, astonished. My adoptive mother seemed, well, hung over. But the All Hallow's Eve coven sabot wasn't exactly a Tupperware party I supposed.

"Dang Margie Blackwell," Sarah muttered. "She always uses too much nightshade and Dandelion."

"Here, baby, eat something. You'll feel better." Charlie pushed a platter of eggs, canned meat, and cheese at his wife.

Sarah shot Charlie a doubtful glare but picked up a fork anyway. "Thank you…maybe."

"You too, Kitten. All that dancing and flirting and flitting around probably burned up all your reserves."

The smell of the food reached my nose as he set my plate down. My stomach growled in response. Charlie couldn't be more right. I felt ravenous. Unlike Sarah, I attacked my meal with gusto.

In between bites, Charlie asked me more questions about the dance, wanting more details than when I had come home. Sarah began to perk up, commenting about this and that tidbit or detail.

I shared the part about Joliet offering me wishes for my fur but quickly added that I said no thanks. I told about my dancing with Larry the Leprechaun and Challen Parks too. That got a response from both of my parents.

"Maybe a wolf can change his colors after all." Sarah considered.

Charlie's response was more skeptical. "Or maybe he's just trying to get Harmony to let her guard down."

Sarah mumbled a protest about looking for the best in people, but Charlie interrupted. "I'm not saying Harmony should be mean or impolite to the young man, Sarah. I'm just saying that it would be wise to use caution. He wouldn't be the first guy to use a girl's more tender sympathies against her. He hasn't exactly been the soul of kindness to her all these years."

Sarah reluctantly nodded in agreement. "True. Maybe you should listen to your father on this one, sweetie. My judgment is a little cloudy this morning."

I looked at her haggard face and mussed hair and giggled. It felt strange to see Sarah as anything less than completely put together. "Witch's Brew, huh? Did you get the recipe?"

"Oh, shut up." She responded without heat, a ghost of a smile hovered on her lips.

I also filled them in on the things Ms. Idlewilde had to say over me to Tesch. Sarah's warming smile faded into an icy glare. "That over-proud, prejudice, short-winged, shallow bitch!"

Sarah went on to add a few more words that would have made a sailor blush. Who knew Sarah had such a vocabulary? Her anger for my cause paled next to my wonder at her imaginative four letter adjectives. My eyes went wide, astonished.

For once, Charlie acted as the level headed, peace keeper. "Sarah, calm down. There's a right and wrong way to handle this. Going to the school and tearing her wings off isn't it."

"I've just about had it with her, Charlie. When she started teaching her biased version of Fae history, I let you handle it. I've watched Harmony study her brains out for that class and barely scrape by, knowing she's a much better student than that creature is giving her credit for. Now, come Monday, Harmony is supposed to spend an extra hour a day being subjected to her crap! I don't think so!" Her cheeks stained red with anger, and her eyes flashed dangerously bright.

"You're right. I couldn't agree more. Monday morning we'll talk with Bellfwigg. If necessary, we'll get Harmony a Fae tutor. Pay for it ourselves. But either way, we will be taking it up with the school board."

Being agreed with took some of the steam from Sarah's wrath. "Fine then, but I still want to give her a piece of my mind."

"Let's see how it goes with Bellfwigg, my love. Then if all else fails, you can 'rip those scrawny, moth flappers off and kick her narrow behind back to Never-Never Land'. Did I get that part right?"

Sarah blushed slightly, but a predatory gleam lit her velvety brown eyes. For a second I had a glimpse of the other side of Sarah that could have spawned the term evil witch.

I blame the time spent with her old coven or her feelings that I'd been slighted in the educational department, but on Sunday, Sarah began my witchcraft lessons in earnest.

We had already gone over the basics of spell craft and herb use. Having been raised in her kitchen, I had a passing familiarity with many of the ingredients as flavors in cooking. Today, she wanted to put some of them to another use by teaching me a warding spell and seeing if I could make it work.

"First, you are going to need this." She passed me a leather bound book across the breakfast table. It had been put together with traditional lacing rather than a binding.

I opened the pages to find them all blank. "What is it?"

"It's your Grimoire. Every witch has a recipe book, his or her spell book that they write their spells in. No two are alike because no two witches cast exactly the same spells."

"I don't understand."

"Think of it like cooking. Remember when you made lasagna from my recipe for my birthday last year?"

"Yes." Lasagna was Sarah's favorite food. I had followed the instructions in her cookbook exactly. It had been good, but not quite the same. I had asked what I had done wrong, and she had told me nothing, I just cooked differently. "It came out different even though I did it just like the recipe said."

"Spells and craft are the same. The witch or warlock has their own flavor that is developed over time into a signature. At first, your spells will be, pardon the word, bland, because you'll be copying my recipe. Eventually though, you'll find your own special touches and add them for more power and effect. When you do, write it down."

I sighed heavily. I had never been much of a cook and feared I wouldn't be much of a witch either. "Sarah, is this necessary? I mean, we don't even know if I will have any witch craft in me. I thought I just had to learn how to recognize a spell, like for general knowledge."

Her voice remained firm but not unkind. I recognized the tone as one that could not be argued with. "It's true that the school only requires a basic knowledge of herbs, their uses and recognition of the types of spells cast for non-witches. Whether or not you have any talent for the craft or power for casting, we are going to find out. I believe doing is the best teaching, so let's get started already."

We tied on aprons and set to work. Sarah's was a yellow, traditional number with the ruffles and lace that would make Betty Crocker proud. It had been sweetly embroidered with the words 'the Witch is in'. Mine resembled more of a mad scientist apron of denim material that covered me from my chin to my knees.

Sarah got out a kitchen step stool and went to a tall cupboard above the sink. From there, she took down her own spell book. It had been wrapped in cloth and had not a speck of dust on its cover.

She lovingly laid the book on a recipe stand out of harm's way then turned to me. "I've taught you before now that the first rule of the craft is 'Harm ye none.' The idea is more than a philosophy. It's an anthem or a prayer for us."

"Witches believe the force we borrow from the universe to make a spell work will forever change that energy. Once the spell is finished and the power captured for its use released, if the intent is for evil, that vitality returns tainted, bringing harmful intent back to you. It's a snowball effect because like gathers like."

"The threefold effect," I answered. She had taught me this all my life.

"Right."

"So first, I want you to close your eyes and clear your heart. Let go of any bad feelings or ill wills that may be in the back of your mind. I always imagined a clear lake stretching as far as I could see as I floated on my back under a warm sun."

The idea of a lake brought Tesch to mind, and while the thoughts were pleasant, they didn't Zen me out the way I thought Sarah wanted. I tried to find that place in my mind and heart where everything felt calm and right.

I traveled back to my dream last night, to the wheat field. With the echo of Gaia in my mind and on my skin, like the brush of wind and how right it had felt to agree to her will. Even if only a dream, those moments when she warmed me with the fingers of a breeze had been the center of goodness. My body swayed with the touch of the Goddess.

In my ear, I heard Sarah coaxing. "Good. Good, I think you are there. Now, when I tell you, I want you to open your eyes slowly, and don't focus on any one thing. Just let your mind's eye see without your worldly eyes getting in the way."

I felt her beside me, close but not too close. "Don't startle yourself. Just relax and open your eyes."

With a contented sigh, I relaxed and slowly let my lids drift open. As she had said, I didn't look to any particular object, letting my eyes settle on nothing, and I saw everything.

All around the room objects glowed with soft colors and rays, like coming out of the water on a sunny day before blinking away the haze. Things that had once started as living had faded hues. Live objects pulsed and had vivid colored auras, like the plants in the window boxes.

I turned my gaze slowly to Sarah in wonder. The halo of warmth surrounding her shimmered the way heat comes off the asphalt in the summer, in a beautiful deep green shade. I raised my hand to touch this glowing field.

My fingers encountered a throb of energy, the same feeling I always felt when magic had been done around me. Now I could see what I had known to be there, power.

"You have a glow, Sarah. It's faint, but it's there." My voice held awe.

Her smile shone proud and pleased. "That's the energy, the power of my life force. Every living thing has it. But the more magik a being possesses, the brighter or more vivid the aura."

"What do I look like?"

"I honestly don't know. Since I gave up my powers to live human with Charlie, I can't see the energy anymore. I still feel it sometimes, but I can't see it." Her voice sounded wistful. "Sometimes I wish I could see like that again, see you just once like that."

"It's amazing." I agreed.

She turned from me. I saw her wipe away a tear before she began bustling about her domain. From the cabinets she removed a pestle and mortar, copper pots and pans, a gallon of distilled water and a stash of her own preserved herbs.

"Fresh herbs and ingredients are best of course. If there are any we need from the window boxes we'll pluck them out. But everything you might need isn't always in season, so it's best to learn how to dry the plants at their peak of potency, and dry them whole if you can. You never know if you will need the whole plant or just the leaves or stem or flower parts."

Distracted by this new field of vision she had revealed to me, I found I could touch the rough cotton of my apron and find a faint pulse of energy. "Not that I want to, but how do you make it stop, Sarah? How do you not see this twenty-four seven?"

She shrugged. "You get used to it, and then it seems to melt into the background until you need to see then you focus your mind, and it's there again. Now, pay attention."

I did. What I had thought would be a learning chore became very interesting indeed.

"There are two basic types of warding spell. One that repels a certain person or type of energy; for instance, say you don't want door to door salesmen knocking and disturbing your Saturday. You can ward against interruption or even strangers. Then there is a warning warding. It's like a boundary spell that lets you know when someone crosses over the territory you don't want them in."

I could see practical uses for either. Suddenly, I felt eager to try. "Which one are we doing today?"

"Well, there's also a third warding that will actually do both. It's a bit trickier, but I thought we might try it."

She looked so enthusiastic and hopeful as if this had been something she had wanted to share with me my whole life. I realized that she had.

Sarah loved me as much as she would have a biological daughter. She would have shared her secrets and craft with me years ago if I had shown an ounce of aptitude for magik. I acknowledged her chance to fulfill a need of her own, to pass on the years of knowledge she had, if not the actual talent.

I wouldn't deny her. "Let's give it a shot. What can it hurt to try?"

"That's my girl!" she beamed like a kid opening an unexpected present, clapping her hands with delight.

"So what are we going to ward and against whom?"

"Oh, I've got just the idea for that." A spirited grin on her face, she handed me a large copper pot. "But first, you need to get your cauldron going."

"A copper pot is a cauldron?"

"Hey, times change. What did you expect? A big black iron kettle? As long as the pot is made of a natural metal it will work. No Teflon or modern alloys. And it has to be an open flame. That's why witches are always cooking with gas these days. No electric ranges."

Good to know.

"Now put that gallon of water on to boil and come over here and look at this spell, and I'll tell you what I have in mind."

I learned a lot over the course of the next four hours. Witch craft was packed with symbolism for the elements of life that allow the witch to borrow power from the universe. Sarah taught me how to plant my feet, center my body to the world, face the due points on a compass and pull energy from the earth, the air, the water and the flame.

Once I held the energy inside, a feeling much like having a heavy stomach after a huge meal, she taught me how to slowly release it into the spell components I mixed, crushed, ground and boiled. It empowered the concoction, sending the energy where I intended it to go, fueling the event I wished to make happen.

"Are all spells this much work?" I asked as a trickle of sweat ran down the back of my neck. I put a lot of effort into making a clump of dried bull nettle into powder with the stone pestle.

"Good potion work can be invaluable. It's a way to save magik for later. You can bottle it with a cork stopper and wax and it will sit on a shelf for years and still be as potent as the day you mixed it."

"That didn't answer my question."

"I know. But the answer is harder than the question." Sarah watched me work with pride. "No, there are spells that require a lot less physical material and some none at all, but those spells require the pure force of the will of the witch to set in motion."

"I don't understand." I continued to pound the nettles, wanting to get the powder as fine as I could manage.

"When a witch or warlock makes a potion, they are channeling energy from one thing into another thing to get an altered result. Nothing is lost. The force has just been moved. When we cast spells of will, some of our own life force has to go into the spell. We use a piece of ourselves either physical or metaphysical as the battery."

"So too much casting by will alone and your battery runs low?" I wondered aloud.

"Or dies."

"Dies?" I yelped in mid grind. "As in dead tired, or dead-dead."

"Both, actually. A witch can exhaust herself from casting by will alone, or pushed too far...be killed."

Wow. That put a different face on this side of the magik, a scary face.

"But that kind of drain usually happens only in battle, or in some cases, to very stupid witches."

"What kind of battle would a witch be in any way?"

"Well, centuries ago, witches fought wars among themselves and against other paranormals. We haven't always gotten along as well as we do now. Truthfully, most paranormals only tolerate each other for the sake of keeping the humans unaware of us."

"But more important, there are those of us that believe we are more than just paranormal. We are Americans too, as much as any other person living in this country. I'm a registered voter, honey. I pay taxes. I love baseball. This is my home, and I'd defend it with whatever means I have."

"Do you think that every soldier who fights for his or her country this day is human? Witches fight for America in battle every day in this world. So do Weres and Fae and many others. They use their special gifts to save lives and protect this country. And sometimes they die like any other soldier."

"I'd never thought about it, Sarah." I replied honestly. "I mean, I know we live in the United States of America. But our world is so closed to outsiders, to humans. I never thought about being a part of it, of them, when they're not a part of us."

"Harmony, the powers that rule us, the Council, may not want humans as part of our world, but like it or not, we are a part of theirs. What happens to them affects us too. Their wars, their laws, their governments can have a big impact on us. At some point paranormals are going to have to recognize this and stop living with our heads in the sand."

"So what, all the paranormals in the world should just get up one day and yell, surprise!? And tell the human world here we are paranormal and proud of it?" I asked incredulous.

"I don't know. Maybe?" She shrugged with a smile.

"No offense, Sarah, but they'd crap themselves, en mass. The only question would be if it happened before or after they tried to wipe us off the face of the planet."

"Now that's just Council talk, pure paranormal propaganda."

"How do you know?"

"How do you?" She countered. "Think for yourself. I deal with a lot more humans in my business than you realize. Charlie is a teacher at a public university. His students are human."

"I like to think we are decent judges of character. Truthfully, most humans are just like us. They want to live their lives with the freedom to choose their own path, to have the opportunity to be healthy and happy in their own way."

"Sounds dangerous to me."

"And it sounds to me like Charlie and I have kept you too isolated. I'm thinking we should start broadening more than just your magikal horizons."

"What do you mean?"

"I'm not sure yet. I'll have to think on it and discuss it with Charlie."

"Oh Goddess."

"Watch your mouth, young lady. Now how's that bull nettle coming?"

"Done, I think."

The subject changed back to my potion work. We used repellent ingredients for the warding, such as nettles, thorns, stinkweed, and bee venom to turn the trespasser away.

For the part of the spell to alert me to the presence of our intended victim, Sarah had me choose a special ingredient that I felt a kinship for. She had me pick something that I felt a strong energy signature with.

My hand went right to the crushed cat-o-nine tails, but then hovered over dragon root too. In the end I used them both. Why not?

The potion lesson had been fun, and I had learned a lot. I could see energy fields and draw power into me from the earth, valuable lessons for any paranormal. But who was I kidding, I was no witch.

We drew up a portion of the potion into an atomizer, like the old perfume bottles with the spritzer on top. I went to put it in the spray bottle she used for misting the house plants, but Sarah said no. No plastic, it ruined the potion, we had to use glass.

I dutifully followed her into the den, holding the potion in front of me like a bomb that might go off. With my cooking skills, it would probably melt the wood floors if I dropped it.

"Okay," she said, indicating a particularly old and dilapidated olive green recliner. "Fire when ready."

"Are you sure about this?" I whined.

"Oh, I am very sure. I have been trying to get this thing out of the house since before you were born. It's awful, and it doesn't match anything else here. I'll never understand how a man so dedicated to restoring this house to authenticity would allow this 1970's atrocity through the front door."

"But it's his favorite chair. He swears it's lucky. He sits in it and watches OU play OSU in the Bedlam game."

"We'll get him a new one in crimson. Besides, what are you afraid of? You don't think it will work anyway." Sarah countered.

True.

I took a deep breath and began pumping the spritzer with gusto. A misty vapor filled the air and covered the chair.

"I'm glad you suggested the lemon peel for scent." I choked out trying not to breathe the fumes.

"Make sure you get the back and the sides."

I dutifully spritzed away for another full minute. We stood back and let the fog settle. Nothing happened.

"Now what?" I asked.

Sarah stood with hands on hips, arms akimbo. "Now we go clean the kitchen and wait for Charlie to get home. You can help me make dinner."

Having just spent all morning in the kitchen, the offer didn't sound that appealing, but Sarah had a strict clean-up-your-own-mess policy. I shuffled behind her back to the kitchen, less and less enthused with each step. Oh well, I supposed it could have been worse. She could have made me sing the Brady Bunch theme song while we worked.

I lost track of time in the kitchen. After the cleanup had been done, Sarah put me to work peeling carrots and potatoes for the stew she had planned for dinner. Actually, I had a pretty good time with it. We kept laughing and cutting up about the simplest things.

She'd asked me some very straight forward questions about my feelings about Tesch and me. Where I thought we were going and to my mortification, how far we had been?

Sarah believed in honesty is the best policy when talking about sex and life stuff. She had always let me know that there were no taboo questions, and I'm grateful for that. Still, it felt awkward saying some of the things I felt out loud.

Close to dusk, we heard Charlie's key hit the front door. He called out in his usual good-natured tone. "I'm home, ladies!"

"We're in the kitchen, babe." Sarah responded. "Dinner's almost ready!"

He sauntered into the room with a relaxed grin and came to slide his arms around Sarah's waist as she stirred the contents in the big copper pot. He gave her a resounding kiss on the cheek. "Hmmm, what's cooking, good looking?"

"Stew." Her head turned to press her lips against his for a proper kiss.

"Sounds great. Hey, I'm going to wash up and catch a bit of the five o'clock news. Will you call me when it's time to eat?"

"Sure."

Charlie wandered back out of the kitchen. He whistled as he went back down the hall.

"Sarah?" I began. "Since we're done for the day, I mean with the lessons and all, can I call Tesch and see if he wants to come over and eat?" I knew my voice sounded really hopeful.

"I don't see why not. Maybe later we can play a game or something together, the four of us."

"Great!"

I held a stack of bowls in my hand where I had been preparing to set the table. A fissure of static electricity crackled from nowhere, and all the hair on my arms and the back of neck stood up at once. It startled me so, I dropped the bowls and they crashed to the floor making an awful racket.

I knew. I knew it just as well as I knew my own name.

"The chair!" I gasped to Sarah.

As if on cue, Charlie bellowed from the den. "Sarah! Sarah! Did you move my chair? It doesn't feel right!"

Sarah and I stared at each other from across the room, looks of wonder mirrored on our faces. I couldn't believe it.

"Oh my Goddess!" I breathed.

"It worked! It worked!" Sarah did her own version of a touchdown dance in the kitchen as she cheered softly. "Yes! It worked!"

Charlie came into the kitchen from the front of the house. He looked both confused and cross. He rapid fired questions as he stalked into the room.

"What's going on in here? What worked? Sarah, did you do something with my lucky chair? I tried to sit in it to watch the news and well, it just didn't feel right to me. It smells like lemon. I asked you to not clean my chair or move it. I like it the way it is."

Sarah and I straightened in tandem to beard the lion in his den.

"I'm sorry, honey, I didn't hear you very well. Harmony dropped the bowls and startled us half to death. What were you saying?" Sarah asked innocently.

Charlie's scowl deepened. "I asked if you did something to my chair. You know the one in the den that I always sit in? I sat down in it to watch the news, and it's uncomfortable, like it doesn't fit me anymore."

"I haven't touched your chair, Charlie. Why would I?" She told the Goddess' honest truth. I'd done the dirty work. Sarah had never been near it.

I could read the suspicion in Charlie's gaze. "Then why is it sitting wrong?"

"Charlie, that chair is as old as the hills plus a day. Do you really think it's going to last forever? For star's sake, you've been holding it together for years with duct tape and bailing wire. Maybe the springs and the padding are just finally giving out."

"Maybe." He agreed reluctantly, not wanting to believe it. "But you promise you didn't do anything to it?"

"I promise you, Charles Phillips, that I have not touched your chair in any way, witch's honor." She held up a hand with the vow, her face a composed picture of truth and serenity.

If I hadn't known the whole truth I would have believed every word. I almost did anyway. Who knew Sarah had such a calm and cool face when it came to deception?

"Then I guess I have to take your word for it." Charlie grumbled. "It is getting pretty old. Dammit, the Bedlam game is this month. How can I possibly watch without my lucky chair?"

Sarah moved smoothly in and put her arms around her husband's waist for a comforting squeeze. "It'll be all right, Charlie. We'll get you a new one and have a splendid bonfire to give the old chair a proper farewell."

His only answer came as a rather rude sounding snort before he left the circle of her arms to go back the way he had come. I know I heard him mutter words like 'women' and 'witches' under his breath as if they were foul.

Sarah watched him go, making sure he went all the way out of sight before she crossed the kitchen to give me a big hug. "You did it, sweetie! You did it! I knew you had it in you."

"What if Charlie finds out what we...I did?" I whispered into her hair.

"He won't, I promise. Besides, even though he won't admit it, I've seen him looking at furniture ads in the newspaper more than once. He's been checking out the new styles of recliners. Sometimes men just have to have a little push in the right direction for things to work out."

"If you say so." I replied skeptically.

"Oh, I know so. Charlie and I have been married thirty-eight years now. When you've been with a man that long, you come to know him better than he knows himself." She gave me a wise wink.

I knelt to pick up the pieces of broken crockery from the floor. Sarah joined me on hands and knees, gathering shards of stoneware.

I'd have to take her word for the whole understanding men better thing. Tesch, I had realized recently, had many revelations up his sleeve. Would I know him as well in four, fifty, a hundred years from now? That thought gave me pause.

A future with Tesch assumed he would want to spend his life with a Fae-Were-Witch, whatever I had become. Awareness crashed in on me. Oh sweet Gaia!

"I'm a witch!" My voice came out in a horrified whisper.

"Yes, isn't it awesome?" Sarah beamed, not quite in line with my thinking yet. "I'm so proud. You packed a good punch into that warding spell too, if your reaction was any sign."

I dropped the pieces of bowls from nerveless fingers. They clattered softly back to the kitchen tiles. I grabbed at Sarah's hand for a lifeline. The force of my grip caused a shard of glass to cut us both. The pain compared nothing to my panic.

"No, Sarah, don't you see. I'm a witch. A Fae-Were-Witch! If the Council finds out, they'll have my head on a pike outside their chamber door for sure!"

"Harmony, didn't we cover this ground when you first shifted into a Were? We realized the danger. I thought you did too." She looked so concerned and understanding. It wasn't the right look to have. She should have been as horrified as I.

"Well, yes. But no, I mean, I hoped for a fluke. I haven't even felt a glimmer of glamour or illusion around me since that thing with Challen. And you said that it used to be kids with different spectrum parents would eventually take after one or the other. I wanted to be like that. That I could be just Fae, or be just Werelynx, but not both! And now I'm three things! It's getting worse, Sarah. When's it going to stop? What kind of mixed bag of genes thing am I? I'm a freak! What am I going to do?"

I felt the palm of her hand make stinging contact with my cheek. It hadn't been a hard slap, nothing that would leave a mark, just an attention getter. I gulped for air. I had been talking so fast, I had run out.

"Now take a breath and hold it." She commanded and took a deep breath herself, encouraging me to mimic the action. "Let it out slowly then do it again."

We did this a few times until some of the tension slid away. She held my hand tightly even though they were slick from the blood of our mutual cut.

"That is what you are going to do. Keep breathing. Because there's nothing else you can do. Panicking will solve nothing."

She stood and pulled me along toward the porcelain double sinks. Sarah managed the faucet into a steady flow of lukewarm water. With gentle hands she washed our cuts with soap and water before wrapping each in a soft linen dish towel.

"Now, look at that." She held out her injured palm to mine, small spots of bright blood dotted the white towels, hers and mine. "Your blood is as red as mine. You are no freak. You are a paranormal child of Gaia and no more and no less than she intended you. And you're my daughter, in all the ways that matter. Your blood is now in me and mine in you."

Tears filled my eyes. "But…" I began to protest.

"No buts. This is the way life is, it goes on. You can either make a choice to live it to its fullest with the gifts you are given, or you can waste it wanting what isn't going to happen."

"I'm scared." My voice sounded small.

"Good, that means you're no fool. Only an idiot is afraid of nothing. Harmony, there are always going to be challenges, blind corners and the big, bad ugly hiding under the bed. What are you going to do? Not try, stand still, wet your pants?"

She shook her head at me, disapproving. "No, not my daughter. I've taught you better than that. Charlie has taught you better. What you are going to do is fill your head with knowledge and your heart with hope so when the challenges come, you'll be ready to meet them."

I swallowed back my fears and nodded. "I'm sorry, Sarah. I just felt wild with terror for a minute. Like a trap had been sprung on me. This is really happening, isn't it?"

"Yes, I'm afraid it is. I told you the Goddess might not be finished with you, and it looks to be so. Sometimes her blessings are a mixture of pleasure and pain."

What could I say? Not much.

Chapter 15

I'D SEEN THE *WIZARD OF OZ* a dozen times or more. It was one of Sarah's favorite films. She loved it even though it was pure fantasy. I didn't get it.

Real witches didn't float in bubbles or have green skin. The closest things I'd ever seen to a munchkin were dwarves, not the human kind, but real dwarves. Only they were not all sugar and sweetness and sang verses at you. They tended to be rather dark and wrinkled and had a very nasty attitude if you trespassed on their property.

However, as October passed into November, I began to feel a lot like I imagined Dorothy felt when first seeing the Land of Oz. My world had been gray and flat. One dimensional, much like the movie's portrayal of Kansas. Now, the sheer variety of color sometimes overwhelmed me.

I would begin even the most mundane tasks; washing dishes, folding clothes or brushing my teeth and find new colors, shades and hues that I wanted to savor and commit to memory. There were so many variances of yellow, red, green, pink, orange and brown. Blue and purple still eluded me, though I didn't know why and didn't want to guess.

I found beauty and wonder in the simplest things. Tree bark and pine needles fascinated me. The changes in the sky at dusk and dawn left me breathless. Sunlight hitting the expensive paint job of a fancy car could keep me staring for more than a good five minutes. I had to be nudged more than once by Tesch, Charlie or Sarah when caught gazing at things for too long.

True to their word, my parents had a conference with Mr. Oliphant, the principle, about their misgivings of Ms. Idlewilde. Turns out, for an Elf, he's not a bad guy. I had always thought elves intractable and reluctant to change.

He couldn't get me out of her class altogether, it was required. But he did agree to review my class work and test scores and make sure that I received a fair grade in Paranormal history.

As an alternative Fae studies instructor, Mr. Bellfwigg volunteered. He was a Brownie, and while considered one of the lesser Fae by the Daoine Sidhe, he still had more practical Fae magik experience than anyone else we could have found, about four hundred years' worth. He also had a good sense of humor and made learning fun.

He commandeered the art room for our lessons. Mr. Bellfwigg

mentioned that any mistakes we made would be no great loss to the art community here, if anyone could tell the difference.

"Now Ms. Phillips, remembering what we've been talking about, how is glamour and illusion alike?" He asked.

"Both, either, need a real object to be attached to."

"Correct, and how are they different?"

"Glamour is typically temporary and can be dispelled if someone is too aware of the truth. It's a smaller scale of energy, only visual and only able to be maintained while the Fae is awake."

"Illusions are more permanent, or can be. They are an entirely fictional creation of the Fae casting the illusion, and will feel, sound and taste real to all but the Fae who made it."

"Exactly!" he beamed at me behind round spectacles. The parts of his cheeks that weren't covered in coarse, dark brown hair colored with the pride of a teacher when a pupil learns from them.

I wondered about something, and it felt as good a time as any to ask. "Mr. Bellfwigg, when I had my, uh, accident with Challen, if the illusion feels, looks and sounds like the real thing, then how could you understand him when he spoke?"

"Oh, caught that one did you?" He took his spectacles off and polished them, appearing a bit uncomfortable with the subject. "Well, it's, uh, a family trait. I speak dog."

"Really? Wow, that's cool! Is it a Fae thing? Will I be able to talk to animals too, someday?"

That sounded fun. Being able to actually go out and talk to birds and deer and other wild animals. I wondered if I would be able to do it as a Werelynx. A new thought opened up. I could have an awesome career as a game warden or a zookeeper or as a veterinarian. I could be a real Dr. Doolittle.

"Um, no. I don't think so, Harmony." Mr. Bellfwigg ended my new college plans quickly. "You see, and I don't share this with many people, but I have a good feeling about you, that you can keep a secret."

"Yeah, sure, Mr. Bellfwigg." He'd always been nice to me. If he wanted to tell me something, between us, I would keep my mouth shut.

"A couple of generations ago, my grandmother was a Pooka, what the humans sometimes call a hell hound. They look very much like large hairy dogs, only with a lot more teeth and regular hands and feet, very intelligent creatures too. They speak canine as well as many other languages. Because of my grandma, Aniline, I speak dog; she taught me."

"Oh." I digested that information. Then asked, "But why keep it a secret? You may not be a pure Brownie, but you are pure Fae. So what's the difference?"

"There shouldn't be any." He agreed with a sad smile. "But nowadays, you'd be surprised at how many of our people think less of someone who isn't pure blooded, even within a spectrum."

"No, sir, I wouldn't."

Mr. Bellfwigg smiled sadly. "No, I guess you wouldn't, child. You've felt the sharp end of a lot of prejudice in you short life, haven't you? Starting out colorblind and all."

I could only nod. I didn't like to think about all the birthday parties and classmate outings I had not been included in over the years because of my defect. It hurt to always be the odd man out, to not belong.

"Anyway," he cleared his throat. "Back to our lesson. Glamour can be a powerful and useful tool for the Fae. It has helped some of us, like Dr. Heckerman, blend into the human world when necessary. Not that you would need it to blend in, your appearance is quite satisfactory to do that already, but it's still a basic Fae talent, and we are going to work on yours."

I would've believed those words were an insult coming from anyone but Mr. Bellfwigg. His voice held no snide innuendo or eyes that implied I looked more human than anything else. From him, it sounded almost complimentary.

"I believe your adoptive mother has shown you how to see the magikal field of light, yes?"

"Yes." I could admit that and not betray any of my own secrets.

"Okay, then. I want you to close your eyes and do that, first." He instructed. "When you open your eyes I want you to look for the yellow spectrum field and imagine it being drawn into you until you are full of yellow. Grab that power and wrap it around you like a blanket."

I closed my eyes. When I opened them I could see all sorts of things around me that glowed in various shades of color, I searched for a strong source of yellow and found golden sunlight spilling in through the shades and splashes of egg tempera paint.

I closed my eyes again. As he'd suggested, I pulled the color to me like a metaphysical comforter from a bed, draping it around my shoulders and arms until it covered me warmly down to my toes.

"Very good, Miss Phillips! Very good." He coached. "Now the harder part. Open your pores and allow the power to soak into you.

Imagine what you feel outside and want it inside, keeping you warm and safe and protected."

It took a little concentrated relaxing. I had to imagine it in parts, first my toes, then my feet and legs, working my way up. When I felt like I had taken in all I could hold, I opened my eyes again. The whole world had a golden glow.

"I am very impressed, Miss Phillips." Mr. Bellfwigg sounded genuinely in awe. I saw his face in a haze of the energy glare. "Being able to absorb that much energy and hold it is not always as easy as it seems. Most can only hold it in their hands and maybe some in their minds, but you have managed to saturate every inch of yourself with power. Usually only the Daoine Sidhe can do such a thing. That's why early men thought they were angels."

He walked around me, inspecting my yellow aura of power. I felt as conspicuous as a hundred watt light bulb.

"I had intended that we would try a bit of personal glamour, but I think before we do that, I need to teach you about shields."

"Shields?"

He nodded wordlessly to himself before explaining. "A shield is a mental guard we can put around ourselves to hide, well, to hide a lot of things, including how much power we have. Think of it as a shade over a lamp, or a curtain on a window. Depending on the shield, the light can be seen as dimmed, or not at all."

"How do I do that?" I could see this being very useful someday, at least the hiding part.

Mr. Bellfwigg took a seat in one of the student chairs scattered around an oval art table. He crossed one short leg over the other at the ankle. He had to slump in the chair or his feet would have dangled like a child's. Not that slumping didn't have its own adolescent similarity.

"You know that white light is the reflection of all the colors of the spectrum and that black is the absence of all color?"

"Yes, sir. We started learning that in fourth grade art and basic color theory." I stood there soaked in yellow light and wondered where he would take the lesson.

"Okay, to build a shield, the idea is to take the yellow power you have and camouflage it in black. The blanket you have mentally wrapped around yourself, keep it close and hold it tight, nice and cozy. But think about it as if the blanket has two sides, one yellow and one without any color. The yellow side, keep close to you and the black side, you turn out."

One of the things I really enjoyed about Mr. Bellfwigg being my Fae instructor came from the visual and sensory imaging concepts he planted. It gave my physical and mental self a clue as to what to do.

He'd told me during our first lesson that magik worked similar to what humans called neural mapping. If you could do something once, the body and mind created a blueprint to follow the next time, like what Charlie had told me about becoming a Were. Each time it would become easier until certain things just came naturally.

I closed my eyes again to attempt the description he had provided. I pulled my psychological sunshine and lemon coverlet tight about my body, snuggling in deep then tried to conceive the flip side of the protection as black cotton.

I heard a chuckle from my mentor and took a metaphysical glance at my perceived shield. It had come out as polka dot black and yellow, a weirdo lady bug. I still glowed in irregular round patches.

"Consider it a homework assignment." Mr. Bellfwigg told me with good humor. By next week, I want you to be able to make a good shield. I think that's enough for today. We will work on your glamour techniques tomorrow."

I stood there and nodded. Believe it or not, all this mental visualizing tired me out. And it certainly worked up an appetite. But I also felt disappointed. I had a lot of questions about so many things.

"Um, Miss Phillips, you can let the power go now."

"Oh, right." Just as I had absorbed the energy into myself from foot to head, I loosened my grip on my mental blanket and let it fall to the floor around my feet where it disappeared into where it had come from. "I'm sorry, I forget sometimes. I had a stray thought."

He shook his head with one of those ironic smiles adults sometimes had. "Don't be sorry. It's actually quite commendable that you don't lose the power you gather when other thoughts intrude. That's a hard lesson to teach and one you have sailed through with natural aptitude."

I glowed again, not with power but with pride at the words. I hadn't heard a lot of praise from my teachers over the years, especially for natural aptitude in anything. "Thank you."

"You are welcome, Miss Phillips." Mr. Bellfwigg answered formally, giving me a gracious nod of his head. "So what stray thoughts were you having that you didn't release your power at once?"

"Oh. Well, I wondered about the shield lesson."

"Yes."

"Well, what would happen if instead of having the outside of the blanket be black, if in my head, I made it white?"

One bottle brush eyebrow cocked while deep, immeasurable eyes regarded the question. "In theory?"

I shrugged my shoulders. In theory or for real, it didn't matter. "Yeah, sure."

"In theory, then, the person who could build a white shield, a truly white shield, would shimmer like a mirage. For all intents and purposes, they would be invisible magically and possibly in the physical sense as well. But it can't be done."

My shoulders drooped, dissatisfied. "Why not?"

"Because white is the perfect balance of all the colors in the spectrum. To achieve white, a paranormal would have to be well, in harmony with all the spectrums of magik. They would have to have white magik."

"I've never heard of white magik, Mr. Bellfwigg."

"That's because it died out almost a thousand years ago with the dragons."

"Dragons?" It came out a hoarse sound. Cold and hot flashes passed over my skin.

He sighed and this time it sounded almost angry. "I suppose with her Fae are holier than thou attitude about history, Ms. Idlewilde conveniently skipped over the story of paranormal creation with you kids. Of course, it is a touchy subject; creation versus evolution."

"I have no idea what you are talking about." And did I want to?

He seemed to weigh his thoughts. "It's like this, Harmony. Some paranormals believe that we, like humans, crawled out of the primordial soup, but that we discovered the Goddess that from all life stems and that she taught us her ways and gave us her blessings and made us into her creatures and servants. That's why we are different from humans. But even humans have a spark of magik in them, because we all come from the original source, which is the Goddess herself. It's a circular form of logic."

"I don't understand."

"Then here is an analogy. Imagine twins separated at birth. Both go looking for their birth mother. One finds her. The mother is so grateful to have her child back that she lavishes gifts and special talents upon them. The other child is lost to her but still part of her. The missing child had the same potential as the twin that found his way home, just not the teaching and advantages, so his would-be magik faded away."

That I could imagine well, having never known my real mother. "Okay, now I follow you."

"All right, that is one theory of how we paranormals came into being. Another is that the Goddess' first children were dragons.

Wonderful, intelligent, fantastical creatures of almost unlimited strength and power, they were all that is magik. Our Goddess Mother had many, many sons, but of all her offspring, only one daughter."

"A favored daughter with all the beauty and gifts of her mother, she could have had her choice of any of the male dragons in the sky, on the earth or below for a mate. Instead, Osmyrah became fascinated with a human."

"Osmyrah?" I asked, pronouncing the word as Mr. Bellfwigg had, *oss-mir-a*. It gave me goose bumps saying it aloud.

"The female dragon's name." he supplied smoothly. "Anyway, Osmyrah became enchanted with humans. Many times she would shift her form into something humanoid and walk among them. Even though they sensed strangeness, with her pale beauty and different skin, they allowed her presence."

"I don't get it, allowed her presence? She was a dragon. She could go anywhere she wanted."

"True, but these were early men and very superstitious. They saw omens and signs in everything. She might have been able to go where they went, but she could not have been a part of their group if they had not allowed it."

I thought bitterly that high school worked the same way. You could show up, go to class, spend day after day in the presence of a group of people and still be on the outside if they didn't want to let you in.

"So, what happened?"

"She fell in love with a human man. Of course it caused quite a fuss. Every male dragon in creation had hoped to win her heart and be her mate. Many threatened to rip the man apart. But the Goddess understood that taking the man from the picture wouldn't change Osmyrah's heart."

"She encouraged the male dragons to be patient, allow Osmyrah one lifetime with her chosen mate. For what is the span of one human's life compared to that of a dragon?"

"Osmyrah married her human and lived as a woman with him throughout his lifetime. As men often do, her husband wanted sons to carry on his line. But while a dragon in human form looks like a woman, she is still a dragon and unsuitable to breed with a man."

"How sad." I murmured. Mr. Bellfwigg had talent as a storyteller. I'd been sucked in by the drama in his voice.

"Just listen then." Mr. Bellfwigg chided gently. "Seeking a way to please her husband, Osmyrah called upon her magik to make her husband's sons grow in her womb. She gave birth six times, and each time the child was endowed with certain dragon powers. To her first son she gave the powers of the shape change, the Were's red magik. To the next she passed the yellow magik of illusion and glamour, the first Fae. The third son had the blue power of sight or far seeing, and so the first Seer. The fourth had the green of nature magik. The fifth son she gifted with orange spectrum magiks, the ability to draw power from the earth's underground treasures and enchant them. Finally, the sixth with violet power to move object through space and time."

"So that's how the spectrum magiks came to be. These sons took wives and had children and passed their gifts along. So you see, in the end, all paranormals are the children of a dragon."

"But how does that mean white magic has died out? Didn't Osmyrah go back to being a dragon after her human husband died?"

"Well, that's the rest of the story. You see, in making her sons, her magikal sons, Osmyrah used the very essence of herself, what had made her a dragon. When her human husband died, she didn't have the power to change back. So, there were no female dragons to carry on the dragon line. The male dragons lived for thousands and thousands of years, yes, but once they were gone, they were gone, and their white magik abilities went with them."

"And Osmyrah?"

"We're not sure. Though not able to take her dragon form again, I think she remained a long lived creature. I like to believe she went on to live many years. Who knows, maybe after a time, she found love again?"

"And you believe all that about dragons and the spectrum races and stuff?"

"My grandmother, Aniline, did. She told me that story so many times when I visited as a child. She heard it from her grandmother, and so forth. It's a very old tale, and most old stories, no matter how fantastic they seem, usually have some truth to them."

I had heard that before from both Sarah and Charlie. Whenever we watched human fantasy movies about paranormal creatures we would often see small bits and pieces of the truth beneath the Hollywood effects and bad acting. It remained a running joke in our home.

"Well, thanks again, Mr. Bellfwigg, for the tutoring and the story." I said, stooping to pick up my heavy backpack. Thanks to my new Were strength, I didn't even grunt while lifting it onto my shoulders.

"You're most welcome, Miss Phillips. See you tomorrow."

I left the art room and turned left, heading for the east end of the building. Our school had been built in the shape of an E, with exits at either end and in the middle. Lockers, painted bright red, lined white walls.

The cafetorium, gym and parking lot had been built separately and had to be walked to in all kinds of weather. This was Oklahoma. We had those 'all kinds of weather' days often. Today proved no exception.

The morning had begun cool but mild and sunny. Now, as I moved through the hallways toward the exit, I could hear the unmistakable sounds of thunder and hard rain. Great, I'd be soaked by the time I made it across the campus to the parking lot where Tesch waited to pick me up.

Funny, I hadn't noticed any sounds of rain in the art room. Sunlight had shone through the windows. I assumed I had been too focused on the stuff Mr. Bellfwigg had been telling me and teaching me. An autumn thunderbuster had sneaked in while I listened to the sad tale of Osmyrha. No help for it, pulling the hood of my now favorite red sweatshirt up, I got ready to dive in and make a run for it.

"Wait up! I've got an umbrella!" A feminine voice called from behind me.

I turned to see dark hair swirling an exotic face. No OU cheerleader uniform today. Just figure hugging skinny jeans in Day-Glo green and a black t-shirt with a logo for some band called *Blood on the Dance Floor*. The logo matched the jeans.

"Joliet?" I questioned seeing her in the school after hours.

"No, I'm the Easter Bunny." She grinned widely. "Want to share my umbrella to the parking lot?"

The quip threw me off, and I stuttered. "No, I mean, yes, I mean..." I stopped to get past my disbelief at her presence and the offer. Until recently, I would have suspected she'd let me drown rather than acknowledge my existence.

"I'm just a little surprised to see you here. I thought everyone had gone home already. But, yes, sharing the umbrella would be nice."

"I'm taking some extra language lessons, French, from Mrs. Dubois. It's a deal I made with my parents. Extra courses of their choosing, and I get to wear the clothes I want to school. I just started." Joliet explained. "What are you doing here so late?"

"Fae studies with Mr. Bellfwigg. I just started too."

"That's right, now that you've got magik they're making you catch up on stuff, huh? How's that going? Learn any more powerful illusion tricks like you pulled on Challen Parks?" She asked in rapid fire as she pulled an extendable umbrella from her large, carry all bag.

I blushed, uncomfortable with the questions. Being so new at everything, I felt centuries behind everyone else. I didn't want to share where I was on my path to enlightenment. "Like I said, I just started. It's too soon to tell."

Joliet didn't ask anything else as she pushed the button to release the nylon cover that would protect us from the worst of the wet stuff. The way it poured beyond the doors, our feet and legs would still get a drenching, but it beat being soaked to the bone.

Sarah and Charlie accused me of having elemental powers and controlling the weather. Fat chance.

If I could do that, it wouldn't be raining cats and dogs right now. I'd slow it down to at least puppies and kittens, a gentle rain instead of a gully washer.

"Hey, I think it's slowing down a bit." Joliet commented. "Let's make a break for it."

Sure enough, the rain let up enough that I could actually see farther than twenty feet beyond the door. Holy cow!

My knees shook as Joliet took the lead and opened the door to the outside. I swear if I heard one meow or woof outside, I would have crapped biscuits.

Thankfully, I didn't have to say much as we hurried across the school property to where a few lone cars and trucks waited. Joliet chatted away while I busily argued with myself about being paranoid.

The rain had slacked up because of the nature of rain storms not because I had wanted it to. Storms come and go. They rain hard then get lighter as the clouds move around overhead. Just ask Gary England, the weather guy on the channel nine news.

I looked ahead and found Tesch's beat up green truck and pointed in that direction. Joliet never missed a beat, keeping up a steady flow of gossip and nonsense as we moved together toward his vehicle.

She covered me around to the passenger door. Tesch leaned over and opened it for me since the windows were rolled up against the steady droplets from the sky.

"So, how about it?" Joliet asked.

"What? I'm sorry." I'd been paying very little attention to what she had been saying. Now she knew it.

She made a small pouting frown with her full red lips. "I asked, since we both have to be here after school now, would you like a ride home tomorrow? You know, we can kind of commute together."

"Well, uh, Tesch usually gives me a ride." She'd surprised me again with her offer. Why would the reigning high school queen want to give me a ride?

"I understand." She shrugged a bit, acting disappointed. "If I had a guy to ride home with, I would too. I just thought maybe, I don't know, we could get to know one another better, and well, it would give me a little more time out of the house. My parents keep track of me like that. You know, come straight home and don't be late."

She seemed sad, standing there in the rain beneath her red and white umbrella. "I swear they read the odometer on my car every night just to see if I go anyplace else."

Dang it! I felt sorry for her. I looked at Tesch, and he shrugged at me as if to say, 'it's a girl thing, you deal with it.' I stuck my tongue out at him.

"How about on Tuesdays and Thursdays?" I offered. "It'll give Tesch a chance to do some moronic guy thing like work on his truck without having to wait for me to get out of school."

Joliet perked up despite the heavier drops starting to fall again. "Great! That's great! Give me your number just in case something happens and my parents veto the idea."

We exchanged numbers then she headed off to her car, a new looking compact in a color I didn't yet recognize. I did know enough about cars to identify the body type as a Mini Cooper.

Tesch started his engine and let it warm up. I slid across the seat next to him to ward off the chill of the rain. He put a long arm around my shoulders, and I cuddled against his side, enjoying the closeness. His unique scent filled my nose, and I relaxed.

"Tough day at the office?" he joked.

"Tough enough, I'm beat. I feel like I've been going full tilt for a month now."

""You have been. There's been more than enough going on to make anyone worn out. You need a break."

"Really? You think?" I laughed. "Got any ideas about when that might be on the schedule? Right now I have mornings with Professor Poff, then regular classes, afternoons with Mr. Bellfwigg, then on Saturdays Charlie takes me to the woods to work on my Were magik and on Sundays Sarah has me in the kitchen cooking up potions and dinner."

"I promise you one of these days we'll find I've mixed up my poppy seeds with my poinsettia pollen and we are all going to be spilling our deepest, darkest secrets over muffins."

"Poinsettia pollen?"

"Yeah, it's part of a truth sayers potion I'm learning." I informed him.

Tesch sighed and hugged me close. My head tilted back to look into his light, jade colored eyes. "I can't do much about the pace, but I can try to put a smile on those sweet lips of yours."

"How?" I breathed the word out like a prayer.

He leered awkwardly. "We have the parking lot to ourselves and some time to kill before I take you home."

My own smile came with a flush. I asked. "Any ideas what we can do with our time?"

"One or two. Want to fog up the windows?"

I answered by pressing my lips to his for a soft but heated kiss. Answer enough.

Twenty minutes later we came up for air. The windows of his old truck had indeed fogged over heavily. The rain continued to fall steadily, drowning away any sounds from the outside world beyond the constant patter on the hood.

We had stopped short of doing anything that would get us in trouble with our authority figures. We'd shared passionate kisses and some petting that made my bones melt in a good way.

I supposed Charlie wouldn't consider petting exactly a virtuous pastime. I thought, almost positively, he would disapprove of some of the places our hands strayed occasionally, but I had a clear conscious for my behavior. Well, pretty clear.

I found new appreciation for the endless talks Sarah had with me not just about sex but about the feelings and the emotional consequences of love. I recognized what occurred between us as new and wild and exciting. It thrilled me to my toes and had my stomach doing flip flops when he kissed me. His touch had my wiring ready to blow a fuse. I had a clear cut case of first love.

As I straightened my hair and zipped my hoodie back up, I stole shy glances at my boyfriend. That still seemed like a foreign word.

He wiped his palm across his lips before rubbing both hands over the thighs of his jeans. It did me good to see I had wrecked his composure too. He gave me a guilty but radiant smile. This feeling of power in our relationship felt great. I basked in the glow of his grin.

Sarah's voice echoed in my head, not Charlie's, telling me that if the feelings we had for each other were the real deal, there would be plenty of time for the more physical side between us to follow. We could take it slow and savor each new page of the story as it unfolded.

"I guess I better get you home. Charlie and Sarah might be worried with the rain." He defused some of the tension with his words.

"That's probably a good idea." I agreed.

I scooted over by the door to give us both a little breathing room.

The defroster cleared the front window. I contented myself with drawing H.P. + T.W. inside a big heart on the passenger window. Girly, I know.

He dropped me off a few short minutes later, having walked me up to the house. On the wrap around porch, we shared a short kiss goodbye. He touched my cheek tenderly.

"You know it's a good thing that Joliet wants to give you a ride sometimes. It'll give me a chance to cool my jets and, uh, think about other things than when I can kiss you again in the parking lot."

I felt the blush heat my face. "There are still Mondays, Wednesdays and Fridays." I teased.

"And don't forget Saturday nights. You have to go with me on dates on Saturday nights. Pencil me in. Wait, don't pencil me in; write it in ink. That way you know it's important."

"You are always important to me."

Tesch enveloped me in his arms, his lips brushing my temple with gentle affection. "I hope so."

He stepped away, forcing distance between us. "I got to go. Wight needs my help with some stuff this evening. But you can call me later if you want."

"Okay. I will."

He backed away from me then, down the wooden steps. Our hands clinging to each other until the last moment, craving that last touch. Then he jumped down the bottom step of the porch and bounded across the yard to his truck.

I could hear the ground squish beneath his steps as he went. Under the overcast drizzling sky, my vision of his retreating back seemed sharper and more defined.

His wide yet slender shoulders were hunched against the weather. His spiked hair had begun to wilt a fraction from the rain. Black jeans hugged long legs that ate up the ground, sending him away faster than I liked while yellow, orange and brown leaves blew across the yard. The deeper greens of the pine trees lining the property gave the world a quality of life.

When he swung his lanky frame into the driver's seat and his truck roared to life, I turned and went into the house. I removed my soaked shoes by the door and wandered up to my room to get started on my newest collection of homework assignments.

Tesch agreed Joliet offering me rides sometimes would help relieve some of the romantic tension we were building. My head knew the truth too. Breathing room, some occasional space for perspective would be a good thing, a sane and reasonable act. But my heart complained about my accepting the offer.

Sometimes being sane and reasonable really sucked. Crazy and unreasonable seemed like more fun.

Chapter 16

JOLIET GAVE ME A RIDE home on Tuesday after tutoring. She talked happily all the way to my house, about people I really didn't know and from the sound of it, didn't care to know. It took me by surprise when she asked if she could come in for a few minutes.

"I'm really not in any hurry to get home. Actually, I try to avoid it when I can." She confessed.

Today she wore a short red skirt with fishnet hose and heavy black boots that buckled all the way up to her knees. She had another black band T-shirt, this one advertising *Bullet for My Valentine*. She also wore some studded leather bracelets and a belt. She looked rock concert ready rather than just having finished a French lesson.

"Sure, *entrée vou*s." I didn't want to be inhospitable after she had given me a ride.

Joliet gave me a questioning look, her forehead wrinkled with confusion. "Huh?"

"It means come in, in French."

"Oh." Her brows smoothed out. "I haven't gotten that far yet. I didn't know you spoke French."

"I had Ms. Dubois for two semesters while everyone else had basic Witchcraft and Were studies. Now it's a reversal of fortunes. I'm studying the things everyone else got to take, but I *parlez vous français*, well a little anyway."

"Cool. Maybe you can help me study sometime. I know I need the help. In return, I can teach you about Djinn. Deal?"

"Okay."

Again, Joliet astonished me. She seemed to be making a real effort to be my friend, connect with me on some level. I wondered about her story, her home life.

I showed her around the house. By way of the kitchen first for some iced tea. We drank an herbal brew of Sarah's own making. I admitted to being happily addicted to the stuff.

In the den she noticed Charlie's horrid old recliner and commented. "What is that ugly thing doing here? It doesn't match anything in the room."

I don't know if my cheeks were red, but they felt warm. "It's my dad's favorite chair from college. Or it used to be. He's getting a new one very soon."

"Well, I hope so."

We went on up to my room. For the first time, I felt a little embarrassed by my cluttered chaos. I had yet to redecorate since acquiring color perception, and I now understood that "eye-popping" and "jaw-dropping" didn't even begin to describe the sensory overload.

When my world had been entirely shades of gray, I had over compensated to fill the void. You name it and I had the pattern to match. As if zigzags, paisleys, stripes, polka dots, checks, zebra, leopard and plaid all in one environment weren't enough, texture competed too. Velour, satin, faux fur, velvet, tweed and vinyl competed for attention as well.

Now that I could see the colors for myself I was aware of the clashing yellows, reds, greens, pinks, probably blues and purples too with splashes of black and white. My room looked like a Hobby Lobby exploded.

For the first time since I had known her, Joliet appeared speechless. She stood in the doorway gaping at the sight while I sneakily kicked a pair of dirty underwear beneath the bed. Have I mentioned I'm not so much the clean freak Sarah is?

"Well, this is my room." I stated the obvious as I flopped down on my unmade bed. "What do you think?"

I could see Joliet struggle for something polite to say. I had to repress a giggle.

"Uh, well, it's…um, it's…it's unique. It fits you." She finally managed.

I laughed out loud. "That's a nice way of putting it."

She looked embarrassed and unsure, so different than a prom queen should. "I'm sorry."

"No, it's okay. Really. Come on, sit down." I indicated the zebra print, pink and lime beanbag chair, still laughing. I tried to think of the best way to explain.

"Before I could see color, I used to collect prints and things that had different textures to kind of make up for the lack, you know? I couldn't see these colors to know what a wild combination it all was."

"Oh. Okay, I understand that." She sat down and looked around some more, her face a bit skeptical. "So, um, why not redecorate? I'd be happy to help. My mom could hook you up with a couple of designer friends she has. I recently had my room re-done in a Greek revival style; lots of white pillars, a fountain and wispy drapes everywhere."

Joliet seemed to have found her voice again.

I shrugged as part of my reply. "I've thought about it, sure. But I've been so busy since this all started happening to me. I haven't had time to catch my breath, much less decide on how I want to decorate."

"Tell me about it."

"Yeah, I imagine you have a lot of pressure, too with your dad being the mayor and your mom on the school board." I thought she sympathized with me, that she also felt overwhelmed with life. Oops, wrong again.

"No, I mean tell me about it." She clarified. "About being colorblind, and then the entire, sudden POW, you see it all in Technicolor. That must be like going from an AM pocket radio to a BOSE sound wave system playing KJ103 at full blast."

KJ103, a popular music station out of Oklahoma City, played all the club mixes of the latest songs. Joliet made very good analogies; I had to give her that.

"Well, yeah, it was a bit of a shock. But it didn't happen all at once. I started seeing yellow first, and then some of the other colors started coming in. I still don't see them all." .

"Hmm, that's interesting. What colors don't you see?" She seemed genuinely interested.

"Blue and purple." I replied. "Or I assume blue and purple because they're the only ones I haven't identified yet."

"Why do you think that is?"

Revealing a small amount of the truth, I answered. "Emotions. It seems the colors come when I experience strong emotions. I don't know what kind of feelings blue and purple are yet."

"Oooh, this I got to hear. Start from the beginning and tell me everything. What emotions and did they involve that hunk of a boyfriend you have?" She leaned forward, eager for details.

This time I had no doubts I was blushing. I hid my face in my hands, embarrassed.

Joliet pounced on me verbally. "It did! It did involve Tesch! Now you really do have to share. Give it up. So what happened? I'm not leaving until you do."

I had a feeling she wouldn't either. So I told. Not everything, of course.

I recited how I had first been angry with Ms. Idlewilde. Then I repeated the visit to Mrs. Tyck's office, then waking up the next day and seeing egg yolks for the first time.

Joliet actually proved a good listener. She commented and laughed in all the right places to let me know she paid attention.

I told her about how the illusion on Challen had been an accident, seeing red. I had to hide my face while telling that. I left out the part about becoming a Werelynx. I did share about the carnival and seeing green and eventually browns pinks and oranges. I very specifically left out my potion experience.

"So now I'm playing catch up to everyone else, learning how to control my Fae powers and use them on purpose rather than by accident. And learn the basics about other magiks too." I concluded.

Joliet sat back on the beanbag when I had finished my tale. In an astonishingly mature tone, she observed.

"You've had some big changes lately. That's no doubt. But it seems to me that you've also been really fortunate. Your parents are supportive. Your best friend is your boyfriend and also supportive. And now you have what's been missing from your life, color and magik. It would be easy to hate you, you know, just for being so damn lucky."

She gave me a half smile, half grimace. Her eyes slid around my room again, falling upon the brass clapper bell clock lying on its back at her feet. The talkative, rocker girl persona slid back into place. "Oh my Goddess, is that the time? Crap! My mother is going to have a cow! I have to get going. Sorry I have to rush. I'll see you Thursday."

In a whirlwind of energy she got up and went running down the stairs. I followed at a less frantic pace. I had only made it halfway down when she threw open the front door.

Charlie stood there, his key out as if he had been about to open the door as well. A look of mild shock crossed his face at the strange girl in his home before he registered me on the steps behind her.

Joliet stopped short. "Uh, hi." She offered, then on the heels of the greeting blurted, "Well, bye."

She went around Charlie like quicksilver and hurried down the steps to her little car. Charlie watched her go with confusion.

"Um, Harmony, was that Joliet Coombs?"

I walked the rest of the way down the stairs to stand beside him as Joliet tore off in her car. I nodded my head. "Yep, it was."

His confusion became concern. "Is she a friend of yours?"

"Maybe." I shrugged. "I'm not sure yet."

"I've had some dealings with her mother and father, especially her father. He's a... shrewd and very intense man. He also seems rather narrow minded. If his daughter is anything like him, I'd be careful what you say to her."

I thought about Joliet and couldn't manage to see her as either intense or narrow minded. Shrewd? I thought about her assessment of my life as being lucky. She did have some of her father in her I supposed.

"Don't worry, Charlie. I didn't tell her anything I shouldn't. I barely know her. She gave me a ride home today."

He gave me a patient, loving grin. "Just be careful, honey."

"I will."

The next few weeks became a pattern of that first Tuesday. Joliet would come in, and we'd go up to my room for a bit. She gossiped, and I listened. She definitely knew all our classmates' dirty little secrets. I had to wonder if she had shared mine with others, and Charlie's warning came to mind.

"Joliet, can I ask you something?"

"Sure." She agreed, taking a sip of her iced tea.

"Why me?"

"What? I'm not sure I understand the question." I thought I saw a trace of a blush tone her caramel colored cheeks.

"Yes, you do. Why suddenly start a friendship with me? We've been going to school together for years. I know you are ahead of me in the grades, but until the dance, I would have believed you didn't know I existed." I gave her my best pointed stare.

She had the decency to turn away. "I've always been curious about you. Everyone has been to some point. I wondered what it would be like to be colorblind, to not have magik. But I couldn't like, you know, talk to you about it, mostly because of my parents. They are really old fashioned and strict and honestly, prejudiced about people they think aren't pure paranormals."

"So what's changed?" I wanted to know.

Her lips thinned, and a guilty look crossed her face. "My mom, she's on the school board, you know. They are having kittens wanting to know what's changed with you and if the Challen Parks incident is a sign of things to come."

"So you are spying on me, for your mom."

"Well, yes. But it sounds really bad when you say it that way."

"Get out."

"Excuse me?"

"I said, get out. Get out of my room. Get out of my house and out of my life. I don't need rides or anything else from you again." I felt my anger bubbling and stood up, pointing at the toxic waste decorated door.

"Wait, Harmony. Please wait!" she begged, coming to her feet. "My mom may have wanted me to find out more about you, yes. But I wanted to do it, not for her, but for me. I'm like you in some ways. I don't have any real friends either."

She rushed to explain herself. "Sure, everyone wants to know me and hang out with me because I'm the mayor's kid or because I'm a Djinn and can grant wishes or because I look good standing next to them. None of them really give a damn about me or what I like or what I want to be. For once, I wanted hang out with someone who didn't care who I am or what I could give them."

"Poor little rich girl who has everything and is still lonely, has found out that money and power can't buy her love or real friends, so I should feel sorry for you?" I intended for my sarcasm to cut to the quick.

Tears filled her striking dark eyes as she looked at me, imploring. "Yes, you should."

A naked ache echoed in her voice. She seemed so genuine, sincere in her plea. Dammit! Sarah always said I had a soft heart.

I gave Joliet a hard stare. "What exactly did you tell your mom?"

"I lied and said you were nothing special, that you were just a late blooming Fae girl." My face must have registered that I didn't care for the comment. Joliet hurried to continue. "Nothing special in the way that counts to my mom, but that's not what I think. I can tell that there is something different about you, something unique."

"She's more concerned about Challen's parents petitioning the Council for were-gild damages and it coming out of the school budget since it happened on school property. And of course of it happening again with someone else."

Were-gild came from an old English term for the monetary price paid for damage done to a clan member outside of war or open challenge. The packs still used it for when one of theirs got hurt by an unprovoked attack by another paranormal.

"But I was provoked!" I sputtered.

"I know, you told me, and I believe you. And that's what I told my mom. She already knew about your lessons with Mr. Bellfwigg. I just confirmed that you are learning how to use your Fae powers and aren't running amok with them. So, you see, I was trying to help you out, even if you didn't know it."

"Running amok?" I raised an eyebrow at that.

"You know, out of control, a danger to other kids." Joliet supplied.

I rolled my eyes. "I know what it means, Jo."

"Jo?"

"A nickname, a shortened version of your full name."

She rolled her eyes back at me. "I know what a nickname is."

"Yeah, well, if we are going to hang out and be friends, I'm giving you a nickname. You don't hear me calling Tesch, Teschandarian all the time. I only use his full name when I am ticked at him."

Her face brightened. "So are we going to hang out and be friends?"

"On two conditions; One, you are honest with me and don't spy on me for your parents from now on. I don't like being used or lied to. And second, you tell me your middle name."

"Sure, absolutely." She agreed. "And it's Kali. Why do you want to know?"

"So I can call you Joliet Kali Coombs when I'm ticked at you."

She laughed at the joke I made. "Thanks, Harmony, for forgiving me and giving me a second chance."

"You're welcome, Jo. Don't make me regret it."

Her answer came as a tight, awkward hug. So I got another new experience, having a girl as a friend and one that hadn't known me all my life and been privy to every detail of it already. I found it kind of fun sharing stories about why we thought this or that on a subject or a song on the radio or our favorite things.

Our new relationship caused a small stir at school. One day, Joliet invited Tesch and me to the cool kids table for lunch. That got us some strange and envious looks, but no one argued about it.

She hadn't lied when she said everyone wanted to be around her for their own reasons. None were willing to give up their place in her circle to dispute our being included.

The conversation around the table became stilted and awkward at first. Tesch hung back and didn't say a word. That he did not want to be under this much scrutiny showed plain as day. Then some wizard guy asked him about his truck.

That broke the guy ice and from there on cars and engines and the best way to fix this and do that dominated the conversation. Trust the universal male language of horsepower to save the day.

Joliet just smiled serenely and roped in the feminine interest with talk about the next school dance, Prom. She informed everyone that they couldn't start too early to discuss themes and as president of the dance committee, she wanted to hear our ideas.

Everyone agreed to rule out a costume dance since we'd just had one. Some suggested popular songs. One girl suggested classic romance movie titles. I sat and listened and had a stray thought.

"What about roses?"

"Did you say something?" A junior grade Fae girl gave me a bug-eyed look.

"I said roses. I read somewhere that different colored roses have different meanings. Like red is love, yellow is friendship, white is pure love or true love, I forget. But I know there is a whole list."

"That's stupid." The junior rolled her eyes at me.

"No, it's not." Joliet countered. "It has some merit, and it's as good as your suggestion, Maelin. I'll write it down and think on it. Besides, you know that ultimately the dance committee votes on the theme."

"We are the committee, Joliet." Another young witch supplied.

"True, and after all suggestions have been thought out we will vote but not at this moment. We're just bouncing ideas around for now."

Joliet's word fell as law in the group. She definitely claimed the leader position or at least functioned as the sun they all revolved around. With her protection firmly in place, no one else had any snide remarks to make to me after that.

Chapter 17

THEY SAY THAT TIME FLIES when you are having fun. It also flies when you are as busy as an ice water salesman in Hades. Between Tesch and Jo, my social calendar mushroomed. I talked to either one or both every day.

With my extra lessons and my parents giving me the benefit of their experiences, my educational career reminded me of a runaway train. I fell into bed each night exhausted, content but exhausted.

In early December I got a Saturday off from Were practice for the Bedlam game. Charlie spent the afternoon cheering like a mad man from the comfort of his new, custom, OU crimson Lay-Z-Boy.

Tesch joined him for some male bonding. Before the game they shared a special ceremony for his old chair. Painting old scores and team symbols on the olive green monstrosity, they doused it in gasoline and set it on fire in the driveway. A fond farewell, I think Charlie cried.

My Were abilities were definitely improving. I could affect several stages of partial change. This proved useful because it gave me the Werelynx talents of strength, hearing, sight and smell and tree climbing, without losing myself to the change. I could still think as me and not just respond with animal instinct.

Sarah continued to pound me with potion work. I had a good two dozen potential spell catastrophes bottled and corked in the pantry. Warding spells, sleep spells, memory spells, truth spells and charm spells just to name a few.

She also began to teach me some spells of only will. That turned out to be much harder, more exhausting work. Since she didn't want me to wind up magikally drained, these lessons were much slower paced and infrequent. Already running on empty, I hadn't had much success with them.

I still had no talent for sorcery, maybe because I didn't see purple. As a result, my classes with Professor Poff, while informative, interesting and occasionally weird, remained generic. Frankly, I felt relieved. I had enough on my plate and could do just fine without more.

I had not come up with a correct answer for his question, and my deadline approached. I wondered if he would at least pass me for my efforts alone.

In opposition were my lessons with my vice-principal. I didn't know if because yellow spectrum came as my first revealed magik or because he showed himself to be such a terrific instructor, but my Fae studies with Mr. Bellfwigg went great. I mastered simple illusions like making a stick appear as a tree and a window as a fish tank, complete with tropical fish.

Mr. Bellfwigg exposed a twisted sense of humor one day when he had me make the janitor's closet look like the boy's restroom door and the restroom appear as a blank wall. He claimed he wanted to test my illusions against what people knew to be the truth and what they saw. Only the janitor didn't fall for it.

Glamour revealed different. I began small. I changed my eye color to a soft, doe brown like Sarah's. Of course Tesch saw through it right away, Sarah and Charlie too. They all gave me double looks. Once they realized the change, it melted away for them. Jo noticed too, but she took a few hours.

As I got better with it, I went a little wild at school one day and glamoured myself to be Jo and her to be me. She thought it a great idea until no one realized I wasn't her. Tesch and Mr. Bellfwigg recognized the difference almost immediately.

With glamour, people have to be truly aware of the real object or person to see through the magik to the truth, like the janitor and his closet. No one at the popular table had known the difference but my boyfriend. Jo wanted to wear the glamour home to her parents. Wisely, I vetoed the idea.

Christmas came, and I enjoyed the lights. Our town tried to pass as a standard human community to the world, not an Amish village, so we decked the halls for the holiday. For once, I got the fascination with all the twinkling bits of color and tinsel.

The days of winter were short and cold. I began to get bored with indoor activities. Being captive to the weather made my instructors a bunch of zealots about my learning. I could hardly wait for spring.

Every day I searched the ground for the first blooming jonquils to poke their heads up. This year I would get firsthand experience of their color, not just their sweet scent.

March roared in like a lion, bringing heavy rains, but leaving a scent behind that promised new life to follow. Patches of green grass sprouted as the temperatures started climbing into the fifties and sixties. A little more than two weeks later, I gazed out of my bedroom window with longing while Jo prattled on about prom.

"Have you thought about a dress yet?"

"I can't go, Jo. I'm still a sophomore, and sophomores aren't allowed. So Tesch and I are off the roster. But I'd love to hear about your dress." I lied.

Jo called me on it. "Liar. I've already told you about my dress twice, and you still don't remember my flower selection."

The prom committee had voted on the theme and "A Rose by Any Other Name" had won the vote. A girl would personify a flower with dress. The guys had it easy, they just had to match cummerbund and tie to their lady's fair blossom. Oh, and get the right corsage.

"You're going as a lily, right?"

"A tiger lily." She corrected.

"Right. So who's the lucky guy that gets to carry your train or crown or whatever?" Jo remained a shoe-in for prom queen.

"You know my parents. There's only one other Djinn in school, Aloysius Benjamin. To them, he's the only suitable escort, so I'm stuck with him."

"Did he ask you?"

"Yes. He always does. I think his father and mine have an agreement or something. And Ally doesn't rock the boat with his parents either, though I suspect it's so they will leave him alone about his…preferences."

"Preferences?"

"Let just say that on prom night, Ally will be more interested in my dress than you've been. He loves fashion and design. In fact, he'll probably wish he could wear my dress. He's gay."

"You're joking! Really?"

She gave me a conspirator's grin, eyes sparkling. "Yep, we tried a kiss once, years ago. You know, just to say we had. There was absolutely no spark whatsoever."

"That doesn't mean he's gay, Jo. It just means he may not have been into you like that." I offered.

She leveled a 'you've got to be kidding' look at me. "Please, Harmony. I'm hot, and we know it. A guy would have to be dead or gay to not want to make out with me. And afterward he kind of hinted that he had kissed another someone, a male someone once, and got more out of it."

"I feel kind of sorry for him. His parents are going to freak when they know for sure. I wouldn't be surprised if they put him in a lamp for millennia."

"Can they do that? You've never really explained the whole Djinni in a bottle thing to me."

"Yes, they can." Her face had an unusually gloomy cast. Jo paused as if to gather her thoughts. "Let me try to explain."

"You know that Djinn work violet magik, like sorcerers. But there's a catch with us. Don't ask me why, I can't tell you that. The catch is we can only summon what already exists by request."

I turned away from the window, sitting cross legged on my bed, giving my full attention while she enlightened from her usual bean bag spot. "Okay, I'm listening."

"For instance, let's say you were cold and wished to be warm, I could summon your sphinx fur for you. Or I could summon a fire right here in the middle of the floor and burn the whole house down. Either way, you got your wish; you'd either be warmed by the fur or the fire."

"Well, that's not very nice." I huffed. The thought of my house going up in flames left me shocked and unsettled. "How could you suggest such a thing?"

"I didn't. I was just giving an example, because Djinns are bargainers, traders, deal makers. We have to exchange magikal services for what we need or want. We can't use our power for ourselves unless in defense."

"What does that have to do with the whole bottle or lamp issue?" I wasn't afraid to admit that I didn't understand. "I don't get it."

"Bottle service, as we call it, is supposed to be training on how to get the best deal possible. Part of getting a good bargain is being able to see the flaws and loopholes in a trade and how to give the least for the most. We learn from the mistake others make in their wishes by not being specific enough or exact enough. Trust me, many a Djinn has gone on to have successful careers in corporate law, car sales and politics."

I frowned at her description. It seemed so… underhanded. "That sounds wrong and unfair, to deliberately twist around someone's words and wishes. I'm sorry, I don't mean to criticize, but it does."

Her demeanor changed. Her shoulders became rigid, and she sat up straight. Jo's eyes narrowed at me.

"Well, I think it's unfair that every other paranormal is allowed to use magik to make their lives easier if they can, but we can't. I think it's unfair to have all this potential power and not even be able to summon myself a Cherry Coke on a hot day. And I really think it's unfair that I am expected to be a slave to the innocuous wishes of countless others while I earn the right to make my own choices!"

Jo's eyes burned with indignation and contempt. Her face had become a mask of hot anger. I'd never seen her so passionate about anything.

"Okay. Okay. You're right, that is unfair, all the way around. I apologize for making a snap judgment."

She huffed and puffed a moment more before settling back against the bean bag stuffing. Her head tilted back while she appeared to get control. To the ceiling, she said, "You're right too. It sucks all the way around. I'd do almost anything to get out of it."

"So can you? This bottle service thing, do you have to do it?"

"Among Djinn, we are not considered adults until we do. We have no rights in the Djinn community. We can't marry or even leave our parent's homes. When a jinni is old enough for service, our parents broker our contracts to the Dali Djinn, he's like our leader, the most powerful deal maker. For us, everything is a bargain hunt."

"Our parents market our services for a term of years, and in return, get a promise of items like money, a home, the right spouse, the necessities for a chosen career when our time in the bottle or the lamp or whatever is up."

"So, you see, when it's time for our deal to be negotiated, Ally and I both want to be on our parent's good side. Otherwise, we could be stuck granting other people's wishes for a very long time and not have much to show for it."

"Oh, Jo, that's awful. I had no idea. Couldn't you go to the Council? Appeal to them. I mean, that's slavery. You're an American citizen; you have rights!"

Jo laughed scornfully. "Our Dali Djinn is *on* the Council." She stressed. "Come on, Harmony, don't be naïve. We may have been born on American soil, but we aren't really a part of all that. What am I going to do? Go to the Department of *Human* Services and tell them I'm a Djinni and that my parents are selling me into indentured servitude for a hundred years for my own good?"

She had a point. Who would believe her? And if they did believe? If she proved it? Well, her life wouldn't be worth spit with the Council. Any more than mine would be if they found out I had more than one spectrum of powers.

"There's got to be a better way." I said more to myself than to her.

"Well, if you figure out a way to mainstream paranormal society to the humans, without starting an all-out panic or slaughter, while at the same time keeping us intact as a people, you can have my vote for Head Councilor, if we were allowed to vote on it." Jo's voice spewed bitterness. I couldn't hold it against her.

"I wish I could."

"Won't ever happen, Harmony." Jo sighed.

"Don't say that. No one knows everything the future holds."

I thought of Madame Osza's predictions about my own prospects. Of the High Priestess card of wisdom and knowledge and the many factors can influence what will happen. The future is always about the choices made in the present. That I believed whole heartedly.

"Normals would freak out if they knew we really existed. We are the stuff of their dreams and nightmares. They'd either try to take what paras can do and use it for their own needs, something any Djinni can tell you about, or their jealousy and fear would have them hunting us into extinction." Jo replied in a fatalistic tone. "Accept it."

"No. If we had a strong and powerful leader who could negotiate a truce before we revealed ourselves completely, and we could be integrated in stages... it could happen."

"And I might grow wings and fly to Bora Bora. Even if we had a leader like that, and that's a big if, do you really think the Council is going to give up control over our world, just like that? They like running the show, having us under their thumb. They'd kill anyone who threatened their hold on the para world."

"I didn't say it would be an easy thing." I grumbled.

"Why are we talking about this stuff anyway? It's making me depressed, and I don't like being depressed. It makes me hungry. Now I've got the munchies."

We meandered downstairs to the kitchen. Standing by the pantry doors as we entered the room, I asked. "Organic or inorganic?"

"Do what?"

I giggled. "Sarah grows produce for a living, remember? So we always have lots of organically grown, pesticide free fruits and veggies. But Charlie is a diehard Cheetos fan. Sarah calls them cheese flavored chemical sticks or orange poison, but we have them."

"Set me up with the chemical sticks. I like to live dangerously." Jo smiled as she slid into the breakfast nook. "And I'll take another glass of that herbal iced tea. It's divine. She should be selling that stuff."

"I'll let her know you said so."

I opened the pantry doors and stepped inside. I raised my voice a notch so Jo could hear me. "This may take a minute. Sarah buys the things for Charlie, but then hides them from him. I think she hopes he'll get tired of looking and choose something healthier."

"Is she having any luck with that?" Jo's voice came from a distance.

"Not really."

Farther away and faint, my Werelynx hearing picked up the ring tone of "As Long As You Love Me", the Bieber song. Tesch called my cell phone, still up in my bedroom.

I poked my head out of the pantry. "Um, Jo, I forgot my phone upstairs, and Tesch is supposed to call any minute. The tea is in the fridge, help yourself. I'll be right back."

"Sure."

I turned and sprinted back the way we had come, up the stairs and to my room. The phone had stopped ringing, but Tesch stayed number one in my speed dial. I hit the button. He answered on the second ring.

"Hi, gorgeous, I was just leaving you a voice mail." He answered.

"Well, now you don't have to. What's up?" I couldn't keep a smile from my lips that he called me gorgeous. I didn't think I'd pass as pretty on a good day, but why argue.

"A little bird told me that your pal Madame Osza will be in town again very soon. The carnival applied for city permits today. They'll be back in about ten days."

"Really? It's too soon. The weather is still crappy. They don't usually show up until late April or early May."

"You're complaining!" Tesch laughed into the phone. The vibrations tickled my ear. "I thought you loved the carnival."

"I do. I just wonder why they are coming early this year."

"Who knows? Who cares? I figured as hard as you've been working on everything, you'd welcome the chance to put it aside and have some fun."

"I'd jump on the chance to have some fun!" I assured him.

"Great! I'll be right over." He teased.

"Perv." I teased back.

"You don't want me to come over? Jumping on me is optional, I promise."

"Sure, come on over. Jo's here too."

"Aw, talk about spoiling a perfect opportunity. Do I have to? If I hear one more word about that damn tiger lily dress of hers, I think I am going to throw up."

"We've already covered that, so it should be safe."

"All right, be there in a bit. Love you."

"Love you too." I whispered softly and hung up.

I bounced back down the steps two at a time, floating on air. Rounding the banister and into the kitchen, I stopped short as my bubble burst.

Jo stood in the pantry door holding a glass, cork stoppered bottle in each hand. The contents swirled liquid gold in one and deep rose in the other. The independently moving liquid spoke loudly that they were full of active magik. I had forgotten that Sarah stored my potions in the pantry.

"What are you doing in there?" I asked.

"What are these?" Jo inquired at the same time.

"You said to help myself. I was looking for the Cheetos." She answered simply.

I had no simple answer to give her back. I searched my brain for a plausible lie but couldn't do it. I had demanded honesty from her as a condition for a second chance at being my friend. To lie to her now would make me a hypocrite.

I chewed on my lower lip, a nervous habit since teething. "They're potions." It wasn't a lie.

Jo narrowed her eyes at me with a perturbed look. "I know they're potions, Harmony. I'm not stupid. What I want to know is why there are over two dozen different potions in your pantry, with recent bottle dates and your initials in the wax that sealed them."

Damn. Damn. Damn. Jo might be vain, even narcissistic at times, but no one could accuse her of being dense. She had the mind of a born prosecuting attorney when she wanted.

I took a fortifying breath and told the truth. "I made them."

Her look said I'd caught her off guard, that she'd expected me to deny it, ready to call me a liar. In disbelief, Jo queried. "You made them? You?"

"Yes."

She stumbled away from me, still carrying my potions. By the sink, she tumbled them onto the counter as if they were poison instead of potions. I cringed at the clinking glass against the tiles. Goddess, please don't let one break.

"Harmony, those are active potions. I can see the magik in them moving. They look like freaking pink and gold Lava lamps! That means they work. That means you are a, you're a…" Her voice faltered.

"I'm a witch." I confirmed.

"But, but you're Fae." Jo argued like it couldn't be true.

"I'm that too."

"Oh Goddess, oh my Goddess, that means you're a half breed."

She clapped her hands over her mouth after the last word as if it were the worst curse words ever. Maybe to her, it was.

Eyes as big as the dark moon; Jo made her way to the nook and sat down. Her skin had gone pale beneath her natural tan. She stared at me like a monster zit on her nose.

"Jo, calm down. It's okay." I tried to use a soothing tone of voice.

"No, it's not!" She protested. "Half breeds are dangerous. They have no control of their magik. They could expose us all to humans."

She recited standard Council propaganda to me. Something I had heard a hundred times over in school and by pure blood adults in the community. It had even been something I had once thought true, until I became one.

I tried reason. "Do I look out of control or dangerous?"

I stood there in Sarah's spotless kitchen, all of five feet nothing, in sock feet and a pony tail looking, I hoped, harmless. My arms hung loosely at my sides. I made no sudden moves.

I watched her eyes rake over me, measuring me up. "How long have you known that you're a...," Jo paused. She didn't even want to say the words. I didn't want her too either. The way she said it sounded ugly. "That you're mixed."

"Since the carnival came last time, maybe a little after. Since I started seeing the color green."

She hung her head in her hands. I thought she might cry. Instead she croaked out, "This is so awful!"

"What's awful? Someone ruin your dress for the prom?" Tesch asked as he came in the back door of the kitchen.

We'd been friends so long and didn't stand on ceremony with each other. He often came in the house without knocking when he'd been expected.

Picking up on the tension between us from the moment he stepped in, he looked from Jo to me and back to Jo. He quickly came to my side.

"What's wrong?" A worried frown creased his brow. His jade green eyes were filled with concern.

Jo jumped up from her seat. "Did you know?" She demanded her tone accusing. "Did you know she's a half breed?"

Tesch looked at me, astonishment written all over his face. His threw the question back to me. "What is going on here?"

I continued to try and be calm, though inside I felt anything but. "While I was upstairs on the phone with you, Jo found some of the potions I made. When she asked, I told the truth. I had to. Friends don't lie to each other. So now the cat's out of the bag, and Jo needs some time to adjust."

I will admit that turned out to be a poor choice of words.

If possible, Tesch's wide eyed look got even wider. He swallowed as if a bug crawled down his throat. "You told her you're a Werelynx and a witch, as well as Fae?"

Damn. Damn. Damn.

"No, but you just did."

Absolute horror colored Jo's face. "A Were! You're a Werelynx too. My Goddess, you're not just a half breed, you're a freaking mongrel!"

"Joliet Kali Coombs!" I gasped. Hurt and anger filled my chest.

"I have to get out of here. Now!"

Common sense told me I needed to stop her from leaving, to make her see reason. That while, yes, I had a mixed heritage; I was still me, still her friend, Harmony.

The wounded part of me, the part her words had injured, said who needs friends like that. How could she have said such a thing to me? Let her go.

The hurt won the contest. I crossed my arms over my chest and fought not to cry as she stormed by on her way out. The slam of the front door echoed through the house.

Tesch didn't say another word. He folded me into a warm embrace, forcing my cheek gently against his chest while his long fingers soothingly smoothed my hair. I wrapped my arms around his waist and hung on.

It took a minute before I gulped a breath, then another and another. Hot tears rolled from my eyes and over my cheeks to wet the front of his shirt. I cried openly for five minutes before I got a grip.

"I'm sorry, Tesch."

"For what, baby?"

"For getting your shirt soaked. I thought I had grown up enough not get upset just because someone called me names."

Tesch sighed. I felt his lips on the top of my head in a feather light, comforting kiss. "I don't think we ever get that old, Harmony. Maybe we get better at hiding the pain but better at not feeling it, no."

He held me a moment more before he began. "I hate to point it out, but we are going to have to tell Charlie and Sarah what happened today. We need to make a plan."

"A plan?" I asked confused. "What kind of plan, for what?"

"Seriously, Harmony, think about it. What if Joliet tells somebody, anybody? What if she tells her mom, or worse, her dad? Think about the consequences."

"She wouldn't do that!" I protested. "She promised me she wouldn't tell on me to her parents again."

"Was that before or after she called you a half breed mongrel?" His voice had a harsh edge I didn't like.

I pushed away from him. "You don't have to be a butt about it."

He pulled at his hair spikes and let out a frustrated growl. "Argh! Yes, Harmony, I do! You are too trusting for your own good. You believe in the best in people. And while I love you for your sense of honor and justice, your sense of self-preservation stinks! Someone has to look out for you, and I took the job!"

"I don't need a keeper!" I yelled at him.

"That is a matter of opinion!" He shouted back.

"And you can take your opinion and go to straight to hel…"

"Whoa! Whoa! What's going on in here? We could hear you two yelling on the porch." Sarah came through the kitchen arch with Charlie a step or two behind. They each carried plastic bags of takeout Chinese.

"First your friend, Joliet, nearly runs us over peeling out of the drive and now you guys look ready to tear each other's heads off." Charlie commented. "Something's wrong, so spill it."

Tesch and I stood apart, glaring at each other, hands on hips, not willing to give an inch. Charlie circled around us, putting the food on the counter. Almost on top of the potions Jo had discarded.

"Someone had better start talking, now." My dad growled.

I turned away from Tesch angrily to better face my parents. "Jo and I had an argument." I began. "And now Tesch thinks he can dictate to me what I need to do it about it."

Tesch snarled behind me. "Don't think you can gloss it over that easy, Harmony."

To Charlie, Tesch said. "Harmony told Joliet about being a Fae-Were-Witch, and the prom queen freaked out. And I tried to explain to Harmony.."

"I did not!" I interjected. "Not about the Were part. You did that!"

Tesch's jaw clamped and I heard his teeth grind together. "I stand corrected. Whatever. Joliet knows the whole scoop. And as I said before someone interrupted, this could be very bad for Harmony, for all of us. We needed to talk with you two and make a plan. If worse comes to worst and Joliet spills her guts, we need to know what we are going to do."

"And as I was telling Mr. Know-It-All, Jo wouldn't do that to me. Then he goes and accuses me of being so stupid that I need a babysitter."

"I did NOT say you were stupid, Harmony."

"You implied it! That I can't take care of myself and my instincts about people stink! Tell him that's not true. Tell him." I looked to them both for support.

Charlie looked at his feet. Sarah shrugged at me. They were no help at all.

"You think I'm stupid too?" I asked, feeling let down and hurt again.

"Not stupid Kitten, just naïve about some things." Charlie answered his tone apologetic. "You know that people can be mean and cruel and petty, but since you aren't that way, you don't expect them to be either. It surprises you. And given that you don't expect it, you're more likely to be hurt by it."

"You know, I am getting really tired of people calling me naïve."

What else could I say? I huffed and crossed my arms again, sulking. I wanted to argue, but I didn't see the point. I'd just be voted as naïve again.

From there, we dug into the Chinese food and hunkered down around the table for what could only be called a war counsel. I hoped I never had to be on the opposite end of a strategy game with Tesch or Charlie. I discovered Sarah could be insightfully devious when needed as well.

"Whether we decide to run or hide or both, we are going to need cash and credentials." Charlie opened.

"I'll start liquidating what assets we can in the morning. First the bank for our savings then I'll take my jewelry to the pawn shops." Sarah offered. "Then maybe some of the antiques."

"I just wish I knew a way to get good credentials in a hurry. I'm sure one or more of my students know how to fake an ID, but birth certificates and stuff like that are different. And obviously we can't go ask the Council for new ones." Charlie mentioned.

When paranormals had frequent dealings with the Normal world, the Council provided credible documentation for them. Birth certificates, social security numbers if needed, even death certificates. It provided one of many ways to keep control.

"Hold on folks." Tesch broke in. "First, if you start emptying bank accounts and selling off the family heirlooms it's going to look suspicious. Harmony knows I've got a stash I've been saving for a rainy day. It's more than enough for running or hiding. Second, I know someone who can handle the papers we might need, no problem."

"Tesch, we appreciate you wanting to help, but we can't ask that of you." Sarah told him. "We can't let you endanger yourself for our sakes or take your money. Besides, I don't think the amount you have would be the kind of money we are talking about."

"Also, I know how you feel about Harmony, but it wouldn't be right for you to just up and leave your family and friends on a youthful whim like this."

I know she meant well. I am sure Tesch did too, but the stare he leveled at Sarah burned ice cold and looked in no way adolescent.

"Sarah, I understand where you're coming from, but let me be clear, I'm going where Harmony goes. My mind is made up about that, so let's not even go there. She's the only family or friend that I truly care about."

"As far as the money goes, I've been collecting jewels, coins, cash and anything else of value off the bottom of every lake in the county for almost two decades. I may be young, but I know what it's like to be without resources and need them. My stockpile is worth a lot, as much as this house and contents, maybe more, and it's portable."

Charlie's eyes widened with shock. Sarah's looked equally stunned.

"Son, we definitely can't take that much from you."

"Yes you can, and you will, for Harmony's sake."

Charlie and Sarah exchanged looks. Then Charlie nodded in that firm way he did when he'd made a decision. "Fine, then. We'll say no more about it besides thank you. Now, tell me more about the person you think might be able to help with the legal papers. Is it someone we can trust?"

Tesch looked a little shamefaced, but answered. "Yes, he can be trusted. It's Mr. Bellfwigg."

"Bellfwigg!" The three of us gasped together.

Tesch nodded. "Mr. Bellfwigg, he uh, well, he has connections. I think it's safe to tell you now; Mr. Bellfwigg is a member of the Wizened."

"I'll be damned! Bellfwigg? Are you serious?" Charlie exclaimed.

"Really?" Sarah sat back, taking it in.

"Um, excuse me, naïve person at the table. What the heck is the Wizened?"

"A rumor, or they're supposed to be." Charlie answered.

"The Wizened," Sarah elaborated, "Are a secret group of paranormals that are dedicated to legalizing, nationalizing and integrating all supernatural creatures into the mainstream world."

"They also believe that all paranormals, whole, half or mixed should have full rights within our society. That instead of hiding from the human world, we should be working with them to better all of us. They think that by segregating our magiks, we are making ourselves weaker and declining our populations."

Tesch and I regarded her like she had grown another head. Charlie gave her a speculative look.

"And may I ask how you came to know the Wizened's agenda so well, my love?"

Her face colored a lovely cherry red. "I dated a boy in college. I think he was trying to recruit me. But then I met you and lost interest."

"Uh huh." Charlie smiled. "We'll talk about that one later."

Tesch seemed eager to move on. "Okay, so we've got the cash and a connection for credentials. What next?"

"I think we all need to pack an emergency bag, three basic changes of clothes, essential toiletries and maybe a few personal items not to be left behind. I'll also pack a goody bag of the potions that Harmony has made, our Grimoires and basic spell components. We may be on the road for a while and not be able to get a ready supply of stuff." Practical Sarah advised.

"My Suburban is the vehicle of choice for traveling. We can load the bags in it and still have room for all of us." Charlie planned out loud.

"Does it have a trailer hitch?" Tesch asked.

"No. Why?"

"Because a travel trailer at some point could be a good idea."

"I'll get one put on in the city tomorrow."

"Aren't you all getting a little ahead of yourselves?" I asked. "You're talking like you are prepping for the end of the world. You are going to feel really silly when nothing happens."

"And if that's the way it turns out, sweetie, all three of us will stand still while you say I told you so as many times as you want. But I'd rather feel silly later than lose you or Charlie or Tesch because we didn't prepare. So for my peace of mind, play along, please." Sarah gently scolded.

"Fine, I'll prep, and I'll pack. But I don't think it's going to be necessary. I think once Jo has time to think about it, we'll make up as friends."

"I sincerely hope you are right, Kitten."

They talked more about details and such. Sarah decided we needed two emergency bags of clothing, one in the Suburban and one at home that could be easily grabbed if the Suburban wasn't available.

Charlie decided to go to an ATM over in Harrah and draw out as much cash as it would allow to have on hand. Full dark had fallen when Tesch left to go contact Mr. Bellfwigg about our papers and to start hauling up his treasures from the bottom of the reservoir.

Still angry with him over our argument in the kitchen, I only let him kiss my cheek goodbye. Then I went upstairs to pack.

Luckily, I still had several worn, but sturdy backpacks in my closet from school years gone by. As I prepared the two bags of clothing, I felt caught in a bad spy movie. Ridiculous. Tesch and my parents were overreacting.

When packing my personal keepsake items into the second bag, I paused. What would I not be willing to leave behind if I had to go?

The first item I reached for, the sphinx stole Sarah had passed on to me. It had magikal value, yes, but more sentimental value. Next came a faded OU sweatshirt Charlie bought me years ago on one of those 'bring your kid to work' days. I packed Gil, the cheap, brightly colored parrot Tesch won for me at the carnival in October. I always wore the topaz heart he had given me from his cache of watery wealth, so I didn't have to worry about that.

Finally, I packed a picture of Charlie and Sarah holding me as an infant and another of Tesch and I dressed up for the Halloween dance. I looked at all of their faces, so happy and proud. Sarah and Charlie were beaming new parents of their baby girl. Tesch smiled with genuine pleasure to be escorting me. The people in my life were willing to give up all they knew or had to call their own for me.

In a moment of doubt, I closed my eyes and prayed to the Goddess.

Please Gaia, please. Let Jo be a true friend. Don't let the ones I love, who love me, suffer on my account. They don't deserve that. I know your will is not always our way, but I don't want them to lose everything because of me.

I thought I felt the warm pressure of wind tickle my face with a whispery caress. I stayed perfectly still, keeping my eyes closed.

They only lose everything, if they lose you, an inner voice answered then faded away.

Well, that happened to be deeply reassuring. Not.

I opened eyes that felt heavy with worry and fatigue to get ready for bed. One way or another, time would tell if I was proved right to have faith in Jo or if I remained the Fool after all.

Chapter 18

I WENT TO SCHOOL on Wednesday feeling like I had a target painted on my back. Any minute the men in black, actually the guys in gray, Council henchmen, would jump out and grab me. My full-on case of nerves had me spilling my books in the hallway just before first period.

Someone stopped to help pick them up. I had a moment of astonishment discovering Challen handing my abused copy of *History and Anatomy of Were Beings* back. The one I threw at Tesch, eons ago.

"From the looks of this book you've been studying way too hard, Phillips." Well at least he didn't call me Gray.

"I've had a lot of catching up to do." I answered.

"So much you've darn near ripped the cover off." He chuckled.

"I guess so. Thanks for the help."

The words felt awkward. I'd never dreamed I'd thank Challen for anything, except maybe falling off the planet. I took the battered text from his hand.

"If you ever need any help with the subject, let me know. I kind of know Were Anatomy inside and out." He gave me a half grin and a wink.

Anyone else I would have accused of flirting. But Challen? Ew.

"I'm getting it, but thanks for the offer anyway."

We stood from our stooped positions, facing each other like wary adversaries in peace time. I turned to head for class. His large hand placed on my shoulder held me back with a soft touch, very non-threatening.

My head rotated, looking over my shoulder. I wondered what he else he could want. As if my attention were the cue, he took his hand away.

"Seriously, Phillips, I know you don't trust me. I can't blame you for that. But I'm trying to work through my issues and feel like I need to make amends for being a jerk for so long. If you ever need help with something, just ask, okay?"

His hazel brown eyes looked sincere. What could I say?

"Thanks, Challen. I appreciate that, and I'll keep the offer in mind."

He smiled openly at me then. "Good. Great. Then I'll talk to you some other time."

"Sure."

He headed off the opposite way from me. I shook my head in wonder. Boys. I'll never understand them. They accuse girls of being hard to comprehend just because once a month our hormones go all wonky; we're cranky and emotional and crave chocolate. At least we have a legitimate reason for being weird.

My morning classes passed in a fog. I didn't have an opportunity to see Jo until lunch. She passed by as I waited in line. I caught her eye and smiled cautiously. She hurriedly looked away, nothing more or less.

I didn't push it. If she wasn't ready to make nice, I could deal. At least she hadn't been nasty about it. She didn't stand up on a table and reveal my secrets to the whole world right then and there.

Finding an empty table, I sat down, away from the popular crowd. It happened in high school, people noticed.

Anytime there's a change in the social hierarchy of such a closed environment, people see it. Having been briefly 'in' with Jo's approval, now I was definitely 'out' for the time being.

I wondered if any of her entourage would have the guts or the curiosity to ask their queen why. And what would she say?

My appetite disappeared, all nerves again, as my stomach whirled with anxiety. Looking at my plate of Salisbury mystery meat and potatoes with gravy, I decided not to chance it. If I got hungry later I had an energy bar in my bag.

When no axe fell on my neck by three o'clock, my stomach decided the coast was clear. Munching greedily on the granola, I headed to the art room for my lesson with Mr. Bellfwigg. He waited, already in the brightly lit room.

"Oh, Harmony, there you are. I am glad you could make it today." His wrinkled face gave me warm smile before turning meaningful as he continued.

"I understand that you and your parents are planning a vacation for next week while spring break is going on. However, I want you to continue your studies during the time you are away. I wrote down a lesson plan and some things I want you to work on while school is out."

Mr. Bellfwigg passed me a large manila envelope that felt too heavy to contain only a lesson plan or homework assignments. One eyelid dropped in a wink as I picked up the package. I caught on to what he meant without actually spelling it out.

These were the documents Charlie, Sarah, Tesch and I might need should we make a run for it, if the Council men showed up for me. A lot of bad possibilities were connected to the envelope that I hoped would never happen. All the same, I picked it up and put it in my bag.

"Thanks, Mr. Bellfwigg." I muttered. I didn't know what else to add.

"You are very welcome, Harmony. I hope the lessons I planned for you will come of good use." He nodded sadly then appeared to mentally shake himself.

"Now, today I want to show you something completely different than what we've been working on."

He clapped his hands together tightly, closed his eyes and began to draw yellow magik into himself. Since he didn't try to shield, I figured he wanted me to watch.

The golden glow began to center in his shaggy fingers. Slowly, he cupped them as if holding water. I could see a wonderful globe of the size of a baseball resting in his rough, calloused palms.

"This is a sphere of magik. It can be used for defense. All paras can call their energy into their hands and then throw the ball at an adversary. Unfortunately, there is a catch. It won't work on an enemy of the same spectrum."

I stared in amazement at the orb of pure power he held. I'd never seen anything so stunning. It looked as solid as any other ball, but the surface moved and swirled with the essence of magik.

"Excuse me? What do you mean?"

"If I were to throw this ball at you, you being Fae, your body would absorb the energy, just offering you more power to call your own."

"And if I wasn't Fae?" I asked cautiously.

"Then the magik might cause you to see an illusion. It might glamour you to look like me and a fellow soldier would attack you instead. Magikal spheres are unpredictable, but they do tend to stay true to the color that called them into being."

"So what are we going to do with it today?"

"Play catch." Mr. Bellfwigg smiled with a wicked grin.

Oh, boy.

"Um, Mr. Bellfwigg, I don't know if that would be such a good idea."

More than a little worried about being glamoured or having an illusion attached to me, I stepped back. I appeared as no great beauty to be sure, but I did not want to look like a four foot five, heavyset man with thick dark hair everywhere except the top of my head. It wasn't vanity to be reluctant to have skin that looked like worn boot leather.

I may have been Fae, but I existed also as Witch and Were and maybe more. His magik might not be absorbed by body.

My face must have registered my panic. Mr. Bellfwigg dissipated the ball of energy, walking toward me.

"Miss Phillips" he began, his tone very low to not be overheard by anyone in the hall. "Finding out your weakness in battle is finding out too late."

His words let me know that Tesch had revealed all about my peculiar, mixed bag of talents. Mr. Bellfwigg offered me a safe place to find out ahead of time what I needed to be afraid of, and maybe what I didn't.

"Sure, okay." I nodded, sounding more confident than I actually felt. "What do you want me to do?"

"First, call your power and your shield."

We had practiced this so much it had become second nature, taking me less time than blinking. "Got it, now what?"

"Now push the power toward your hands. Not all of it, just enough to make a sphere the size of the one I showed you. Imagine yourself forming a snowball; cup your hands for the right size around the energy until your palms feel full. Then pack and press the power the way you would snow until it becomes solid."

I closed my eyes and tried to grab the imagery as I moved the power from the center of my being into my hands. Controlling the flow went much the same as Sarah had taught me about pushing power into potion ingredients.

I compressed my hands, consolidating my magik snowball into the right size. When I felt as if there were actually weight and mass in my hands and not just my head, I opened my eyes to see what I'd done.

There it was. My own Fae-made ball of energy in my palm. It felt heavier than it looked.

"Excellent, Ms. Phillips. Though why I am surprised I don't know. You have shown yourself to be an exemplary pupil, a very fast learner indeed." Mr. Bellfwigg beamed at me.

I returned the compliment. "I think it's because you are such a good teacher, sir."

I think he turned a little pink, hard to tell beneath all that facial hair. "Thank you. It's nice to be appreciated."

"Now that I've got it, what do I do with it?"

"Throw it at me." He stood a mere ten feet away now.

"Throw a ball of energy at you." I repeated. "What if I miss?"

"Nothing. The magik will dissolve back into the nether it comes from and you make another."

"And if I hit you with it?"

"I think that is the point. What good is a weapon of defense if you can't hit a target with it? I promise Fae energy will not hurt me. In fact, it tickles a bit as you'll see for yourself."

I remained very nervous about that part and wished he hadn't reminded me. Oh well, here went nothing. I wound up like a pitcher on the mound, reared back…and missed.

"Sorry. Gym class was never my best subject." I told him as I watched my orb metaphysically shatter and fade away.

I heard him mutter 'obviously' with his head turned away to where the sphere had gone a good five feet behind him. He turned back to me and smiled brightly. "No matter, just make another, and try again."

I spent the next half hour forming balls of magik and lobbing them, inaccurately most of the time, at Mr. Bellfwigg. I had hit him maybe three out of seven times when he decided to start dodging, his reasoning sound if not frustrating.

"Do you really think an enemy is going to stand still for you while you toss magik at them, my dear? I doubt it very much."

I did too, but my aim stunk. I mean like dead skunk, road kill kind of stunk. I only hit him maybe seven out of twenty times once he started moving. Depressing.

When I threw sphere twenty-two, he fired one back at me. The yellow circle of energy hit me square in the chest. I stepped back with the impact. The power passed into me feeling like ants running under my skin as it spread out and melted.

I giggled. Not just from the sensation, which did tickle, but with relief that I hadn't sprouted coarse hair all over my face. At least, I didn't think I had.

My eye came up to look at Mr. Bellfwigg who casually bounced a ball of power from hand to hand. His look screamed I told you so.

"You could have warned me." I stared him down.

"I could have." He agreed. "But most opponents don't tell you what they intend to do before they do it. Kind of like they won't wait to see if you give as good as you get." He threw the ball he held at me, and I haphazardly darted and ducked for cover.

From there, the battle raged. Mr. Bellfwigg and I pitched magik at each other like the last two kids on a dodge ball court. As I dipped behind a chair after chucking one of my few accurate throws his way, I found myself smiling. This had turned out to be fun.

"Okay, time is up. I think you have the hang of it."

I stood up from behind my protection. Another sphere of yellow took me full in the face.

"Hey, no fair!" I cried. "You said the lesson was over."

"Always suspect your foes, even when they hold up the flag of truce. It could just be a trick to draw you out. And that *is* your final lesson for the day." Mr. Bellfwigg replied in a slightly breathy voice. I think we had both got a workout with the game. "We will work on it more tomorrow. Your aim is atrocious."

"I told you I wasn't any good at sports, sir." I reminded him.

"That's something I have always admired about you, Ms. Phillips. You always tell the truth, even when it's unfavorable about yourself."

I lifted an eyebrow at him, not sure if he intended sarcasm or not. Mr. Bellfwigg had already shown me he had a warped sense of humor with the bathroom illusion.

"Be ready tomorrow for round two, Mr. Bellfwigg. I might surprise you."

"Of that I have no doubt."

It was Wednesday. Tesch picked me up. He offered to help me fog up his windows again, but I had a different game in mind. I told him about my lesson with Mr. Bellfwigg and asked if he could make the energy orbs as well.

"Sure, Harmony. It was a cool game in the fourth grade while everyone figured out how to call their powers. But teachers put a stop to it when too many kids went home sprouting leaves from their eyebrows or with a tail they didn't come with originally. Now, guys horse around in the locker room sometimes, but that's all."

"Why didn't you tell me you could do that?" I felt hurt that he hadn't shared his abilities with me.

"Harmony, haven't you figured out yet that I do as little magik as possible around you. Or I did. I never wanted to make you feel bad that I had powers that you didn't." He smiled and put an arm around me for a gentle squeeze.

Seeing his point of view made me feel better. Tesch remained a great guy and a terrific friend.

"Okay, well you don't have to do that anymore. Today, I want to play tag with magik. I need to get better, more accurate."

"Anything my Princess commands, so shall it be." He teased.

"Jerk." I replied with a smile.

Tesch showed me that he could indeed call a ball of magik to his fingertips. Pleased, I noted I could do it much faster. He also demonstrated that the size could vary, from the size of a nickel to the size of a basketball.

175

"After gym, it's nothing to get pinged in the back by one of these." He held a glowing circle as big as the end of my thumb in his palm. With practiced ease he flicked it with a finger and sent it flying into the bark of a tree in the yard.

"It stings. Sometimes if I get hit by a Were-ball, I sprout some hair on that spot, but it only lasts an hour or two. That's why the balls are small. No permanent damage."

"What about the ones as big as dinner plates?"

"Self-defense only, you could incapacitate someone with one of those. They'd be useless for hours or more. Did Bellfwigg show you elemental orbs?"

"No. What are those?"

"Well, besides calling an energy ball of color, paras can call balls of elements too, though the element is limited to the para's wavelength."

"What do you mean? Show me."

"Were's can call fire, sorcerer's lightning, Seer's wind, Witches and elves can call rain or water for example. Orange magic can call the earth or precious metals."

"What about the Fae? What do they call?"

"Light. It's like a ball of sun or a star. But those kinds of energy are purely for fighting. If someone calls that kind of energy, they want to hurt you, maybe kill you, so get out of the way if you can."

I instantly began to wonder if I could call elemental magik orbs and if I could, which ones? But that kind of practice would have to be done in secrecy; when absolutely sure no one would see.

Tesch and I played energy tag in my front yard, using the bushes and tall pines for cover. He had good aim, and I had to work not to get hit even at a distance.

It's been said that practice makes perfect. I needed a lot more practice because I continued being far from perfect at this but getting better. By the time it became fully dark, I had clipped Tesch with my yellow orbs more than I missed, at least at distances less than twenty feet.

I felt exhausted. Tesch stayed for three bowls of Sarah's delicious beef stew and cornbread. I on the other hand fell asleep before even finishing one. With mumbled good nights and hugs all   around, I dragged my body upstairs and fell into the bed, clothes and all.

Thursday came and went. No gray cloaks appeared to haul me off to wherever. Joliet ignored me as if I were see-through. Mr. Bellfwigg and I played his version of catch again.

I scored much better this time. My accuracy improved to an average of fifty-fifty. I did something probably because no one had told me I couldn't and made two energy orbs at a time, one in each hand. When I rapid fired at Mr. Bellfwigg with a barrage of golden balls, he seemed genuinely impressed.

"Very good, Miss Phillips! Your speed counter balances your precision. You can hit one out of every four, but can throw four in less than a minute. You are bound to hit something you aim for."

If he intended praise, it needed work, but after all the other nice things he had said to me recently, I didn't take it too hard. I just reached into the nether for another energy orb to lob his direction.

The only difference in my routine included Sarah picking me up from the school. I hadn't seen Jo after school Wednesday or Thursday and wondered if she ditched her extra French lessons to avoid me.

When Friday ended with no Council henchmen dragging me from class or an overhead announcement naming me a freak of nature, I started to breathe a little easier. Surely if my friend planned to rat me out she would have done it by now.

Spring break arrived. No school for the next ten days. And at this point no impromptu vacation either.

The packet from my Fae mentor had indeed contained the necessary documents for me and Tesch and my parents to start over anonymously. His sense of humor, or something else had the forger of these documents turning Charlie and Sarah into Michael and Kerri Lyons with two children, Darian and Hope.

My feelings for Tesch were far from brotherly, so how would we make that fly? I still hoped to never have to find out. So far, so good.

Just because school was out didn't mean my lessons had taken a break. If anything, Sarah and Charlie doubled their teaching efforts, feeling they had my undivided attention for a change.

I spent my mornings with Sarah in the kitchen whipping up some wicked brews. We produced a choking spell, designed to cut off a person's air supply until they passed out. She showed me the forget-me potion, that if used, the victim would never remember the wielder, ever. Even if they met them a hundred times or spent one thousand days with them, walk out of the room once and bam, no memory.

Sarah's Coup De Gras concoction made me wince. The green liquid made food poisoning sound fun by comparison. Sarah swore that whatever resided inside a man or woman's digestive track made a speedy and violent exit. Anyone of a mind to harm or pursue us wouldn't be out of the bathroom for a month. The makers of Pepto-Bismol would pay a fortune for the recipe.

I spent afternoons with Charlie. He decided to expand on Mr.

Bellfwigg's lessons. The reason behind the object for a partial change, to have the advantages of my Werelynx senses while calling energy orbs. So far, I could call red orbs when I had whiskers and fur but no other colors.

With my lynx vision and reflexes, my aim improved greatly. My red orbs demolished targets like Russian cruise missiles. I used targets with Charlie because without magik to protect him, even his kindred red spectrum could cause an injury.

Tesch didn't get off so lucky. Him I pinged with impunity nickel-sized energy orbs of red, yellow, green and orange.

Orange orbs were the hardest for me to work with. There'd been no opportunity to try them before. It may have been related to the heavy, solid nature of the magik. Powers in the orange spectrum are related to precious gems and metals and stone craft.

Or maybe it was the maleness of the magik. Orange spectrum users were in a fashion the mules of our community. There were no females.

Dwarves, gnomes and leprechauns were born to any spectrum colored parents, pure or not. They were a genetic fluke, like albinism in humans. Some paranormals treated them as badly as I had been treated. Others considered them a blessing for without them the orange spectrum would be useless and their skills lost forever.

If a para desired an enchanted sword or chalice encrusted with talisman gems, Dwarves were where they went. If a magikal doorway or arch was needed, Gnomes were the best supernatural stone masons. And everyone knew about the pot of gold at the end of rainbow. What they didn't know? Each piece turned out had been charmed by the Leprechaun that minted it for good luck or ill will.

But the weight of the orange energy, after the feather lightness of Fae magik, felt like trying to pull rocks from the earth with my bare hands. I felt I could barely lift it. There had to be some kind of learning curve that I had not yet met to wield the orange spectrum energy.

The days melted into each other. I found myself flabbergasted to discover the week almost gone already.

Tesch and I were sitting on the sofa in the den while some sitcom episode about geeks and a pretty girl droned. Honestly, I fell asleep.

A hard nudge in my side as Tesch jostled my head on his shoulder ruined the view of the back of my eye lids. I yawned lamely.

"Hey. Did you hear what I said?"

"Mhmm" I mumbled, sinking back into the drifting tide of relaxation, snuggling my head back into the curve of his shoulder. The soft rhythmic thump of his beating heart lulled me.

"So, do you want to go?"

"Sure."

"And afterwards, we will coat ourselves in honey and set our hair on fire. Does that sound good, too?" He asked.

"Fine with me." I answered sleepily.

My brain reacted slowly to his sarcasm. It took a couple of moments for the nonsense factor to register. My eyes opened more fully to take in his teasing smile. "Wait. What?"

"So, I finally got your attention?" Tesch chuckled.

"No. Yes. I mean, what did you say about setting our hair on fire? Who's hair? Why?" Sleepiness had left me utterly confused.

"Relax. I was just trying to see if you were actually listening."

"I was relaxed. Didn't my snoring give that away?" I snapped, giving him a halfhearted punch to the ribs.

"Touchy, aren't we?" He commented. "I wanted to know if you would like to go to the carnival tomorrow. They rolled into town Friday, we missed that and Saturday. Tomorrow is the last day. I thought we might actually try to wring some fun out of this Spring Break. Since it doesn't look like we are going to be fleeing for our lives anytime soon."

"Fun." I grumbled. "I'm sure Sarah and Charlie outlawed that. They haven't wanted me out of their sight for more than five minutes lately. There's no way."

"Yes, way. I already talked to them and pointed out that all work and no play makes Harmony a grumpy girl. You need a break or you are going to break or snap or go bonkers or whatever you want to call it."

"I'm not grumpy!" I pointed out grumpily.

"Fine, then. If you don't want to go, we don't have to."

"Hold on." I interjected. "I didn't say I didn't want to go. I'm just a little surprised they agreed."

"Well, Charlie did mention something about you giving him a serious kitty growl over the last piece of bacon this morning, and Sarah said you chucked a potion, pot and all, into her rose bushes when it didn't come out right. I think they agree with me. You need a day off."

I didn't argue with that. All the recent tension and lessons and one thing after another had left me feeling drawn tight, like a bow without an arrow.

Perking up at the idea of going out on a fun break, I needed to do something for no other reason than just because I want to. I didn't think I could wait for the next day.

"Yes, tomorrow!" I agreed eagerly.

"No problem. What time do you want me to pick you up?"

"Noon. Don't be late or I'll go without you." I warned with mock fierceness.

"When was the last time I arrived late?" He asked, incredulous.

"Not since I started telling you to show up half an hour early for everything, so I guess the fourth grade. But your internal clock always needs winding."

"And here I thought you were just one of those rare girls who were always ready. Now I find out you've been playing me all along. I'm wounded." Tesch comically placed a hand on his heart.

"Sorry babe, you always hurt the ones you love most."

His eyebrows pulled together in a serious frown. Tesch muttered under his breath. It sounded ominous, but before I could probe deeper his face relaxed, and he gave me that green gaze that made my heart flip and my stomach flutter.

"If we are going to be up and going by noon, you need to head for bed, and I need to go home. Can I have a good night kiss?"

He didn't have to ask me twice. Or the third and fourth time either. I did eventually find my way upstairs to my pillow, having forgotten all about his gloomy mumbling. A dreamy smile stole over my swollen lips as I sank into the downy bliss of my bed, glad tomorrow promised a change of pace.

Chapter 19

"Straight up noon as promised, Princess." Tesch smiled lazily.

I had found a spot to wait for him on the front porch steps that morning while I took in the spring green grasses and sweet damp smell of fresh growth. The first jonquil had bloomed.

"My watch says twelve-ten." I said, teasing him about his tardiness.

"What can I say? I forgot to wind my internal clock. You're still here, I see."

"You lucked out. I find I like watching the grass grow sometimes."

"That sounds entertaining. Maybe we should forget the carnival after all? Just sit here all day and watch flowers bloom." He made to sit beside me on the stoop.

Before Tesch could plant his butt or anything else he had a mind to, I stood up, took his hand and started moving toward the driveway. "I don't think so, Aqua Man. Get in the truck, already."

We were by no means the first to arrive at the carnival. In fact, the ticket lines were as long as I'd ever seen them. A lot of people in the area had the same idea as us, wanting to squeeze the last bit of entertainment from spring vacation. Also, we discovered at the window, the carnival offered a pass special.

Usually an all-day pass for the rides went for twenty dollars. They were offering a one day armband for fifteen bucks.

Tesch pulled out his wallet and handed over the cash. The ticket girl gave us a good looking over. Then in a speech that sounded rehearsed, she informed us. "Today every one hundredth arm band sale also gets a free pass to either the tent show or a visit to Madame Osza's to have their future revealed. You are one of the lucky. Which attraction would you prefer?"

I knew what Tesch would say. He didn't put much faith in card reading. Before he could answer, I cut him off. "Madame Osza's please."

He gave me a look that landed somewhere between disgruntled and queasy, before shrugging. "Madame Osza's then."

The young woman with unremarkable features reached forward through the ticket booth window to attach a bright red plastic band around our wrists, first Tesch and then me.

The moment her skin touched mine, I knew she glamoured herself. The nondescript features and mousey brown hair were camouflage but covering what truth, I couldn't say.

Light brown eyes that wouldn't be remembered met mine. She had felt her magic waver at my touch as well. The slight tremble in her fingers as she snapped the hospital type bracelet around my arm betrayed her. Her gaze revealed awareness that I knew at least some of her secret.

I gave a small I-mean-you-no-harm, smile and turned away, pulling Tesch with me. I didn't know if he had felt or seen anything, but I didn't want him asking questions with a hundred other people milling behind us waiting for their turn.

An appropriate distance from the crowd, he turned me to him. "What was that about?"

"What?"

"Picking the trip to the fortune teller's over the tent show? You know she gives me the willies. Besides, tea leaves, tarot cards and palm reading are all bunk and bull."

"Teschandarian Monroe Wight! You know as well as I do that true seeing exists. Seers, sphinx, centaurs and lamia are part of our world. They were prophesizing before our grandparents were even thought of." I felt vexed with his stubbornness to believe.

"And when did you last see a sphinx or a centaur running around, hmmm? They died out with the dragons almost a thousand years ago." He responded pessimistically.

The mention of dragons made me edgy, but I defended. "Not true. Charlie told me there is a clan of centaurs here in America. They are in the Ox Bow Mountains, one of the last true wildernesses. There are lamia in the Carpathian Mountains and sphinx in the Sahara as well."

He gave me a disbelieving look. "Those places are a long way from here, Harmony. Besides, I didn't see any hooves beneath Madame Osza's table the last time we were there. I don't think she's a centaur."

"She doesn't have to be. I'm not a pure anything, but I obviously have some gifts. Why couldn't she?" I argued.

He didn't have a snappy comeback for that one. Instead his shoulders drooped and he groused. "Fine. We'll see Madame Osza. But do we have to do it now? I'd actually like to have some fun today if you can be persuaded."

"Fun is definitely on the agenda." I grinned. "Lead on."

Time alternately dragged as we waited in lines for rides and flew as we shouted out thrills of abandonment. We were rotated, spun, zigzagged and whirled at top speeds. The day grew short despite the recent daylight savings time change. Darkness spread quickly, and temperatures dropped as the sun sank westerly.

It seemed the whole town, or at least most of it, had turned out for the carnival. Laughter, the screams of thrill riders, children crying over sticky treats lost to the dirt, voices shouted from all directions. All the while hawkers encouraged one and all to try their luck on the Midway.

Challen and his pack were there. He waved merrily at me from the top of the Ferris wheel. What the heck, I waved back.

I saw Jo and her group of suck-ups from a distance. I know she saw me and Tesch at least once because she made a point of going the opposite direction.

It made a sad statement to me that the person I had once most loathed in school now made it a point to be friendly and the person that I had let into my life as a trusted confidant deliberately ignored me. After that, my steps slowed and my enjoyment was half-hearted.

Tesch noticed. We stopped walking halfway through the Midway. Warm arms wrapped me in unconditional acceptance and love.

"Hey, forget her." He advised. "She'll never have as true a friend as you again, Harmony. And that is all her loss, not yours."

"You say it, I hear it. I might even believe it. But it doesn't make it hurt any less." I agreed, feeling those darn tears prick at the backs of my eyes.

"Only if you let it, babe. Don't allow anyone to steal your joy, Harmony. There's always someone who will if they can, simply because they don't have any of their own."

I pulled away from him just enough to look up at those amazing green eyes. "How'd you get to be so wise?"

"Years of watching you take an emotional beat down by jerks and bigots like Parks and Idlewilde. All the times they made you cry and I wanted to pull their heads off but couldn't. I had to listen to old and wiser heads tell me about the higher path and doing the right thing and crap like that. It stuck with me, I guess."

"Older and wiser like who?" I wanted to know.

"My guardian Mr. Wight, for one, Sarah and Charlie for two. And Bellfwigg; he's had a definite input."

"Speaking of Mr. Bellfwigg..."

"We were? I thought we were talking about how wise I am. I like that much better." He gave me a little squeeze around the middle.

I laughed in spite of myself. "Seriously, Tesch. I want to know how you came to know him. Or about him at least."

Tesch looked uncomfortable with the subject. He released all but my hand and started walking, towing me in his wake. "You could say he played an instrumental part in my coming to McLoud. He and his people are very interested in the welfare of the younger generations."

"So they helped you find a home after you lost your family?"

"You might say that." He stopped short and turned back to me. "Look, Harmony, I really don't like to talk about the past. It's done and gone. All that matter is I'm here now, and as luck would have it, I get to be with you. That's enough for me. So are you ready?"

"For what?"

"You picked the free pass remember. I'd just as soon skip it." He tilted his head to indicate the familiar pavilion with golden stars and moons we stood in front of.

I looked at the tent, surprised to find Madame Osza's palace of wisdom. Now that I stood here, I wasn't sure I wanted to go inside. My instincts said it needed to happen, but another part of me dreaded what I might learn from her this time.

Five months had passed since she last gave me her predictions. Strangely, some of her forecasts had found their mark. Not all, but then when is anything one hundred percent accurate. Surely my turn for happily ever after had come around.

Tesch registered my hesitation. "Really, Harmony, we don't have to use the dang pass. I'll just throw it away." He pulled out the printed piece of paper and made as if to tear it into bits.

"No." I grabbed his arm, stopping the first rip in time. Prying the ticket from his grip, the words tumbled out. "I want to go in. I need to. Call it a gut feeling."

"Need to?" He eyed me skeptically. "That's a bit creepy. Don't you think you're overdoing it? I mean, I'll go. You know I will. You don't have to go all mystical forces at work here on me."

I gave him my best peeved look. "Shut up, and go inside already."

"After you, Princess." He made an exaggerated sweep with his arm.

I ignored him and moved the tent flap aside, stepping from the lights of the Midway into the candle lit glow. The softer illumination of flames made deeper shadows inside. It seemed we had stepped back into last October. Not much had changed.

Madame Osza sat at her table dealing cards in what could have been an elaborate game of solitaire but for the faces on the postcard size rectangles. Without looking up from her game, she spoke to me. "I am glad you have come back to see me, young Fool. The time for your journey is at hand."

"Excuse me?"

"For what should I excuse you? Have you done me or mine some wrong? Or do you apologize for simply being what you are, a Fool?" She continued to casually turn cards over.

I stiffened. "That's not what I meant."

"I know what you meant." With a sigh, she looked up from the table to give me the full attention of her one dark eye. A red silk patch covered the other tonight.

"You meant for me to explain what I said about your journey. But you seek new answers to old questions. Your future has been read. While some choices are still yours to make, others have already made theirs, setting the wheels of fate in motion."

She looked over her my shoulder to Tesch who waited a step behind me. Her stare felt heavy even though it fell on him instead. "And that one, he made his choice long ago to tie his fate to yours. Nothing can be changed for him. He will see it to the end. This he knows as well. There is nothing more for the cards to tell."

I crossed my arms, indignant. "So you won't tell our fortune."

"I already have. And I don't care for repeating myself." She went back to turning the cards.

A hard knot of gall filled my chest, burning all the way down as I swallowed bitterness. I had believed, really thought, that a higher purpose guided me to her tonight. There would be answers, information, and clarification from Madame Osza for me. I needed her to fill in the blanks with something other than the uncertainties I possessed. Now, she declared she had none.

"So this ticket isn't worth spit. You know we could report you to the authorities. Have you arrested or run out of town for false advertising." I flung the battered square of printing onto the table, onto the top of the tarot deck spread before her.

She chuckled at my temper.

"This is good for a free *visit*, child. And you are visiting, no? It says nothing about a reading. But we will be leaving soon enough. There is a storm coming. We will pack up early and go from this place, for the last time I think. The caravan leaves tonight." Madame Osza raised her face once more to pin that black stare on Tesch. "Your journey is at hand. Don't be late."

My lips sputtered with angry disbelief. I couldn't make the sounds into coherent words.

"Come on, Harmony." Tesch placed a hand on each shoulder and pulled me backwards from the tent. "We're going home."

"I need answers, Tesch!" I complained with angry tears in my eyes.

"To what?" He snapped back at me with exasperation. "Is Joliet worthless as a friend? You can answer that for yourself. Is your life in danger? Maybe, only time will tell. But we've planned the best we can for whatever may come. Do you have people in your life that love and care about you? If you don't know the answer to that one yet, then you haven't been paying attention at all."

The heat and anger left him as he took my hands in his. "I love you, Harmony. I have always loved you. And nothing you can do or say or become is going to change how I feel about you. Do you need a better answer than that?"

I felt a sob building in my throat. Tesch had given me an answer to the most important question. He loved me, and that should be all that mattered. "I'm sorry. I've been so worried about what is going to happen to me, to us and to Charlie and Sarah. No, I don't need a better answer. And for what it's worth, I love you too."

"To me, it's worth everything."

Tesch's hands let go of my fingers to cup my cheeks. His head bent to give me a soft but meaningful kiss. My own lips clung to his for the comfort and warmth he always provided.

We stood, exchanging silent promises with our mouths. Without words he promised to love, honor, cherish and protect me all the days of his life. I returned the vow, offering my heart, my loyalty and my trust. We came apart, breathless and silent. Anything spoken would have fallen short of the feelings we shared in that moment, so we said nothing more.

Tesch took my hand again and led me slowly and carefully over the rocky ground to where we had parked earlier. I climbed in on his side and slid over just far enough to let him in.

The warmth of his body had become something I craved at my side. The comfort his strong arm around my shoulder as we drove away from the noise and lights gave me peace within. My eyes closed, and I drifted away without thoughts.

Chapter 20

I FELT A CHANGE in the tension of Tesch. His body stiffened. He lifted his arm from around my shoulder, placing both hands on the wheel instead. We were almost to my house. The truck slowed to a crawl ten yards before the driveway.

I raised my head from his shoulder, coming alert to the change in his posture. "What's wrong?"

"I don't know." He replied. "All the lights are off, even the porch light."

I swiveled my head to peer between the trees that lined our property. Tesch seemed right. There were absolutely no lights glowing through the windows or from the sconce by the front door.

A tremor of apprehension ran through me. Charlie and Sarah always left a light on for me. Even if they had gone somewhere themselves, the porch light and the small lamp in the foyer would be on.

The black Suburban and Sarah's silver Prius were still parked in the drive. With both cars at home I had trouble believing they'd gone anywhere.

"Maybe the power is out." I offered as explanation.

"Maybe." Tesch agreed. "But I am going to circle the block. Use your cell and try to call."

I fished my phone from the pocket of my hoodie and went to hitting the speed dials. The house number beeped in ominous repetition with a busy signal. In today's world with call waiting, a busy signal was almost unheard of.

Next I tried Sarah's cell, then Charlie's. With each I got the same pleasant sounds of my parents explaining that they couldn't answer just then but to leave them a message. My worry ratcheted into high gear.

"No answer, Tesch. Not on the house phone or their cell phones. What should we do?"

We were cruising at a snail's pace down my street again, but the house waited at the other end of the block. Tesch pulled over near some overgrown shrubs in the yard of an empty house. He killed the engine.

Unbuckling his seat belt, Tesch warned, "Stay put."

"Are you kidding?" I asked in shock. "Why? What are you planning on doing?"

"Nothing. I just want to quietly slip up to the house and make sure things are okay. It's like you said, the power is probably out or something." Something in his face read that he didn't really believe it.

"Then why can't I come with you?"

"Because... well, just because. If there is something wrong, you don't need to be in the middle of it."

"Like hell." I answered, telling him what I thought about that. "That is my home, Tesch. I have just as much right or more than you do to know what's going on. I'm not going to sit here like a good little girl and wait. So get over it."

"Harmony, please, just wait here. I promise I'll be right back." Tesch tried to wheedle me into agreeing.

"Ain't happening. If you go, I go." I crossed my arms over my chest, unmovable.

"Dammit. Why can't you ever do what I ask? Just once, hmm?" Tesch swore softly at me. "You have got to be one of the most stubborn people I know."

I didn't contradict him. Instead, I just gave a hard stare that spoke clearly. If he went, I would be right behind him.

He climbed out of the truck, not even bothering to try and talk me out of following him. Holding out his hand, Tesch steadied me as I slid off the seat and onto the ground. Tesch knew when I made up my mind about something, arguing with me became futile. Right or wrong, I was going home.

We hurried through the dark, hand in hand down the street. It felt silly keeping to the shadows, bent at the waist to keep our heads down. But Tesch walked in the lead. He seemed determined to creep up on the house like thieves.

We came up to the property line and cut back along the hedge row, avoiding the wide open spaces of the front yard, for more tree covered area of the back. Even the back of the house was blacked out. I had hoped when we came around to this side, some kind of light would shine in welcome.

The night held eerily quiet. No insects chirped. No birds twittered from their nests as we passed beneath. Even the neighborhood dogs were silent, not barking their complaints.

Tesch and I slipped across the backyard as silent as the rest of the night. Dew had begun to form on the grass and behind us. We left a wet trail that could be easily recognized as foot prints. I guess we'd worry about that later.

Tesch eased up to the back door. He looked back at me and laid a finger across his lips in a gesture of silence.

Tension coiled in the pit of my stomach. Every slip of sound we made, the creak of the screen door pulling open, the click of the latch as he turned the brass doorknob, even the slight swish of the weather seal brushing over the kitchen tiles as the door swung inward, they all seemed as loud as a fire alarm to my ears.

I practiced being careful, not letting the screen make more than a soft pat as it closed behind me. We stood as quiet as mice in the once homey kitchen with its deep green ivy vines and herb filled window boxes.

If the unnatural silence of the house hadn't given me a clue that something was amiss, the war zone that Sarah's neat-as-a-pin kitchen had become did. I stared in horrified wonder, too stunned to make another sound.

Cabinet doors hung open, askew on damaged pivots. One clung bravely by a single hinge. Dishes lay in a shattered mass on the floors and counters. The refrigerator had been pulled from its nook and lay on its side, contents spilled and broken. By the dim light of the moon the wall by the pantry door looked scorched.

What in the name of the Goddess had happened here?

Without thinking, I went to hurry farther into the house, stepping on broken glass, not caring that it crunched loudly beneath my sneakers. Tesch reached out a restraining hand on my arm.

"Harmony, no." He whispered fiercely. "Let me go first."

"Tesch!" I moaned quietly. My eyes pleaded with him to let me go, to go quickly, to do something, anything besides to stand here not knowing.

"Hold my hand, and stay behind me." His voice almost lost in the quiet. His jade colored eyes were narrowed, serious and stern.

I knew at once if I didn't follow directions Tesch would turn around and walk out, dragging me behind him if he had to. I nodded in agreement, not trusting my voice.

A grim look of determination settled between his brows and across his lips. Tesch moved forward into the wreck of our kitchen. He minded his steps, trying to avoid the shards of glass and pottery, but it proved an impossible task to not make some noise.

Holding his hand in a death grip, I stepped as carefully with about as much success. As we went forward, the small amount of moonlight the big windows provided was left behind.

The hall between the kitchen and foyer became pitch dark. We moved blindly, with hands gliding over the smoothness of wallpaper covered plaster. Every second step I felt the slight indent of a seam where Sarah had worked so hard to match the strips perfectly. My throat tightened with emotions I refused to name.

Tesch stopped abruptly. In the roaring silence, I could clearly hear as the pads of his fingers moved over the wall in a faint glide, stopped and then came back.

"What?" I asked in a frantic hush.

I heard him sigh heavily before answering, his voice a strained murmur. "Holes in the wall."

He started moving again, and my own hand had a moment to pass over the areas he had felt. There were two, no three, indentions and one softball sized gap in the solid plaster.

My courage faltered. The house stood so still, so quiet. An essence of warmth that had always lingered here had departed. It felt as if I didn't belong in my own home. The welcoming of familiar scents and sounds had been stolen.

Tesch moved deeper into the darkness, but I stood still and waited for a hint of presence to touch me, fill me with comfort that I hadn't lost my safe haven. All I felt was cold.

More felt than heard, I noticed that Tesch had stopped moving. My head turned to look for his silhouette in the shadows. His form knelt at the foot of the stairs, seeming to struggle with something large and heavy. Shaking legs took unsure steps forward to help.

The something large and heavy I realized as the huge desk that normally rested at the far end of the living room had fallen or been thrown. The mammoth piece of furniture where Charlie graded papers and planned lessons, but could still catch bits of the news and sports on the plasma screen blocked the door.

The crimson drapes that Sarah had hung across the wide bank of windows at the front of the house had been torn away from their placement, rods and all. The uncovered frames of glass allowed an amber glow from the street lights to penetrate the room. They permitted enough illumination to turn everything to a sepia mockery.

I came to a crouch beside Tesch. The desk rested at an odd angle with a scant four inches between the cherry wood furnishing and the golden hardwood floor.

"Here, let me help." I whispered. My fingers curled around the sharp edges, and I pulled upward against the massive weight. Two things happened at once.

Tesch frantically admonished me. "No, Harmony, wait."

A low moan escaped from beneath the desk. I startled, losing my grip, and fell back onto my butt.

"What was that?" It came out breathless.

"Charlie." Tesch answered in a solemn tone.

His voice bled through the coldness with its devastating candor, filling me with horror. My vision swam before sharpening, taking in the whole of the picture rather than the pieces.

The space between the desk and floor had been created by Charlie's head and shoulders. Now I could see the motionless fingers resting just beyond Tesch's booted feet. A trickle of dark fluid followed the pattern of the wood grain floor. In the half-light provided from the naked windows, it appeared black. I feared in daylight the liquid would stain the oak boards to match the red wooded desk.

"Oh, Goddess." I gasped. My heart beat a frantic tattoo. "Tesch, we have to get this off of him."

"I know." He nodded, placing a calming hand on my shoulder. "But I wanted to prepare you, first. I don't know how badly he's hurt. Moving the desk might make things worse. We have to be easy; quick but easy."

I dry swallowed. My mouth felt full of ash. "Okay."

Together we maneuvered so we could both get a firm grip on the desk. Tesch indicated that we should lift it up and over before turning it onto the side.

I don't remember ever being more scared in my life. What condition Charlie might be in haunted me. No trace of Sarah presented itself yet.

Concentrating on what I could see and do, Tesch gave me a silent nod to go ahead. I employed muscles I'd never known I possessed to lift and pull. Beads of exertion broke out on my upper lip and between my shoulder blades. My low back, arms and legs screamed at me for using them like this. I ignored them and kept my eyes on Tesch for command.

The desk remained a monstrous piece of bulk, but we managed to raise it a foot up and over before shifting its weight to the side and upending the furniture off of Charlie's still form. He hadn't made another sound during our rescue efforts.

As soon as the weight safely rested off and away, I went to my knees and crawled to Charlie's side. Gently as possible, I turned him onto his side then back. Tesch came to me, helping to turn the trunk and legs.

Hot tears ran silently over my cheeks. My vision blurred again as the sorrow wetted my face. Charlie's face showed a bloodied mess.

He'd been beaten. The swelling and bruises made him barely recognizable.

Blood, dried and fresh, darkened his neatly trimmed beard, having run from his nose and lips freely at some point. A deep gash went from his temple to his chin on the left side of his handsome face. I turned my eyes away from what I thought might be exposed muscle and cheek bone.

Tesch moved his hands experimentally over Charlie's legs and torso while I held his head and shoulders in my lap. My best friend's face remained grim with purpose. His assessment of Charlie for wounds had another side effect. My adoptive father groaned pitifully at the searching touches.

His eyes opened to me. "Kitten?"

"Oh, Charlie!" I sobbed.

Raising a hand to my cheek, his face crumpled with a spasm of pain. Coughing harshly, his fingers fell back to his side. Somewhere deep in his chest I could hear a menacing rattle. Fresh blood stained his lips and chin.

Between coughs and gasps, Charlie spat out. "Sarah..upstairs."

Tesch and I locked gazes.

"I'll go." He offered.

"I think there's a flashlight in the cupboard beneath the stairs."

I suppose that would have been helpful to know when we walked down that dark path to here, but my brain had been too scared to offer up anything useful. What I remembered now had to be pure random thought. My emotions were bombarding me with no rhyme or reason.

Tesch just nodded acknowledgement that he heard me and crawled away into the darkness. I turned my focus back to Charlie. I reached for the hand that had tried to touch my face and held it to my cheek. His fingers were ice against my skin.

"Charlie, what happened?" I begged.

Eyes a color I couldn't see, in a pale face, stared up at me. There were lines, small crinkles from age and a thousand smiles, at the corners of his gaze. His voice came to me a strained whisper.

"They came… at dusk. Gray cloaks. We wouldn't tell… them where. They knew…about you, Harmony."

The last came with a gurgle and froth of blood. The rivulet made a slow course from the corner of his mouth down his bearded cheek. I wiped his life's fluid away gently as my tears mingled with the blood.

My heart felt busted up, like the broken dishes on the kitchen floor. The sharp pieces stabbed my chest as if they would poke through me. I couldn't breathe right.

Charlie's words let me know what I had agonized over. Joliet had revealed my secret to someone, probably her parents. The 'who' didn't really matter, she had betrayed me. Sold me out, cut a deal, made a bargain for her benefit with my life as the collateral.

I hiccupped and sobbed quietly. Not expecting an answer, I asked "Oh Goddess, what do we do now?"

The chilled hand I held to my cheek gripped my fingers fiercely, demanding my attention. "Run." Charlie choked out. "Take the bags. You and ...Tesch, run."

"Charlie, I can't leave you like this. I'm going to get you help. Tesch will be back with Sarah, and we will get you help."

Dumb, dumb and dumber! I realized I still had my cell phone in my hip pocket! I used my free hand to reach for the device, fishing awkwardly. I held on to Charlie's hand for dear life. I would not let go.

The metal felt strange and awkward in my fingers. I unlocked the screen with a thumb swipe, ready to dial 9-1-1. Then I remembered.

Paranormal's cell phones were linked to a specific emergency service, a Council operated emergency service. They couldn't let the Normals find out about us accidentally. The Council would come running if I called for help all right, come running to get me and take me away. The phone fell from nerveless fingers.

What can we do? Who would help us?

Charlie's fingers squeezed again. "Kitten. You have to go... run with Tesch. We love you, always... Best thing ever... happened to us. Our baby girl."

His smile for me filled with love and sorrow. Charlie knew what I would not accept. His moments were limited.

"I love you, too. Both of you. Just hang on Charlie. Tesch is bringing Sarah. She'll teach me a spell to heal you. We'll patch you up, and we will all get out of here. We'll run, the way we should have. I am so sorry I didn't listen to you. I'm sorry I argued with you about staying. I'm so sorry!" I babbled with grief.

"Shh." Charlie tried to comfort me. "It's okay...Harmony."

The last word escaped his lips with a sigh. I kept hold of a hand that had gone slack in my grip. Not daring to breathe less I miss the soft intake of his, my tears flowed unchecked.

With growing horror I watched Charlie's blue eyes glaze and stare at me lifeless. In painful wonder I saw their light azure color for the first and last time. My hurt built too great to make a sound. Every breath regretted for the raw agony it gave.

Sitting on my heels, I clung to my father's hand, the silence so heavy around us I feared I had gone deaf. When Tesch's booted feet stepped from the carpeted stair runner onto the hardwood of the foyer, I startled so hard I choked.

His gait, slow and awkward, demanded my attention. I mourned the instinct to look up as he moved into the room. A heart I didn't think could be anymore broken crumbled into dust.

Tesch carried a heavy burden like a child, wrapped in a rose pink blanket. Over the top, long strands of red hair hung loose. With him came a strong smell, something I could only identify as burnt meat drifted to my nose.

Nausea burned my throat. My eyes blurred and watered. My head shook from side to side denying.

No. No. No. Not Sarah too!

Tears fell from Tesch's eyes. His gaze came to me as heartbroken as I had ever seen him. He moved forward with the bundle. I moved back to let him pass.

Tesch knelt beside Charlie to lay Sarah at my father's side. He nestled her into the crook of Charlie's shoulder, placing the hand I had held moments before around her. Gently, he closed Charlie's eyes.

From his kneeled position, Tesch turned to me. He pulled me into an embrace. "Harmony, I am so sorry. I loved them too."

I felt numb in my grief. My arms couldn't respond to his touch, not to hug him back or push him away. The world appeared an alien place. My sun and moon had stopped shining, and I'd never learned to navigate by the stars.

"Harmony, we have to go." He whispered into my hair.

"I need to see her one last time, Tesch."

"No. No, Harmony. It looks like their room got hit by a lightning storm. Sarah…" I heard him gulp loudly. "You don't want to see."

I pulled back from his embrace. Ugly determination filled me.

"I have to, Tesch. I have to. I want to know what they did to her. I know why. Someday…." I couldn't go further with the pain and despair roaring through me. But inside I promised myself, someday, somewhere, sometime, the guilty would be held accountable.

Tesch let me go, reluctantly. On limbs of lead, I crawled around him to Charlie and Sarah. Her face hidden by the blanket he had wrapped her body in, my fingers trembled as I reached to pull it back.

My hands went to my mouth as I gasped in shock. Holding back the gorge rising, threatening to spill from my lips, I forced myself to look at the blackened skin of her once smooth cheek. The flesh had been charred, melted to the bone. Her right eye had been seared closed, her pert nose half disintegrated. I had kissed her today, on that soft cheek that smelled like rich earth and rosemary, before going out to wait for Tesch on the porch.

Shuddering, I pulled the edge of the soft pink material back up to cover the terrible sight. Leaning forward, I touched my lips to the fabric over her cheek for a last goodbye.

Tesch helped me stand. I don't know if I could have or would have if he hadn't pulled me up. My heart lay on the floor there beside them. I longed to just lie down and rest there too, maybe forever.

He dragged me back down the hall we had come through into the kitchen. Tesch had me stand by the kitchen door and wait. "I have to get the bags with the papers for us. Charlie told me where to find it. I'll get yours too and be right back."

I can't say how long he took. Time lost its meaning as I stared blankly out at the night. He came back before I registered he'd gone.

Tesch helped me into a back pack, put another over his own. He hung a satchel over my shoulder. It clinked softly with its contents. I glanced down at it mildly.

"Some of your potions." Tesch informed me. "Sarah... Sarah had them packed already."

I could only nod that I understood. Words were not available to me.

"Let's go."

Again we hugged the shadows like forbidden lovers, stealing moments with each patch of darkness. As we moved closer to Tesch's truck, the night grew darker. Clouds rolled in, covering the meager glow of the moon and stars. Only street lamps provided illumination to guide us.

The wind picked up and brushed my skin with a cool caress. I could taste the promise of rain on my tongue. Madame Osza had predicted a storm tonight. She had been right, on many levels.

Suddenly, Tesch pulled me up short, dropping back into the cover of an azalea tree that had begun to blossom delicate white flowers.

"Be still." He cautioned before motioning for me to look down the street.

Moving slowly, a dark sedan crunched over the patched and crumbling asphalt of my street. It came even with Tesch's truck, stopping.

My breath froze. Exiting the sedan was a dark skinned man in a charcoal gray cloak. He went to the old green pickup parked on the side of the road before melting into the cover behind it. The four door car moved on toward my house.

"What do we do now?" I whispered urgently.

Tesch laid a finger over his lips for silence. He indicated we move away from the road, farther into the brush as quietly as possible. Every sound we made felt as loud as a gunshot.

Not far enough for comfort, but I suppose far enough for safety, Tesch hunkered down to face me. He answered my earlier question smoothly.

"I think it's time for a little glamour, Princess. You are going to make us look like someone from school. I don't care who. We cross this field on foot, come out on the back side of the carnival then try to blend in."

"Then what?"

"I don't know. Find a way out of town I guess. I'd say go to Bellfwigg, but he's always under suspicion. I wouldn't be surprised if one of those Council goons camped on his porch."

Since I didn't have any better ideas I just agreed. "Okay."

I closed my eyes, pulled my shield around me and drew on the yellow power of the Fae. In a matter of minutes I had changed us into a boy and girl I'd often seen in Challen's pack. I think their names were Joshua and Samantha...or Sylvia. I remembered it started with an "S".

Joshua, a ginger, had a bulky frame that looked as if he would be at home on a professional football defensive line. Sylvia/Samantha had black hair and a rabbit face that she made up with too much garish green eye shadow. Good enough to blend in and I had seen them with Challen tonight at the carnival. Goddess that felt like ages ago.

We moved on without further comments. The sounds of our labored breathing as we quickly walked away from the scene of the crime reached my ears. Occasionally, in the distance, a dog would bellow or a cow made a mournful moo. My shoulders cringed as the still dry grasses of winter crunched beneath our steps.

It seemed like forever before I heard the shrill music and laughter of the last fun seekers. The time had to be close to midnight. The carnival would be shutting down and closing up shop soon. We hadn't thought of that. In half an hour there would be no crowd to blend into.

What would we do then? We had nowhere to go and no vehicle to get there even if we did. Tesch's plan had some major holes in it, but I had no room to criticize. That I could put one foot in front of the other came as a small miracle. Escaping seemed low on the totem pole of priorities.

My heart and mind were numb with anguish. Only Tesch's steady pace kept me moving. I followed because I didn't know what else to do. I moved as he moved, stepped where he stepped. Not because he told me to, just because.

We came out of the field on the far end of the carnival. We were able to step onto the Midway between the balloon dart game and the children's Merry-Go-Round.

Tesch stopped to scan the smaller crowd. I stopped because he did. He seemed to be okay with what he saw. Taking my hand again we started walking down the Midway in what would be described as a casual stroll. I trailed in his wake.

"We are going to Madame Osza." He told me.

"What?" Even in my traumatized state of mind, surprise reached me. "Why?"

"I hate admitting it, but she knew something was going to happen. She even told us to not be late. Remember?"

"No. I mean yes, I remember. But no, we can't go to her. Why would she help now when she wouldn't before?"

"I don't know that she will, but right now, it's the only idea I've got." Tesch breathed out the side of Joshua's mouth. We were halfway to Madame's tent when a voice rang out behind us.

"Josh, Yo! Sylvia, Josh!"

The thing about glamour is, if you don't remember you're wearing one, you might not act or move as the person you look like. It had been one of the first things I learned when Joliet had looked like me and I her at school. I had forgotten that tidbit with everything else going on and it had turned about to bite us in the butt.

"Hey man!" Challen chugged up to us from the crowd. "Didn't you hear me calling you guys? I thought you went home hours ago. Dude, since when do you hold hands with your cousin?"

Oops.

"Uh?" Tesch stammered.

I wasn't in the mood to play games. "Challen, it's me, Harmony Phillips."

I let go of the glamour covering my face for just a moment so that he could see the real me beneath. The young Werewolf's face blanched. His eyebrows almost disappeared into his hairline. His eyes darted back to Tesch/Joshua then to me again.

"Aqua boy?" Challen's tone held no malice.

"Yes." Tesch answered through gritted teeth.

Before the machismo could overwhelm us, I broke in. "Challen, you said before that you wanted to make amends to me. If you meant it, you can, right here and now. I just need you to play along. Walk with us. Pretend we are your friends."

"Are you in trouble?" Challen asked.

His eyebrows had finally come down out of his hairline and were now drawn together in concern. His hand reached forward as if he meant to place it on my shoulder, but Tesch/Joshua maneuvered between us protectively. Challen looked as if he might growl, but shook himself like a dog shakes off an unwanted scent in his nose.

"Chill out, Wight. I only ask because there were Council henchmen crawling all around here tonight. They really pulled down the mood, too. Most everyone decided to go home early. The carnival people are already packing up their gear." He looked back and forth between us again. "I may not be the smartest guy in school, but I'm not stupid. You two showing up wearing Josh and Sylvia's faces and wanting me to play along, it seems suspicious to me."

Muscling past Tesch to be face to face with Challen, I asked. "Will you help me? Please?"

"Sure. I think I owe you more than that really. But Monday, I'd like an explanation."

Neither Tesch nor I corrected him that we would not be available to explain anything at school the next day. It remained doubtful that I would ever see Challen Parks again after tonight.

Once upon a time I would have smiled at the thought, but right now I felt too empty, to abused by loss to care.

Our twosome became a threesome that attempted a casual stroll to the dark green tent still a hundred feet away. My stride faltered, and I stumbled when my eyes happened on a sweeping dark gray cloak moving along the edge of the crowd that remained. Two male hands shot out to steady me, taking me by the elbows.

It might have been comical if I hadn't been on emotional overload. I shook them both off with a snarl. "I'm fine. Let go."

We made the tent fine from there. Outside the flap, I halted, unsure. How does one knock on cloth? Never mind.

I pushed aside the heavy canvas and went inside. The candles and candelabra were gone. Instead, an electric Coleman's lamp hung from the center tent pole. It made for a much brighter interior and magnified the shabbiness. Stitching and repairs to the tent were made apparent. The mystery of the unknown had evaporated leaving behind only an old woman in a wheel chair.

Madame Osza sat with her hands folded in her lap, patient. I suspected the table and cards were packed away in the large trunk in the corner.

"You needn't hide yourself in here, young Fool. The gray cloaks have already asked me about you. Did I see you tonight? Did you mention where you were going?"

I dropped the glamour. "What did you tell them?"

"That I was an old woman and not a child sitter for all the young fools in the world." Madame Osza cackled at her own humor.

I wasn't sure what to say. Thank you seemed lame. I said it anyway, lame or not. "Thank you."

"You are welcome, Harmony. Or is it Hope now?"

Pain flashed inside my chest, stealing my breath. How she knew didn't matter. "It's Hope. Harmony died tonight with her parents Charlie and Sarah Phillips."

Behind me I heard Challen exclaim softly. "What the hell...?"

Tesch murmured something to him I didn't even try to follow. Madame Osza gave me a sad look and opened her arms. I didn't even hesitate. I fell to my knees, burying my face into her lap where the soft chenille blanket began absorbing the flow of my tears.

Knotty fingers with their baby soft skin patted my shoulders and stroked my hair as I sobbed my loss and grief. There were no words. Only the primal calls of the deeply wounded echoed from my throat.

Charlie and Sarah were gone. My parents, people I loved more than my own life had been taken from me. Stolen, for what? Because of something I couldn't help? Because I had been born a freak of paranormal nature! They'd died because of me!

"Hush now, child. I see the poisoned thoughts inside you. You did not cause this tragedy. Jealousy caused this. Stupid fear and ignorant prejudice caused this. You are not to blame."

"Why?" I cried bitterly. "Why me? Why them?"

She raised my face from her knees, to look at my tear ravaged face. "I wish I knew, but only the Goddess has that answer. I am not privy to Her plans for you, only to the paths you can take on your voyage to fulfill Her needs."

"What do we do now?" Tesch asked.

"You travel with us for a while. No one notices us. We come, we go. You have your belongings with you; that is good. It would be better if you had a vehicle, something that would blend in, but we will make due." The fortune teller supplied.

"I have a truck, an older one. But it's parked near Harmony's house. There are Council men all over the place there, I can't go back and get it."

"I can."

I had forgotten Challen. I guess Tesch had too. We had spoken openly in front of him about too much. I couldn't help but wonder what he thought went on.

"Challen, I appreciate the offer, but you don't know what you're getting into here. There has been some…" Tesch began.

"Save it water boy." Challen interrupted. "I am offering Harmony, or Hope or whatever she wants to call herself, my help. I'm doing it to clean my slate, get my karma right with her and myself. If *she* needs your truck, and you can't get it right now, then I will."

Tesch bristled visibly. His lips thinned with a cutting remark, I could tell. "We don't need your help."

"But we appreciate it. I appreciate it, Challen. Thank you."

With nowhere to stalk off to, Tesch crossed his arms to sulk. Challen smiled softly at me. "You're welcome."

To Tesch he gave a smirk. "Are the keys in that heap you calling a ride, or do you want me to hot wire it?"

"I'll give you the keys." Tesch glared with indignation.

"No thanks. If those retards in gray catch me, I'd rather be able to say I'm stealing it as a prank. It'd have to be a joke. There's no way I would steal it otherwise." Challen needled Tesch a bit more. Some things never change. "I'll be back in twenty minutes, thirty tops."

"How do you figure? It took us over an hour to walk here."

"'Cause Wight, I'll be going as the crow flies, or rather, as the wolf runs." Challen gave us what could only be described as a wolfish grin before exiting the tent flap.

"That one has some spit and fire in his blood." Madame Osza commented when Challen had gone. "He'll be back soon enough. Now, put your glamour back on. I am taking you to one of the campers for now."

I pulled the magik back around us for a walk across the carnival. My hero, ever the gentleman, placed himself behind Madame's chair to help propel her across the uneven ground.

She directed us to a group of travel trailers that were parked in a purposeful maze, making me think of a rolling apartment complex. The camp enclosed a center courtyard with a huge patio cover and picnic tables. Coffee and donuts were there for the carnies to eat.

A man with a heavy beard and bulging arms sat with his steaming cup at one of the tables. His eyes felt like they were burning a hole in me. When he stood and approached, I hesitated, intimidated by his sheer size. He rose as a moving mountain.

Stepping into our path, he waited; arms crossed a red, plaid covered, barrel chest. "These are the two you spoke of, Mother?"

Mother? I glanced from the petite but regal woman in the chair to the dark giant. Wow. I bet that hurt.

"Yes, Goliath, these are the ones." She pointed a finger over her shoulder, "The young man is Darian. He is a Siren for us. The young lady, well, she is our Hope."

A shiver went down my spine with her words, as if the Fates raised their heads and blew a cold breath down my back. It scared me.

"Show them to Anisa's trailer for now. Their own vehicle is coming. We leave as soon as we can get everything in order."

"It will be as you wish." The behemoth of a man bowed and gave the Madame a gentle kiss on her cheek. Me, he pinned with a fathomless stare. "Follow me, my lady."

The man moved with a grace I wouldn't have thought him capable of, given his size. He led us through narrow passages between trailers, slipping through as easily as a man half his size. I would have been lost in this maze without Goliath to guide me.

Finally, he approached a beaten camper near the edge of the labyrinth. One beefy hand tapped knuckles on the aluminum door. His knock descended light and brief, not the heavy handed pounding I had expected. The door opened promptly.

A human, female little person in a Hello Kitty bathrobe and blonde ponytail answered. Goliath spoke without preamble.

"These are the people we have been waiting for, Anisa. Mother asks if they might rest with you until we break camp."

The short woman brightened with a smile that warmed her tanned face. "I'd be honored. Come in. Come in, please."

She maneuvered the screen latch and opened the portal wide. "The rain is coming. Get on in here and have some tea or something." Her voice held that welcoming, southern charm usually heard only in the Deep South. I smiled in spite of myself.

Tesch and I plodded up the steps and into her home. It turned out neat as a pin and very brightly decorated in sunshine yellow, hot pink and bright orange. Anisa's camper had been given some modifications to accommodate her short stature. Stairs to the overhead bed had been added as well as some built-in steps to the sink and counter tops.

Anisa herself guided us over the threshold and to her kitchen table. "I'm so pleased to welcome you to the carnival and my home. Would you like some hot tea? I've peppermint or chamomile?"

I had my doubts that tea could warm me, but Sarah had raised me to be polite. My chest ached with the thought of her name. "Peppermint, please."

"Sure thing, honey, coming right up." The vertically challenged woman bustled about the tight interior, heating water, gathering bright yellow cups and tea bags. "Nothing like a good cup of tea to steady the nerves. I must say, all the camp has been aflutter wondering if this season would be the one. But I never doubted Osza. She's a keen one. Runs this place in a good fashion, fair but firm."

Anisa set a cup of dark liquid that smelled of peppermint before me, adding a sugar bowl and cream pitcher to the table as well. I began adding a liberal amount of the granulated sweetness.

"Anyway, when she said she saw the Queen getting closer in the cards, that you would need us, the carnival packed up and came on, even if it was a bit early to start the season. Some, like that high and mighty Katarina, didn't want to leave Durant camp that soon. Madame just gave them the stink eye and they shut up and packed along with the rest of us."

I glanced up sharply from stirring my tea, "Excuse me, what did you say?"

Anisa stopped in her motion of cleaning the counter and putting away the supplies. "Oh, I said that Katarina didn't want to hit the road early, but Madame..."

"No, before that. Madame Osza saw who in the cards?"

"The Queen, you know the Queen of Swords. That someone you trusted decided to betray you and because of it, you'd need a rescue."

Joliet!

A burning star formed in the pit of my belly, spreading through the shell of my heart. Anger and bitterness filled my soul and flushed my cheeks. I turned narrowed eyes on Tesch.

"I can't believe I was such a fool to believe in her." I whispered through clenched teeth. I choked on the knowledge that I ended up indeed 'the Fool' Madame Osza had named me.

"Harmony, don't go there." Tesch warned. "There's no good that can come from blaming yourself."

"I'm not blaming myself, Tesch. Not at the moment. I know where some of the fault lies, with that lying, scheming traitor!" I hissed at him.

The rage of treachery done to me boiled so hot! It coursed through my veins, opening channels; breaking through dams I'd been unaware existed inside me. A kaleidoscope opened before my eyes, swirling color and patterns. I saw each color and the emotions that had drawn them to me.

Yellow had been the pretty poison of prejudice that had enraged me. Red a fear of changing the relationship between Tesch and I. Green had come when I'd accepted the new beginning between us.

The orange, pinks and browns of my worlds were shades of learning to communicate, to see another's point of view. The misunderstanding between Tesch and I on the blacktop, Charlie's over the top reaction, even Challen's admission and apology were a part of it.

Blue had come to me in the moment of my greatest sorrow. My grief ran deep because I'd been lucky enough to experience the powerful, unconditional love parents have for their child. Their loss became a razor cutting me to the quick. Their memory would be the rock foundation of my life.

Purple is the shade of loyalty. It is a royal cloak of honor for the true and faithful. It can shroud liars and betrayers of friendship and trust. Both had touched me. I had given my loyalty and friendship to be rewarded with an empty promise and lies.

Understanding dawned. Whatever spells that had chained me; the last link had been broken.

I would never again be blind, to color or otherwise.

"Harmony! What are you doing?" Tesch's frantic voice broke in on my colorful revelations.

I returned to myself to find my hands glowing white hot, grasping the fragile porcelain cup. The tea boiled, almost gone, evaporated! The cup itself had begun to fold inward in my grip. Releasing my hold, the white light in my hands faded.

"Wow. I never saw the like." Anisa exclaimed.

My head rotated sharply toward her astonished exclamation. Something in my look must have spooked her.

Blue eyes wide, she stammered. "Don't worry, my lady. The carnival is kind of like a traveling Las Vegas. What happens among us stays among us. I won't breathe a word. I swear."

"What just happened with you?" Tesch demanded.

"I don't know." I spoke the truth. In all honesty I couldn't be sure, even if I suspected. "I need some air."

Scooting from my seat at the camper table, I stood quickly. Poor Anisa almost toppled over in my rude passing. I mumbled a hasty apology.

"Wait, Harmony, I'll go with you." Tesch began to rise.

"No, I need a minute alone. Please, I'll be fine."

Without waiting for a reply I went to the door, fumbling with the latch before making my way out into the night air. The moisture came across tangible, heavy on the skin of my face. Somewhere in the distance, lightening flashed, lighting up the night, revealing the deepest of blue-violet in between gray clouds. The storm moved in from the west.

Nothing compared to the storm brewing inside of me. Grief, love, sorrow and fear beaded sweat of desperation on my upper lip and forehead. Power filled my head creating the buzz of a beehive in my ears as it had so long ago in Ms. Tyck's office.

A shiver of steel replaced my spine. With deep resolve I pulled magic, *my* magic, around me. All of it! All the colors that I held within I used to call power from the earth, the air, the trees and lights that flashed and glimmered everywhere. Drawing them about me, I made a cloak and did what couldn't be done. I turned my shield white...and held my breath.

Tesch burst from the back of camper a second after. He called softly.

"Harmony?" His gaze scanned. "Harmony, where are you?"

He looked right through me.

I stayed still and quiet. For once, I didn't want Tesch by my side, not now, not for this.

He moved on into the night, heading through the maze of campers and trailers to no doubt search for me. The first drops of rain began to fall, pattering the ground around me, but never touching my skin. My shield kept me protected from more than sight.

In a few hours, maybe less, I would be leaving the only place I had ever really known. I planned on running away with the carnival, how cliché. My parents were dead. My life here over and gone, but one thing had to be done before I could go; one piece of business needed to be finished first.

Tesch would worry until I returned, but that couldn't be helped. Sarah would have been disappointed in me for this, maybe. I think Charlie might have understood if he were there. But he wasn't and never would be again.

Pain. Raw and real clutched me. I ached to fall to my knees, let the change happen, to run off into the night as a Werelynx that would not feel these things. To lose myself in the animal I could become. But I held on and fought for control.

On this night I existed as more than a Were or Witch or a Fae. Under this sky I became a dragon, angry and powerful, and I had a bone to pick.

I walked away from the lights and sounds of the carnival, invisible in my white shield. One thought, one name circled in my brain, around and around with a vengeance.

Joliet Kali Coombs.